Never Wed an Outlaw

Deadly Pistols MC Romance

Nicole Snow

Content copyright © Nicole Snow. All rights reserved.
Published in the United States of America.
First published in September, 2016.

Disclaimer: The following book is a work of fiction. Any resemblance characters in this story may have to real people is only coincidental.

Please respect this author's hard work! No section of this book may be reproduced or copied without permission. Exception for brief quotations used in reviews or promotions. This book is licensed for your personal enjoyment only. Thanks!

Cover Design – Kevin McGrath – Kevin Does Art.
Photo by Allan Spiers Photography.
Formatting –Polgarus Studio

Description

I'M PREGNANT, ON THE RUN, AND WEARING HIS RING...

HANNAH

How the hell did I get here?

Oh, right – Daniel "Dust" Grayson. Scariest, sexiest man alive. The only man who's ever stolen my panties, lured me into his bed, and left me begging for more.

This isn't what you're thinking. Yes, he's an outlaw. Trouble incarnate on two towering legs and the hottest smirk south of the Mason-Dixon line. But I'm not in a world of hurt because he's President of the Deadly Pistols MC, or because my big brother is his right hand man – hello, drama!

No, Dust tried to save me from myself. I can't let my secrets kill him.

It's time to forget everything: his love, his kisses, raising the baby he'll never know together.

Never wed an outlaw. A broken heart was my wedding present, and now it's my only defense...

DUST

Hannah was my biggest mistake. Ain't every day a man claims a girl, shoves his ring on her finger, and tells her she's his 'til the end of time. I had it all, blind to the storm approaching.

Then she disappeared. She forgot about us.

I'll die before I let her. Darlin', I'm coming.

Don't care if my best friend is her kin, and he wants to rip my head off.

Don't care if she's a hostage to the meanest crew I ever laid eyes on.

Don't care if I have to move heaven, hell, and everything in between to bring her home.

If Hannah's a mistake, I'm owning up. Every single inch of her, every kiss, every damned day. She made me crave the whole package, a wife and kids, like a man needs air.

I can't stop. I won't go back. She's coming back to my arms, or I'll rip this wicked world limb from limb.

I: Love's Labor (Hannah)

This baby wasn't coming easy. An hour must've passed since the last labor pain. More than twenty minutes since the small medical team gathered around me stepped outside for a break.

Long enough to wonder how the *hell* I'd gotten myself into this.

Like I had the luxury of dwelling on the past. Right now, through the pain and confusion, a bigger question weighed on my mind.

I had to know how I'd get myself and my new born bundle of joy *out* safely.

We were so close. Just another day or two of driving from Texas to the West Coast, where I had a cargo ship waiting to take us away from everything I knew.

New Zealand. That's where I wanted to raise my son. Somewhere stable, safe, and far, far away from every crushing debt Hannah Davis ever owed.

I'd lived under a new name for seven months. New career. Brand new life.

A more normal one, happier than anything I ever had in

Tennessee, or wherever my coding skills took me.

Somewhere I'd never have to hear Dom breathing his threats in my ear, or watch my back for anyone wearing a Sicilian mafia tattoo.

Somewhere I'd never have to think about Dust again. Did such a place exist on this planet?

Even now, the bastard wouldn't leave my mind.

He was there every time I closed my eyes.

There, every time our son shifted deep inside me, eager to see the world for the first time.

There, when I looked into the empty room surrounding me, knowing he was about to miss his first born's entrance into the world.

There, there, and *there,* whenever I thought I'd hold it together just a little while longer, to get this baby out of me so I could heal and hit the road.

Some men don't know the meaning of *leave.* They're with you in your dreams, your nightmares, and the taste of their lips lingers on yours when there's nothing except bittersweet loss in your heart.

My fingers stretched down, flexed, clenching the edge of the bed. The cold, clinic metal in my fist was a terrible substitute for his hand – the manly, reassuring grip I knew he'd have on me right now if I hadn't taken off months ago, leaving him behind.

It wasn't like I wanted to. I did the right thing, took the only option I had under the gun.

By abandoning him, I'd saved his life, and so many others.

Winding up in this bed alone, about to give birth, was proof positive that I wanted to save *everyone* in that stupid motorcycle club, including my lover, my brother, my precious little niece.

They wouldn't die thanks to my mess.

I wouldn't force the Deadly Pistols into protecting me, and sinking their teeth into more than any little Smoky Mountain biker club could chew. Nobody stood a chance against the monsters waiting for my blood. They were bigger, stronger, easily able to decapitate entire rival groups overseas without a trace, and take everything they had.

Maybe someday, they'd overplay their hand, and a bigger, meaner beast would chew the Sicilian Brotherhood apart. Maybe Dom and his men would just be a bitter memory then. Maybe I'd be able to send a secret note to Knoxville, telling Dusty his son was happy and healthy in a new country, and that he'd always have a piece of my heart.

Yeah, *maybe*.

Hey, maybe a unicorn would come crashing through the wall and spirit us both away to an all-you-can-eat chocolate buffet in the next ten minutes.

Magic horses were a lot safer than those loud, growling Harleys that used to get me hot for the man who'd gotten me pregnant, anyway. I laid back, more painkillers flooding my system, letting them soak in before I had to force my early baby out.

I was still seeing unicorns and motorcycles in my head when the door swung open.

The doctor and the nurses were back, thank God. Then

I looked up, and saw hell itself on two legs and a leather jacket.

Dom paused to smile before stepping forward, wiping his switchblade on his jeans. The stuff staining it was too thick and red to be juice from the pomegranates he always plucked at in front of me.

Blood. Lots of fresh, dark blood, leaving a rust-colored stain on his grey trousers. As if I needed another reminder this man can murder without having to be careful with the evidence.

"Fuck, peach, thought we'd never find you."

We? The door swung open again, and three more goons entered. All of them bigger, balding, and not nearly as happy to be here as their boss.

"Took us on a damned road trip we really didn't have time for. I'll add it to your tab. You can thank me later, bitch," he said, flashing his teeth, before his smile disappeared into a dark scowl.

Crying wasn't even a choice. When I brought one hand to my cheek, it was already wet.

Hot, glassy tears came for Dust, for my son, for the future I'd feared, staring me in the face. I mourned the lonely, safe ones I'd never have, now that the monster had tracked me down.

Dom waited about thirty seconds before snatching at my hair, jerking my face hideously close to his. "You really thought you could run? That I wouldn't fucking find you?" His nostrils flared and his eyes narrowed, fixing on me like an eagle about to have lunch. "Used to think you were smart, back when we first cut our deal. I thought you'd work smart, work fast, and make us all some money. I'm never this stupid. You made a fucking fool of me, Hannah."

He sighed, his fingers shaking angrily. "After I'm through with you, I'll be kicking my own ass for being blind. Believe me. Still, you're a bigger fool than me if you think you'll get away with wasting our time, unpunished. Stop shaking, bitch. Don't scream, or you'll get another one of those sweet little nurses killed on the way out."

Another nurse? As in, he'd already murdered one?

Jesus.

The goon on my right lifted my arm, pulling the IV out of it. Shaking my head, I stared into his deep, dark eyes, desperate to see something human.

"Please. Just let me have my baby first. I'll do anything you say after, if you'll just –"

"What'd I tell you, peach?" His blade moved against my throat, telling me I'd made a huge mistake trying to reason with him. "The time to shut the fuck up was sixty seconds ago. You've pissed away enough of my time, and I'm not letting you take no more. We're walking, while we've got this ward blocked the fuck off, before all those assholes bust in here and call the cops. Let's do this easy. Last thing I wanna do is rip that brat out of your guts and handcuff you to the nearest laptop so you can pay me my fucking coin, all right?"

My tongue pushed hard against the brutal lump forming in my throat. It wouldn't go down.

That rock was my grief, my anger, my self-loathing for

failing my poor baby son and myself.

Christ, for getting an innocent woman killed. The blood on his knife didn't lie. He'd killed her to get to me, taken her life like it was nothing, just like he'd murder anyone else in his path if I didn't shut my mouth and play along.

So, I did. I listened like a good girl through the pain, the regret, the terror. Allowed them to help me up, lifting me away, wincing when another contraction came.

I followed him in a haze with his men's rough arms holding me by the shoulders, escorting me out to the van waiting past the nearest exit. Its windows were so dark they might've been black holes.

I laid down inside on the crappy mattress, trying my damnedest not to completely lose it.

The van's loud engine growled, and the vehicle jerked forward, just as loud Italian rock started blasting from the speakers. The human bulldogs sitting next to me never looked up, messing with their phones, as casually as if they were waiting for drinks at a busy restaurant.

"Told you I'd get everything I'm owed. Every fucking cent, Hannah," Dom rumbled back at me from the front passenger seat. "You're gonna work those precious little fingers to the bone. Don't give a shit if you have to type with that kid on a leash. We both know why you're here. And if you act dumb, give me some shit about playing innocent, you're gonna feel the back of my hand straight through that morphine. The fact that you owe me in the first place means you're guilty as sin."

Innocent? The hot, red tears streaming out my eyes

wouldn't stop coming as the harsh word rolled over in my mind.

If there's one thing I knew, I'd brought this on myself.

I took their loan. Used money I couldn't pay back fast enough to live it up, pretending I had it all, trying to force the premature success I should have earned honestly. I let Dusty take my heart, pull me in deeper, and put a baby in me who didn't deserve to suffer *any* of my mistakes.

Too bad that didn't matter to the bastards around me, driving me off to nowhere. *Too bad* some mistakes were so big they chewed a woman up and spat her back out in pieces, little bits she'd never stitch together again because the damage was irreparable.

My belly twitched, and I put my hand over it. I owed the entire world an apology for how naive and selfish I'd been, but nobody more than this poor, sweet babe, and the man who'd helped make him.

It didn't matter now. The karma train rolled on, loud and furious, heading straight for me.

I'd let her plow through, ruin the last black scrap of a heart beating wildly in my ribs. In her collision, I'd pay for what I'd done.

But I had to keep her away from everybody else. My family didn't deserve to die for my mistakes.

I wasn't giving up, even if Dom's bastards rolled me up in chains. They'd ruined my escape, but they wouldn't stop the hateful, lunatic determination scorching my eyes each time my tears worked their way out, rolling onto the beat up mattress under me on the van's floor.

I couldn't run anymore. I couldn't keep making the same mistake.

I had to stand my ground. Fearless, honest, and alive.

I swore, with only God as my witness, I'd bring my baby into the world, and keep myself breathing.

Opportunity would come, if I just sunk my nails in, and held on.

I'd send these animals back to hell, and give my son a life where the only monsters were make believe.

II: In Control (Dust)

Fourteen Months Earlier

"Fuck me blind as a bat," I whispered underneath my breath the second I saw her, taking a long draw off my beer.

Sure, there were plenty of hot chicks at a club wedding, but none of them looked like *this*. They wore the same skimpy, desperate shit I'd seen a thousand times since I put on this patch. Same stuff that bored my cock to sleep.

Skin tight tank tops and ass grabbing shorts got the younger brothers hard, and didn't do a thing for any man who'd had his fill of sluts over the last couple decades.

This chick was different. Lavender heels, a long purple dress with frills like she'd borrowed it from a palace, designer purse wedged against her tit that must've cost three times the leather on my cut.

Too good to be here at Firefly and Cora's wedding. Hotter than she had any business being. Completely off limits, and my dick throbbed when it wanted the impossible.

I sucked down the rest of my brew and fished out my

pipe. Needed to take in a good, long pull from southern tobacco before I laid my lines on a honey like her.

"Shit, Prez, you look like you had one too many already. Can't believe I'm gonna be next, right?" Skin, my Treasurer, came up next to me and slapped my shoulder.

"Can't believe he beat your slow ass to the punch, yeah. When's your wedding, boy?" I growled, banging his fist.

"Soon as Meg and me sort out the business with the girls at the bar. That business doesn't run itself, you know. It'd sure be nice to knock the Deads flat, too, before we've got any more wedding bells ringing in this club."

"Yeah," I said, blowing a wisp of smoke out my mouth, my eyes never leaving the girl in the corner, laughing while she chattered away with our newly married Firefly and his old lady, Cora. "We'll tear their balls off sooner or later. Don't wait for them, brother. At the rate it's going, you're gonna watch Joker or Sixty tie the knot before you."

He laughed because I'd just told the dumbest joke in the world. Our Veep, Joker, was fucking crazy. If he ever started caring about anything except his dead brother and that big ass Irish Wolfound he just got, I'd swallow my own pipe.

And Sixty? Forget it. That boy never went after anything except the loosest pussy when he didn't have oil on his hands from working in the garages.

"Whatever, Prez. I see where your mind's at tonight." Skin winked, following my gaze over to the little table where Miss Sexy, Purple, and Mysterious sat. "Christ, you know who she is, right?"

No, but you better start talkin', I thought, giving him a

look that said as much.

Skinny boy's grin only got bigger. "Fuck it. I gotta find my old lady and party a little more. I'll leave you to find out. More fun that way."

He knew I wouldn't chase him down and get in his face for screwing around. Not at a brother's wedding, when nothing ever rolled except good times aplenty.

Growling frustration, I put out my pipe and stuffed it back in my pocket. Then I straightened my leather cut on my shoulders and headed straight for her.

Firefly and Cora slipped away just a minute before, leaving me a perfect opening. Not like I needed one. Talking to pussy and reeling it in came easy.

"You look like you oughta have a champagne flute in your hand, not a damned Jack and coke," I tell her, taking the seat across from her.

Turning slowly, I gave her a solid ten seconds to take me in. Fuck, her big blue eyes looked beautiful when they went wide, and liked what they saw.

Women always liked what they saw when I stood in front of 'em. *Always.*

"Why's that?" she said, narrowing her eyes, flicking her brunette hair over her shoulder. "Do I really look so out of place? Like I don't enjoy getting drunk off my ass at my own brother's wedding?"

Brother? Shit.

I thought I recognized those big blue eyes somewhere. I did a quick turn, looking over my shoulder, and saw Firefly dancing in a slow, drunken, lovestruck embrace with his new woman.

The impossible just became un-fucking-thinkable.

"Holy Hannah," I said with a smirk, turning back to her. "So, that's who you are? Little Hannah Davis? Fuck...you must've been going to your first prom last time I saw you ridin' on the back of Firefly's bike."

"Ain't so little anymore, Dusty."

"No, darlin'." *No you ain't,* I think to myself, admiring her like a slow sip of good whiskey.

How that skinny little girl filled out, sprouted tits as big as melons, had to be one of the great mysteries of the universe. Couldn't see her hips or legs, hiding under the table, but damn if I didn't want to.

"Are you just going to ogle me all evening, or ask me to dance?" Her glass went to her hot red lips, draining the last of her drink.

For a chance to see those legs, and feel every hot inch of her pressed against me? I'd dance the fuckin' waltz.

"Come on," I said, extending a hand.

I pulled her up and we walked out to the little patio, where several other couples mingled. Most of the brothers had one or two sluts on his arm, except for the two boys hitched to their old ladies.

Lion and Tin, our two newest brothers, were too busy sucking face with their girls to call it a dance anymore. Insane, really, because they'd both got beaten to shit a little while ago during a run-in with the Atlanta Torches MC.

Classic rock blasted through the outdoor stereo. A swarm of fireflies lit up the night all around us, like they'd come down from heaven to pay homage to Hannah's big brother on his wedding night.

"Firefly talks about you every so often," I said, grabbing her waist and pulling her in, swaying with her to the beat. "You're some hot shot, globe trekking, caviar snorting businesswoman now, yeah?"

"Close." She looked up, bathing me in eyes as big and blue as marbles. "I like to live fast and hard these days. Something you know a few things about with business and all, I'm sure."

"Darlin', I was born in it. You had to learn. I'm impressed."

Just then, my dick was pretty damned impressed with those hips. Turning in my arms, she teased me, pushing my hands back across her belly. Next few beats, and her ass started moving into my crotch, dangerously close to grinding.

Didn't know if I was harder because she looked so good, or because she was a brother's sis. One more wicked, taboo thrill I didn't need to save my ass from trouble.

"Seen your face on some of the billboards," I growled into her ear. "Even here in Knoxville. Every girl with a phone is using your app, prowling for dick. You're something else, using your own sweet face for marketing your hookup machine."

"Mm-hmm," she purred, bending her sweet ass into me again. "It's not for sex, you know. It's for casual, low pressure, flirty and fun meetings for busy professionals and –"

"Yeah, yeah. Firefly sang the jingle for us a few weeks ago. *Need a date? Take a date! Got a minute? Get a drink!*"

Lending her a hand, I watched her turn around as the song wrapped up, reciting her ad's tag-line. "Don't tell me you're using that thing to find yourself boyfriends, too."

She smiled slowly, drifting into my arms, pushing her hands across my neck. "Don't need to. Believe it or not, the straight-laced business guys and marathon runners on there ain't my type."

"No? Then who the fuck is?"

I already had a good idea, but I wanted her lips to do the talking. They did, a second later, when she brought her face so close to mine I could feel her breath on my lips.

"Don't play dumb, Dusty. I like my guys big as trees and fearless, but never stupid. My brother's found himself a girl because she knows he's got a brain underneath the muscles and ink. He wouldn't stay in this club if that weren't true for all his brothers."

"Babe, you know it," I growled. "Any man who's stupid doesn't get far with this patch. Ain't just our fancy app that vets people. We do it the old fashioned way."

Honestly, only thing I wanted to vet right now was how wet she'd be if I pushed my hand up her skirt. Fuck, I couldn't hold back any more.

Whatever had gotten into her tonight, the booze or the break from business, I never wasted time when there was a woman down to fuck in front of me. My hand snaked down her spine, spreading flat at the top of her hips, before gliding lower.

She'd never need any help from a computer to find a man with *these* hips. Hell no.

Couldn't decide if I liked her top or bottom better. One thing's for sure – she had the kind a woman's blessed with when it's her destiny to have a couple kids deep inside her.

'Course, kids were about the last thing on my mind right about now. My dick went full primal while I caressed her curves, imagining how hot she'd get straddling me, gripping her ass, riding me all the way home.

We danced the rest of the tune. Rock turned into Johnny Cash, country and hard beats coming together like the hearts banging themselves wild in the darkness tonight.

When the music died, she tried to pull away, the little minx. Damn if I didn't growl, catch her by the wrist, and jerk her back to me.

"Where you think you're going, darlin'?" I whispered, my teeth against her ear. "We've got a lot more catchin' up to do. This ain't over."

Caressing her cheek with one hand, I tipped her face to mine, saw it was begging to be kissed. I wondered what kind of voodoo shit got slipped into the club's whiskey tonight to make me seriously consider laying a brother's little sis.

"Keep it in your pants just a little longer. I have to see Huck and Cora one more time before they leave. We'll catch up more later, Dusty. Maybe we can talk business," she said, flashing me a wink over her shoulder as she pulled away.

"Business?" I snorted. Only business with her that interested me was finding out how wet she'd be when I slid my hand between her thighs.

"Sure, why not? Maybe I'll make you an offer you can't refuse. Later, Dusty. Promise."

Promise. Fuck, something about that word rolling off her sugary lips turned my cock from steel to diamond.

What the hell would happen if I brought her into my office, threw her across my desk, and reached underneath that fancy purple dress, ripping her panties off?

It'd been too long since I had any fun with a girl I was really in to. Always too much club biz tying me down, too many wars and missing pennies in the club's coffers to worry about. We were just getting on our feet after my old man left us damned near broke before passing me the gavel.

Slowly, I reached for my pipe, sinking my teeth into the wood when I gave it a light. Oddly disappointing tonight.

Tobacco didn't taste half as good as I imagined Hannah tasting on my lips. If I didn't have her scent, her sweat, her cream on my tongue by the end of the night, I'd punch the mirror when I saw myself in it the next morning for letting her slip away.

Normally, fucking around with a brother's family in this club was suicide. Dumber than crashing your ride into the nearest police station. Hannah, though...she might be worth the trouble. Just for tonight.

I nodded to myself, watching the thick, rich tobacco smoke curling out my lips. *Yeah, boy, you're damned near fucked.*

Some boys know a man shouldn't keep stacking his plate high when he's already got more than he can swallow. Not me. Not now. I'd risk the drama and blows to the face from a very pissed off Firefly if it meant having Hannah Sexy Davis' notch in my bedpost.

* * * *

They were busy talking for about an hour. I watched Hannah, Firefly, and Cora at the dinner table outta the corner of my eye while I shot the shit with Joker and Sixty.

My table jerked in between bites of rib. My Veep was doing that damned thing with the knife again, slamming the blade through the gaps in his fingers like a circus freak interviewing for a new job. Or just a fuckin' idiot looking for an express ticket to the emergency room.

"That's enough," I said, looking up at him. "Ain't it time to take that dog for some fresh air, or something?"

He always stared at me with those hazel, almost gold eyes. Looks that made me wonder if there was anybody home. "Sure, Prez."

He stood up a second later while I shook my head. I watched him walk off with the big Irish Wolfound's leash in his hands. If it weren't for that dog keeping him grounded, I'd have a helluva time trusting anything going on in that boy's head.

Wasn't his fault, though. Several years ago, a few mean motherfuckers from the Deadhands MC killed his twin brother and put their grandpa in a nursing home. I promised him vengeance – but only when the club got its balls back, and had the force to make those bastards extinct.

Revenge, you couldn't fuck up. Going against the Deads? Absolute death sentence, unless every single one of your ducks was in a row, and armed to the goddamned beak.

I raised my beer to my lips. Didn't taste as good, thinking about Joker's shit. One more dirty little secret I'd hidden from the brothers for their own good. Trouble with secrets was, they never stayed buried forever.

"Shit, Prez, you've been sitting there all hour like a statue. Don't you want to watch the happy couple kiss?" Sixty smiled, stroking his goatee, clanging his bottle loudly one more time.

Cora and Firefly must've been getting damned tired of it. Or maybe it was one more excuse to lock lips while the whole club looked on. Must've been a thousand wedding kisses already that night, and adding one more wouldn't hurt.

"Give the girl a break," I said. "She's carrying his kid."

"Yeah, yeah, maybe you're right! Easy to forget she's knocked up. Least they're doing things in the right order, or close enough," Sixty said. He pulled out a smoke and putting it between his lips. "Poor woman's gonna need a day to rest up after big boy gets done with her tonight."

I nodded, giving him a dirty look. He might be right, but their fuckin' wasn't any of his business.

"Easy, brother. You're not talkin' about her like she's a piece of fuckin' meat. Cora's an old lady now. Part of the club's extended family. Woman deserves the same respect you give my ma, Meg, and anybody else who puts a brother's ink on her skin."

Deflated, he looked at me, taking a long drag on his cig. "You're the boss. Hell, I'm surprised they're sticking around here so long. They gonna hang out there, chattering away with Firefly's sis all night?"

"No," I said, taking my cue to stand up and stretch.

Not just no. Fuck no.

"She's got business with me," I said, holding in a smile when I thought about calling my balls on her clit 'business.'

I headed over, stopping behind Hannah's shoulder. Didn't say anything 'til I had Firefly's attention.

"What the fuck you two still doing here?" I asked. "Hit the road and get this gal out on her honeymoon, boy. That's an order. Besides, I'm fixing to borrow your sis for a minute. Got something business-like to discuss in the backroom."

Hannah turned around and flashed me a smile, slowly standing with the happy couple. Purple never looked so good. Couldn't wait to tear it off her.

"Club business, or personal?" Firefly straightened, giving me an icy stare. Perfect with those blue eyes in his head, though they look a helluva lot prettier in Hannah's face.

"You wouldn't understand how to mix business and pleasure, Huck," Hannah chirped, giving her brother crap like any little sister should.

Firefly didn't look too happy. For a second, I thought I might be seeing that trouble flirting with me sooner, rather than later. But then he put his hand out, took mine, and gave it the strong grip only another vet wearing the patch wields.

"Whatever. I'm too damned happy today to give a damn," Firefly said. "Come on, darlin'. Let's blow this fuckin' bash."

Soon as they were gone, Hannah pushed into my arms.

Took a long, hot second running my hands through that silky chestnut hair. If there weren't a dozen people around us, I'd lay her out on this table and take everything she offered, just like a starving animal.

"It's later now, ain't it, darlin'?"

"My car, or your office?"

"Office," I growled. My dick jerked in my pants, alive with the fire in my blood.

"Great. I'll meet you there." She pulled away just in time, heading into the clubhouse, leaving me one more full, beautiful view of that ass I needed bouncing on my cock.

Didn't take me long to catch up. I headed through the crowd one more time, slapping hands with several of the boys and saying a few words. Took the long way in, through the garages attached to our building, where I found Firefly and Cora heading to their honeymoon.

I stopped to say a few words to Cora on the way out. Poor girl had been through hell. Her daddy, my old friend Jimmy, offed himself a few months ago. Left her in deep shit when she came to the club for protection. Now, she'd found her happy ending, long overdue.

Marching on in, I moved past the bar, ignoring a couple prospects who'd had too much and passed out on the floor.

Soon as I got into my office, I saw Hannah draped across my desk, her legs swinging off the edge. Perfectly positioned, ready for me to pull apart and sink my tongue into her.

Sweet merciful fuck. "You learn how to look all sexy in between that coding, darlin', or does it just come natural?"

"Why don't you find out?" she said, pursing her lips.

I loved a challenge – especially when it made my dick harder. I stepped up, pulled her into my arms, and finally buried my lips on hers.

Her heat, her sweetness, her kiss…fuckin' divine was the phrase that came to mind. That phrase, plus a hundred more, at least a dozen too crude to say.

Our lips twined together, hungry as hell. When my tongue found hers, I only let it dance for a fraction of a second. When my face peeled away, she had her hand on my cheek, roaming across my stubble.

Her eyes were narrowed, begging, hating me already for teasing so good. "What? You really want it fast and hard that bad? Didn't think you'd be the type to skip the foreplay," I said, raising my eyebrows.

Her hands moved to my chest, pushing against it. "You wish. Actually, a little foreplay is *all* you're getting tonight, Dusty."

She can't be fuckin' serious. I blinked three times before I could move my lips.

"Bullshit," I said, sliding my hand up her thigh, dangerously close to the pussy I knew was soaked a few inches higher.

"Truth. I'm all grown up and I like new experiences, but I don't just lay down with any old guy. I'm Huck's sister, after all. I have standards." She smiled so sweetly I want to bite that damned bottom lip and never let go 'til she got naked. "You're a big, grown man…older than the rest. More mature. You can control yourself, right? Just a little make out session tonight, and then we can decide where we want to go from there."

Growling, I wrapped my hands around her waist, jerking her close to my chest. Two seconds later, I had her pinned against my desk, smashing my lips into hers so hard it hurt.

Control? Goddamned control?! I'd show her who had it, and then some.

My dick ached like hell the entire time we thrashed lips. Couldn't think about anything else except tearing off her clothes.

I wouldn't crack, playing my part in this silly ass game 'til she begged to suck my cock.

How many years had it been? I'd never given her a second look before she had these curves, never saw her as anything except my closest brother's little sis.

In the blink of an eye, she'd become a woman. And *what* a woman with her big, soft tits pressed flush against my chest, two sweet nipples screaming to be sucked underneath that wine colored dress.

We barely came up for air. Her breath grew hotter in my mouth, sweeter by several magnitudes. Layers of sweat rolled off us in the humid Dixie night. Nothing perched on top of my desk survived without crashing to the floor.

Her wrists twitched in my hands toward the end of it. Hannah's hips were grinding on mine again, moving that perfect V between her legs against my cock. All the fabric in the way didn't matter worth a damn.

When her lungs hitched the last time and she bent her

legs around me, digging her heels into the backs of my legs, I almost blew my load in my pants.

She came hard, into my mouth, without even getting naked. I'd done a lot of things with a woman in my life, but this was the first time they'd never come from just my kiss.

Smiling, I watched her break away for desperately needed air. "That was a lot more than just kissing, darlin'. Looks like you'd better work on that control."

I turned around, tucking my shirt back into my waist, tangled up in the heat of the moment.

And *fuck*, what a moment.

"Yeah…sure." She picked herself up from my desk, trying to be sarcastic.

Both our eyes go straight down to her legs. They were trembling, still shaking after the dry, fiery orgasm I'd fucked into her with just my lips on hers.

Christ. Normally, seeing that would be a savage invitation for more, everything we should've done skin-on-skin the first time.

Too bad. I wasn't gonna crack.

She slid off my desk slowly, leaning on it for a few more seconds to replenish her lungs. I walked over, cupped her chin in my palm, running the other hand straight through those long locks that smelled as good as she looked. Her hair looked even sexier when it was messy, with just the right sweat halo brimming on her forehead.

"You're hot as hell, Hannah. Don't know what the fuck kinda game you're playing here tonight, but if you ever want to do this again naked, you know where to find me."

Her smile pulled tight across her lips. Was she really blushing from just my words after all that like an innocent school girl?

"I have to fly out to Seattle tomorrow, Dusty. Business meeting with my old mentor, Ty Sterner."

I cocked my head and squinted. "You mean that rich kid who married his own sister?"

"*Step-sister.* He's more than just tabloid fodder, believe me," she said, running her fingers slowly across my chest. My cock jerked, hornier than ever to be inside her. "You have your business. I have mine. Maybe we can have dinner and see what's next on the menu once I'm back in town."

"Next? Babe, you're gonna have to beg for my tongue next time. Not to mention anything else." Her eyes went wide, making me grin like mad. "Don't give me that look. You're the one who started it. Lucky you, I like being in control. Just as much as I like a challenge with the right woman."

Her lips turned up in another smile, and then she sauntered past me like a cat who'd had her fill on milk. "I'm flattered that you think of me that way, Dusty. Truth be told, I'm too busy to settle down anytime soon. I'm just here to have some fun with you and…well, whoever else I choose."

Whoa.

"Whoa!" I growled, stepping in front of her to block the door. "Easy, darlin'. You know exactly what I meant, and that's nothin' for us to laugh about. We're both gonna play it real cool, real casual, and that's where it ends. I'm gonna have to put a moratorium on playing heartbreaker here because I don't want Firefly breaking my nose when you run to him all disappointed."

She grinned, a little too forced and bitter for my liking. "You think I want my brother worrying about me when he's playing family man? Come on, Dusty, I'm not helpless. I'm just jerking your chain."

What-the-fuck ever, darlin'. Long as you jerk something else in the near future, I thought, my mind racing a hundred miles an hour.

The next growl leaving my lips was angrier. Made her feel it when we kissed one more time, my fist tugging at her hair, bringing her sweet mouth into mine.

"Goodnight, Hannah. You'll be seeing a whole lot more of me soon."

"Oh, I hope."

I backed off the door and watched her leave me with nothing more than another wink, plus the biggest blue balls in the entire world. *Fuck.*

I needed something to take the edge off. It was still a wedding party, after all, so I headed for the bar, grabbing the closest bottle of Jack I could find.

Didn't crack it open 'til after I rode my bike home. My place wasn't much to look at, just a functional little house on the edge of town, decorated with old Harley posters, Deadly Pistols patches in frames, and a few Civil War relics passed down from my great great grandpa.

I drank deep that night in bed, one hand on my dick. Sucked down a shot for every time she'd almost made me blow, setting me on fire like no woman had since...well, fuck, I couldn't remember.

It had been a long damned time. Almost as long as this club was weighed down with its woes, ever since my old man died and left me to clean up his wreck.

* * * *

Woke up the next morning smelling heaven. Eggs... bacon...coffee?

What the fuck? I jerked up, shaking off my hangover, wondering who the hell was in my house cooking up a banquet.

I had one hand on the loaded nine I always kept next to me on my nightstand, ready to switch off the safety, when I heard her singing country to herself. Fuck, it was just Ma, sneaking in early for a breakfast. It had been awhile since the last time she'd done it.

Throwing my legs over the bed, I found a fresh shirt and rolled it on, getting into my jeans. I was still straightening my cut on my shoulders when I walked into the kitchen. Stainless steel caught my reflection, mirroring my patches from a dozen different angles.

Blood red, outlaw black, fiery yellow. Skulls and daggers and pistols everywhere. What I'd earned in sweat and blood, I wore proud, every day of my life I went out on the road or showed up at the businesses I owned.

"Mornin', Dusty," Ma said, loading a plate of good food for me while I pulled up a chair at the counter. "You look like you just peeled yourself off the road. Too much fun at the wedding last night?"

"Something like that." I shook my head.

Forty one years old, and I still took barbs from my mother. Sure as hell didn't mind her cooking for me, though. Woman had a knack for making awesome breakfasts, huge sandwiches, and the best damned stroganoff a man ever had out of thin air.

Ma sat down next to me with her plate and coffee cup while I dug into my food. "Cora looked so pretty yesterday, wearing my dress. I'm happy I could loan it to her," she said.

"Yeah, it did the job. I'm sure she appreciated it, Ma. Lord knows she couldn't have rustled up anything better with Firefly on her ass to get hitched, soon as he found out about the kid."

Ma looked me up and down, taking a long slurp off her coffee. I swear she had more energy than anybody wearing the patch, a scary spark for a gray haired lady pushing seventy, and still working at the hospital part time when she wasn't fixing up wounds for our boys, or bringing us biscuits and gravy on the weekends.

"Joker's gonna be next," she said, smiling like she could see straight into the future. "I just have a gut feeling about that boy. He's hurt too much not to snatch up a good woman the minute she walks into his life."

I swallowed my food and grunted. "Don't hold your breath too long, Ma. He doesn't care about anything except that damned dog and getting payback for Piece."

She stared down at her plate, slowly taking a bite. "You'll be surprised. I think we'll all be real soon. Weddings in this club come fast, like lightning. It was the same for me and your father. Whatever else changes in this club, I don't think that ever will."

I gave her a long, hard look. She talked about my old man too much for a woman whose marriage went to total shit during the last decade.

Somehow, she loved him through it all. She loved him through his boozing, his gambling, his women. Taking on too many debts and making too many enemies, all the bullshit we're still mopping up together as a crew.

"One thing's for sure – it'll be Joker before it's me," I said, helping myself to some more bacon to go with my coffee. "Least we'll have a few kids hanging around the family get togethers soon, thanks to Meg and Cora. Only a matter of time before Skinny boy catches up to Firefly in the baby department."

"*Nope.* You don't get off *that* easy, Daniel Grayson." She wagged a finger at me and I stopped in mid-step.

Fuck, I hated it when she used my real name. 'Course, she was the only woman entitled to call me anything except Dust, seeing how she gave me birth. Still left a bad taste in my mouth.

I hadn't been called Daniel or Captain Grayson since my time in the Merchant Marines, helping protect America's trade ships from pirates in the Indian Ocean.

Yes, *pirates*. Merciless motherfuckers who'd hack heads off with dirty machetes, assuming they didn't get you with a rocket propelled grenade first, straight from their speedboats. Good, dangerous practice for coming home to

Knoxville and taking over this club, dealing with the Deads, the Torches, and other mean sonsofbitches who had all the Somali pirates' greed and none of their restraint.

"You owe me at least one grandbaby sooner or later. The whole wife and family thing, well, that's your choice," Ma snapped, draining the last dregs from her mug. "Look at this place!"

She turned on the stool, motioning toward the Civil War sword I had hanging on the mantle. "Do you really think Early would want his blood going to nothing? While you do – what, exactly? Get your hands dirty fixing cars and riding with the boys? Making money – for what?"

"We both know I don't give two shits about what dad would've wanted," I growled. "Family didn't do him much good when he really went off the rails."

Ma's coffee cup clanked down hard. Fuck, now I'd done it. She never cried openly anymore, but the hurt never died, all the pain he'd given her before he shuffled off his mortal coil.

"Aw, Ma, come on. I didn't mean it like that. You're like a mother to this whole club, you know, and a damned good one to me and everybody else. That's never gonna change." Grabbing her hand, I gave it a squeeze, before heading for the coffee thermos on the counter to refresh her cup.

"Maybe *I* care about your future, Daniel. Just like I care about my poor dead husband's past." She stood up, without bothering to finish her toast or the fresh coffee. "I have to get going. I'm going to be late for my shift."

Part of me wanted to run after her. But I'd fucked up

like this before, and this routine had gotten way too familiar.

"Let's do lunch. I'm taking my yearly trip down to Atlanta soon since everything's quiet up here."

"Okay, fine. I'd like that," she said quietly, halfway out the door. "Just get yourself there and back in one piece."

The door slammed shut on her way out, leaving me alone on a beautiful morning. Wouldn't be the first time.

I knew how it went from here. I'd feel like shit the rest of the day, at least 'til I hit the road and fresh mountain air work its balm. Eventually, Ma would lick her wounds and show up here again unannounced.

Sooner if, God forbid, something happened in the club warranting her medical talents.

I chugged the rest of my coffee and headed into the back for a quick shower before I hit the road. I'd be checking out the Ruby Heel, our new titty bar in town, managed by Meg and Cora.

The club was making more money these days by going clean, or close enough to it. Titty bars and chop shops for cars and bikes were a hell of a lot safer than the black market. If only the clean stuff made as much coin as going dirty.

Our growing gun trade was the ultimate dream. Carving ourselves a route from Knoxville to the sea, one worth gaining our club attention from the bigger clubs out West, the Devils and the Grizzlies MC. If we could get their greedy asses to trade with us and our friends on the coast, we'd be raking in so much money this club would never worry about the vault going empty again.

Just one problem: the Deadhands were still in the way. God willing, I'd hatch the perfect plan to wipe their asses out soon, and claim revenge for Joker and everybody else who'd ever been fucked by their sick club.

Work called, and she was a fuckin' slavedriver. I couldn't afford distractions like Ma's hurt feelings, or getting myself tangled up with any broad. Even if Hannah was a lot better than most.

I had a mission, staring me in the face every damned day I woke up. And when I sunk my teeth into a calling, I never, ever let go.

III: Rock and Hard Place (Hannah)

I told everyone I went to Seattle for business, but that was half the truth. It was several weeks after my brother's wedding, one more happiness cut short by looming hell.

They didn't know me. Not Huck, not Cora, not even Dust, who caused me to tingle every time I thought about the full body collision we had in his office.

They wouldn't believe the truth, even if I told them. I'd lived a lie so long I couldn't remember what honesty meant.

While they sang my praises, I kept that fake smile plastered to my face, showing the world the smart, sexy, highly successful woman they loved. Yeah, they were fucking clueless.

Truth was, everyone's favorite clean cut, bouncy, and brilliant entrepreneur of the year had her work cut out for her with secrets she could never tell. *Dark* secrets that would mean lost blood, not just lost money, if they ever spilled into the open.

So, I'd come to Seattle to face them again.

I sat in a back alley down by the bay, waiting for the scariest man in the world.

The stink of fish markets closing up for the evening wafted around me. A few couples strolled by, hand-in-hand, walking the main path by the docks while the sun slipped below the horizon.

The lucky ones. They didn't have a care in the world.

They didn't have to worry about a madman who might jab a knife in their spine if they said the wrong thing.

When my phone rang, I jumped, my hand shaking as I brought it to my ear. "Hello?"

"You're in the usual spot?"

"Yeah, I'm ready," I said coldly, closing my eyes.

I'd lived what came next many times. My phone clicked dead a second later, and then the black sedan pulled up next to the alley, blocking any escape.

Doors opened. Two angry, stern looking men in suits and ties got out, combing the small space all around me.

"Stand up, doll. This'll only take a second." I'd dealt with the one barking orders before. Tony, one of Dom's lackeys, a strong arm who always enjoyed groping me too much.

I stood up, wanting to get it over with. His hands roamed freely. They went up, down, behind my shirt, before he slipped to his knees to inspect me from the shoes up.

"No wires, no weapons. Bitch is clean," he growled, speaking more loudly into the speaker clipped to his ear than the other goon leaning against the wall.

One more door to the car popped open. My eyes stayed closed for several more seconds, listening to his footsteps, wishing like hell I could just make it all disappear as easily as a bad dream.

"Hannah."

As soon as the bastard said my name, I had to open my eyes and look at my tormenter. There he was.

Dominick Barone, or Dom, for short. A hired killer raised in the Sicilian Brotherhood, who'd infiltrated the multi-billion dollar Sterner empire of legit businesses where I'd interned. An utterly ruthless, heartless, savage son of a bitch who'd made me an offer too good to pass up.

I'd naively taken it. Too desperate, too hopeful, and too damned greedy for my own good.

"I don't know why we need to keep having these face-to-face meetings," I said. "We could save ourselves some travel time and do it over the phone, or online. Ever tried Skype?"

Dom didn't look amused. He stared at me with his cold green eyes, his hair laid down like an oil slick, two jagged scars going up both his fifty year old cheeks. He'd gotten them in a brawl somewhere in Baltimore, back in the days when the mafias were limited to a few coastal cities.

Yes, I'd done my research. Learned everything I could about the monster at my throat, and I knew he was *dangerous.*

"No, peach. Travel has its charm. So does seeing you again," he said, sitting down on the bench next me. "You know how I feel about doing things in person, Hannah. Much less chance you ever fuck me over if you get any sick ideas in that pretty little head."

He never looked at me. Not once.

Instead, as he always did, he reached into his pocket, pulling out his knife and a fruit I'd never be able to look at again without turning my stomach.

Pomegranate. Raw, angry, and always glowing blood red.

Using his wickedly sharp blade to pry it open, he dug in, catching the seeds in between the fingers and stuffing them into his mouth, one at a time.

"Tony, give her the damned file already," he said, staring at a fresh red morsel in his fingers. "Look it over. You're gonna work everything in there into that goddamned app of yours. Another fake account for you to sync up. We'll transfer our cut straight to the shell business, the salons and pizzerias and shit, once you've coded it in. I'm making your job easy, peach, how 'bout a little gratitude?"

I said nothing. Tony stuffed a manila folder into my hands. I quickly opened it, looking through the documents, my heart twisting a little when I saw what they wanted.

They didn't understand software and builds like I did. They might as well have asked me to put a huge red flag on my dating app that said *hello, FBI!*

"Uh…you know this raises the risk of some nosey kid finding you out, right? It doesn't take much for anyone trying to duplicate my app to stumble onto the code you're requesting here. Trust me, there are a lot of copycats trying to be competitors these days."

"Won't risk a damned thing," Dom snapped. "See, that's where you snap your little fingers and pull another rabbit out of your sweet little ass. You've been smart enough to mask our shit up 'til now. Smart enough to make us a cool million in a week to pay back a little debt you owe from our seed money. You'll think of something brilliant, peach. Your magic works for both of us. Me and my boys will go ahead and make more money without Uncle Scam getting wise to it. And you'll get to keep that fancy fucking house, and inch forward, a little closer to the day when we won't have to do this no more."

I still owed him three million. That day wouldn't come for at least another year or two, and only if the app kept making big money on paid subscriptions.

I'd seen new things flame out before. There were no guarantees in this business.

And if the Feds found out they were using me for money laundering, through an investigation or some kind of fluke…oh, God.

I'd end up on the wrong side of Dom's knife, or in a Federal jail cell for knowingly abetting a criminal scheme.

"Why you gotta look so sad? We've come a long, *long* way, haven't we, peach?"

I nodded glumly.

"That's right, so fuckin' far. I remember the night we met after Mister Sterner's company bash. You, fresh out of the slums with a fire in your belly and a little real world job experience in your cap. Me, schmoozing you like a friend of Sterner's, pretending to be your angel investor. You told me how bad you wanted to be the next whiz kid in tech, have your face on every blog and magazine. I said I could make that happen. Shit, when I tossed you the paperwork for the loan, and told you I might want to keep some shit off the record, I never saw anybody sign so fast. Normally, they ask a lot of questions, too, and I have to make up stories. But you, peach…you were good. You trusted me, blind as a fucking bat. You were hungry, Hannah…too damned greedy for your own good."

My stomach knotted, making me want to throw up. I hated him for reminding me how I'd trusted him, ignored all the signs that the flash investment in my idea was too good to be true. He'd stalked me like a wolf, and I'd walked into his jaws.

Why it happened, well, that wasn't a mystery. When a girl grows up dirt poor with nobody except her brother to look up to, she jumps the first time somebody offers her several million and a chance to blow up big.

Gullible? Oh yeah, and now I'd pay the price in blood and heartbreak.

"I'll do what I can." The defeated tone in my voice sounded obvious, even to me.

"Fuck yeah, you will," he growled, stuffing another pomegranate seed into his mouth. "Because you remember what happens if you don't? If you start to panic, take off, think you can cheat us out of our own money?"

"Yeah, Dom, I remember…I don't need another reminder."

I can't fucking handle another one, you sick bastard, I thought to myself. *Please, no reminder.*

"Really, peach? Because your eyes are telling me maybe

you do. Here, let me give you one." Growling, he slammed his knife straight into his open fruit and cut straight down it, spilling red, slippery seeds everywhere. "You fuck up, you die. That simple. But first, before we bury you alive chained up in a drum, we get every goddamned dime we're owed in flesh and blood. We'll keep you chained up and use that rockin' pussy of yours every damned day we want. Hunt down every friend and kin you've ever had. No, that damned biker patch on your brother won't save him. We'll bring you his fucking face skinned off his body and throw it in yours. I hear his new wife's knocked up, about to squeeze out a kid. Maybe we bring your little niece to say hello to auntie, one piece at a time…"

Rage, hurt, and fear churned in my intestines. How he kept such close tabs on me, I had no idea, and I was too sick to care.

My ears stopped working at some point while he droned on about the sadistic things he'd do to me. I couldn't mentally handle the list of atrocities he ran off, and so I shut down, his threats fading into my heartbeat's savage roar.

He was talking about killing Huck, my brother, and his family. The only thing I had left after we both left that shitty trailer we'd grown up. The only one who'd ever cared, who had more to live for than me.

Then he talked about sex, violating me in ways I didn't dare imagine. It shouldn't have been as revolting as the death threats, but it was, because I was still a virgin.

"And when we're all through with that, peachy pie, we'll make sure nobody ever finds your fuckin' body outside the fishes. It's a big ocean. You see that shit out there?"

I refused to follow his knife, pointed over the top of the car. He motioned out to sea, past all the cranes from the loading docks, where the depths were deep, dark, choppy.

"Damn it, bitch, I said *look*. Tony!"

Grabbing my head, his goon twisted it around, forcing me to see where I'd wind up – probably in pieces – if I didn't obey his every whim.

"We've dumped a lot of people out there, Hannah. Made more bastards and bitches disappear in so many underwater trenches it'd make Davy fuckin' Jones himself jealous. This isn't just a debt," he growled, his ice cold face coming closer and closer to mine.

Tony's grip on me tightened. I couldn't move. My blood was officially iced over. A single livid tear slid down my cheek, tracing a fiery trail across my skin.

"None of this has to happen, Hannah. You do what you're told, pay us back with interest, we won't have any problems like figuring out how many fucks it takes to get bored before giving you to hell," he said, extending a finger.

Everything inside me recoiled when he touched me, catching my tear on his fingertip. He brought it back to his lips with a growl, opening those dry lips just enough so he could suck my pain off his finger.

"Let her go, boys. We're done here." He stood, slamming the heel of his perfectly polished shoe on what's left of the pomegranate. "Until next time, my Georgia Peach."

Yeah, *next time*. I tried to stop shaking while I watched

them walk slowly to their car, get in, and drive off like ordinary businessmen.

I never dared to correct them about my birthplace, Tennessee, born and raised. They knew everything else about me, and the one simple fact they'd gotten wrong wouldn't change anything.

Clenching the manila envelope, I stuffed it into my purse, and started walking briskly away from the docks, into the city.

I'd been planning to have dinner with Ty and his family tomorrow, my old billionaire boss from several years ago, but now it wasn't even a possibility. I had to find an excuse to blow him off, anything to avoid breaking down about my plight in front of the man who'd been a mentor to me.

After that, I had to catch the first flight the hell out of here.

* * * *

As soon as I checked out of my room, I called my brother, asking if he had any contacts in Atlanta so I wouldn't have to rent a car for the drive home to Knoxville.

First opportunity, I'd be getting hammered to forget Dom and the mammoth amount of life-or-death coding work he'd dropped in my lap. Too bad a girl can't drink and drive several hundred miles.

"You're coming back already? What the fuck happened?" Firefly growled into the receiver.

"Nothing, nothing! Ty has kids, and our meeting got cut short. You're about to find out what that's all about." I smiled, trying to focus on knowing I'd be an aunt soon, once Cora's baby came. "I'm flying into Atlanta tonight. I don't want to deal with the drive in the dark, so I'm wondering if there are any club assets in Georgia?"

"Not many since shit went down there last time. Just Dust."

Dust. My heart nearly exploded behind my ribs.

Dust, with his strong, quiet, teasing ways.

Dust, with his hands and mouth that set me on fire. I always had a strange fascination with scary body art thanks to Firefly, and the tapestry painted on Dusty's skin made my brother's look like a child's painting.

Dusty, the man I never should've kissed, much less thrown another hook to, who'd known me when I was just Firefly's scrawny little sis. Now, he treated me like a woman, and I ate it up.

Beautiful, dangerous, bossy Dusty.

"You're sure there aren't any prospects?" I asked softly. About a hundred butterflies took flight in my belly, imaging all the things that could happen if I took a ride home with Dust tonight. Alone.

"No. Prez is the only option, take him or leave him. I can't come down and get you with everything going on up here, unless you're in a bind."

"Nah, it's fine. Thanks, Huck. I'll see you soon for the baby shower."

Perfect timing. The agent at the gate to my flight announced the start of boarding, and I had about five more minutes to decide if I wanted to give Dust a call before I got on.

I wanted my ride. Hell, maybe part of me wanted to ride him, but I'd never live it down if I did.

And if I broke down in front of him, remembering my mess with Dom, the double life I'd been leading for the past year as a hostage to the animal I should've been smart enough to avoid...

The club would have open war.

God, I wanted to see him again. Forgetting the mobster's blood chilling threats sounded pretty good just then, too. I needed a distraction.

If there was any man who could make me forget my secret woes, it was the big, gorgeous bastard whose number was staring me in the face on my contacts.

"Attention, attention, attention! We're now boarding rows 17-D," the agent blared into the microphone.

Decision time. I clenched my teeth, letting out the biggest sigh in the world when I pressed the call button, and watched with my stomach twisted in a knot, while my phone connected to Dust.

IV: Past and Present (Dust)

Several Minutes Earlier

I sat on my bike, watching the sun slip down across the horizon. Several thousand men were buried here beneath the tombstones, long lost boys who'd died in every damned war this country ever had since 1830.

Conflict ran deep in my veins on both sides. My great great granddaddy fought for Dixie in a cavalry regiment on my old man's side. Ma's side had my great great uncle, an artillery Major for the North, who'd crawled through hell when East Tennessee became ground zero for all the blood soaked brother-on-brother savagery defining the war.

History buff? Maybe I was, but I'd punch anybody in the face if they ever called me a nerd.

I thought about my family a lot, bloodlines steeped in the country's wickedest turmoil, trickling down across generations. The Deadly Pistols name wouldn't exist for this club if it wasn't for my old man's gun, passed down to me since it did its time killing men on these battlefields more than a hundred and fifty years ago.

The gun was locked up at the clubhouse, stuffed in a wooden box I rarely opened for anybody. Seeing her, touching her, that was just for me.

Every brother wore her symbols all over, inked deep in our skin. I had a whole arsenal scrawled across my back, my chest, smoke curling out of the steel barrels on my arms. Saw them every morning I woke up, every time I shed my clothes, every time I got between some girl's legs and fucked her 'til she screamed my name.

Deadly Pistols Motorcycle Club. So much history, and a lot more blood, wrapped up in a tidy symbol that grinned back at every man who'd ever put on the patch. We'd sworn our lives to the skull, the wings, and the smoking guns. Wouldn't ever change.

This club, this symbol, they went straight to my family, kin my blood and patch alike. Made me who I was, straight to my fuckin' core.

Right now, the club deserved a helluva lot better than it'd gotten.

I took a long pull on my pipe, pinching it between my fingers, thinking about how we were still busy undoing my old man's bullshit, several years after he'd met the reaper.

Early had his fun, and he fucked a lot of people over. My daddy made too many enemies, blew too much money, and left Ma's heart in tatters. Left that poor, sweet woman waiting to join him some day on the other side, but I knew they'd be going their separate ways.

Ma was never bound for hell like him. He deserved every fuckin' lick of the flame for what he'd done to the club, done to his brothers, done to me.

Fuck you, Danny, his ghost growled in my ear, as he did way too goddamned often. *I ain't the only one bound for fire.*

Someday, we'll meet again, boy. Count on it.

Growling, I stubbed out my pipe, wanting to put bad memories behind me. I had my getaway.

I was eager to start the long ride home from Georgia, heading back into the Smokies. I'd take the off roads leaving this state at night so the Deads wouldn't have a shot at getting me alone.

They came around these parts, but they'd been slow to snap up the free territory we'd left for the assholes after killing our old friends-turned-enemies, the Atlanta Torches. Even if they showed, they'd have plenty of street gangs to fight in the city, so many battles it'd stretch a club as big as theirs to the bone.

I had my key in the ignition when my phone went off.

I ripped it out, looked at the screen, and saw a name that turned my dick to stone. "Hannah? Where are you?"

"About to get off the runway and come home, Dusty."

"Yeah? What's wrong, darlin'?" She shouldn't have been calling me from the airport. Adrenaline filled my veins, overwhelming the desire to finish what we'd started at Firefly's wedding for just a second.

When a woman rang this line, she only did it for two reasons.

Either she wanted every inch of me up inside her, or she needed me to bust heads.

Both were plenty valid. I'd never said no to either one, and I sure wasn't gonna break trends with this little minx.

"Why does something have to be wrong? Can't a girl just call to say hello?" Her sarcasm warmed my ears, sharp and sexy as ever. "Listen, I talked to Firefly. I'm coming into Atlanta tonight, and I don't want to deal with a rental. My brother said you're the only club man down there. Honestly, making your head any bigger is just about the last thing I want to do, but I need a ride to Tennessee even more, so...I think you see my dilemma."

"Yeah, darlin', I think so, too." I smiled, feeling the fight-or-flight hornet swarm in blood calm down, surrendering to lust, running in my blood thick as warm honey. "I'll be at the airport, waiting. When do you get in?"

"Four hours or so. Sometime around ten. I'm not much for driving at night, but I'll make an exception if I'm the passenger."

"Gonna have to make an exception for my bike, too, babe. Only way we're getting home." I heard her suck in a sharp breath, and suppressed a laugh. "Calm down. We'll take it slow through the mountains and stop for coffee to stay warm. You can keep those little hands around me as tight as you want. I won't even try anything crazy."

"You'd better not!" she squealed, sucking in another sharp breath as soon as the words are out.

Almost like the sounds I imagined she'd make all red and sweaty, riding every inch of my cock. *Fuck.*

That hard-on in my jeans jerked something fierce. Knew I'd probably have to pull over at a gas station just to jerk off if I wanted to make it home with this girl without losing my damned mind.

"Seriously, babe, just get your sweet ass home. I'll be waiting. Text me wherever you want to meet as soon as you're on the tarmac."

She hesitated for several seconds, saying nothing. I wondered if she'd really take me up on the ride, or take off with that rental after all.

"Okay, Dusty. I will. I appreciate the help here, even if you might be the last man I want giving me a helping hand."

Click. The line went dead, and I saw her name flashing cold on the screen.

Stuffing my phone in my pocket, I started my bike, and headed for the closest bar by the airport. I'd have a couple beers while I waited for her long ass flight to come in.

Perfect timing, really. Gave me a few hours to figure out how the fuck I'd keep a lid on my raging need to screw this girl 'til we both went blind.

* * * *

Several hours later, just after ten, I saw her standing on the curb. Uptight, punctual, and sexy as the last time we'd kissed.

Hannah squeezed the handle on her suitcase when she saw me getting off my bike and coming toward her. White knuckles meant nervous, increasing the odds that her pretty blue eyes liked everything they drank in when they looked at me.

"Been awhile, darlin'. Let's get this loaded up and hit the road," I said, pulling the suitcase from her hands.

Surprisingly, it didn't weigh much.

"You're lucky I traveled light," she said, trailing after me. "Going home on a bike wouldn't even be an option if I'd brought more of my wardrobe."

"You'd be surprised what fits on this bike when it needs to. I'm more than happy to have you tag along with your thongs and handcuffs tucked in this bag. You and your kinky shit are always welcome on this ride, darlin'."

Her eyes flew open, looking like they were about to leave her head. "Dusty! I've only been here for two minutes, and we're already joking about sex?"

"Who said I was joking?" I narrowed my eyes. Extending a hand to her, I wrapped her little fingers in mine, and passed her a spare helmet with my free hand. "Don't worry, babe. All screwing around aside, I'm not getting between your legs 'til you show me you're ready. We both do business. Let's treat this like any other professional deal, something you're entitled to because you're part of this MC. I've got too damned much respect for your brother to do anything else."

That seemed to calm her. Relaxing her grip on my hand, she straddled the bike, climbing on behind me and fixing her helmet.

"Okay, damn it. Deal. But I swear, Dust, if you go back on *anything*...I'll get off first chance I've got and hitchhike the rest of the way."

"I actually believe it," I told her. "Everybody with the last name Davis is stubborn as a mule. Firefly's shown me that a hundred times over, and I know you've got the same spark, seeing where you're at with life."

I watched her in the mirrors. That perfectly beautiful chestnut hair disappeared into the black shell protecting her skull.

Didn't know if the helmet made my temptation better or worse. It had a way of bringing out her other features, outlining her big blue eyes, her rosy lips, those white cheeks I wanted to paint red with fuckin' lust.

My compliments brought a smile to her face, but it seemed like there was something else, too. A quiet, halfway hidden sadness, some secret shit chewing at her, gnawing deep. Any girl who looked like that had secrets beyond her rocking body. I'd pull them out of her, sooner or later, one honest kiss at a time.

"Let's just make some miles," she said, curling her hands around my waist.

We rolled out of the city without another word. Left me wondering why the hell having her hands on my abs felt more electric than anything else.

* * * *

We were about to cross the border into Tennessee just south of Chattanooga, a little after midnight, when all hell broke loose.

Rain. Fog. Lightning. Thunder so loud it shook the countryside.

Hannah had been damned quiet up 'til then. Her hands did all the talking I needed to hear, tensing up against my skin, making her cling to me like a scared cat.

Who the hell could blame her? We were having a good old fashioned mountain storm, crashing straight through the summer sky and rolling toward the Smokies, breaking up the humid summer sweetness.

Too bad we got our asses caught right in the middle.

Another lightning bolt hit the ground off to the side of us, taking out a tree. My old navy senses stabbed my brain, slowing everything down, making me duck and weave like I was back on a speedboat, chasing the sea.

"Dusty!" Hannah screamed my name while we missed a few more hulking fallen branches.

"Hold on with everything you've got," I growled back at her, gripping my bike's handlebars. "We're in for some chop heading down this exit."

At least, I thought there was an exit in front of us.

I took the chance, knowing any side road was safer than staying on this highway. My bike roared down it, away from the poor bastards on the road just as blinded by the rain and chaos as us. Every car passing was a human error waiting to happen.

I couldn't let it. Not with this woman behind me, shaking like a leaf, gone so quiet she must've been praying for her life.

Didn't have a clue if we'd hit the border or not, passing into Tennessee. Just then, I didn't much care. My eyes scanned for neon signs, seeking a truck stop, a motel, anything that'd keep us safe while we waited out the storm.

Several more long, rainy miles passed before I saw it.

ROOMS AVAILABLE! The signed blinked through the

blurry waterfall pouring down on us like a dream. Just a crooked old sign lit neon pink.

I didn't think twice while I swerved in, ramming my bike into one of the empty spaces. Hannah's nerves were too fried to get up when I told her to.

"Let's go, babe. Let me help." She didn't fight me when I reached for her hands, pulled her off the seat, and into my arms.

Practically carried her inside while we moved into the dingy little front office. There was nobody at the register, so we stood there waiting. My arms were still around her, and I swore when I realized it.

"Shit. I'm sorry, I saw the storms coming when I checked the weather this afternoon. Thought we could beat 'em. Also didn't think hell itself was opening up and dumping the whole fuckin' sea on us."

Another lightning bolt stabbed through sky above the parking lot, drowning every other sound in savage thunder. My grip on her softened, sliding down toward her hips, palming that little nook near her belt line, where some man was gonna be lucky to put a kid one day.

"We'll wait this out, darlin'. Won't hit the road 'til it stops and the weather report on my phone says the coast is clear. You okay?" I asked.

"Not if you think I'm getting back on that bike tonight!" She spun, jerking away from me, her back going flat against the wall. She sighed, pushing her wet bangs out of face, big blue eyes softening. "Look, I'm sorry, Dusty. I really am. It's been a long trip. I'm tired, burned out, and it looks like there's no chance I'll get home anytime before four in the morning."

Seeing her freak the fuck out didn't even bother me. I stepped up slowly, a smile on my lips, letting my eyes roam her throat and her face.

This time, I took her softly in my arms. Reached out, cupped her chin, and softly pushed my fingertips into her skin.

"Ain't a problem. We can get ourselves a room here tonight, and wait for mornin'. It's just a short hop home from here. An hour, maybe an hour and a half. None of the boys are gonna miss my ass for a few more hours."

Nodding softly, she pulled away from me, and stepped up to the counter, ringing the bell. A small, older man stepped out of the little room behind the desk a few seconds later.

We made our arrangements quick. One room for us to share, the best he had in this run down pit stop, deserted thanks to the storm. Going for two would've been risking roaches or bed bugs, but Hannah asked about it, telling me she'd pay for everything.

I leaned in, whispering my worries in her ear. Bugs seemed to set her on edge, so she agreed to one. Took every fiber in my bones not to get up in arms about that. But I gave her a pass to soothe things over, watching as she slipped the man her card to run.

I gave the lazy little fuck behind the counter a dirty look. Too many off-the-books shit motels like this had fucked over my club. Not so long ago, we had more dirty bars, motels, trucker spas, and whorehouses in the mountains. Same place Skinny Boy had rescued his old lady, Meg, from.

"It's straight down the hall, sir. Last door on your right," the owner said. Hannah grabbed her bag and walked off before she heard the last part. "Only one bed, I'm afraid. Our spare cots are busted right now, so I can't offer any help."

"Forget it. We'll live," I told him, before I took off, heading for the room with the keys in my hand.

Yeah, we'll live. Assuming laying next to the hottest little ass I've wanted in years doesn't make me have a stroke tonight.

I didn't say shit to Hannah, stepping past her to unlock the door. Let her find out our dilemma once she opened it, tuned on the light, and we stepped into the tiny room.

It was cleaner than I'd expected. I made the rounds, looking for any signs of screwed up locks on the windows that could make it easy for anyone to get in, or bugs waiting behind the headboard.

Nothing. Small favors went a long way tonight.

"Well…this is just *great,* isn't it?" she said quietly, looking at me as I flopped down on the mattress. "You're going to take the whole thing yourself?"

I lifted my head, mischief beading in my eyes. "Nope. We're sharing the bed, darlin'."

"Sharing?!" Damn if her cheeks didn't go rosy red when she turned her head. "You know that isn't going to work. We can't forget what happened at the wedding…"

"I remember just fine, Hannah. Told you, I ain't doing shit to you, if you don't beg. I'm the one in control, remember? You're not getting so much as another kiss 'til you're good and ready. So, you can come on over, take off those wet clothes, and get some shut eye."

For a second, she stood there like a statue. Staring me down, one hand perched on her hip, wondering if she can trust me not to tear off her clothes the instant she laid down next to me.

Truth be told, it wouldn't be easy keeping these hands, this mouth, and this cock to myself. Thankfully, age had its advantages, like helping a man save the fire and brimstone for the times when he finally sunk into a pussy craving every inch of him.

Blue balls had nothing on my word.

I swore on everything I had I wouldn't fuck this chick 'til she was good and ready. Yes, *ready*.

Ready to whimper.

Ready to moan.

Ready to scream my name when I frigged her clit so hard she squirted all over my balls.

"Darlin', the sheets are getting cold. I know you need the sleep. If you're still pondering the ifs, ands, and buts in your sweet head, you can stop. Here's some collateral so you know I'm going by my word."

I sat up and stretched. She watched me stand, throwing off my cut, working on my belt. I stripped to my boxers, only thing I still had on that wasn't soaked, pulling out my knife and gun before I let my jeans hit the floor.

"Here," I growled, stepping up to her, holding out my weapons. "You can hang onto these for the night, if they'll make you feel better. If you think my word ain't good enough, you're welcome to stick a bullet or a blade wherever you think it'll hurt the most the minute I put a finger on you."

She grabbed the weapons weakly, shaking her head. "Dusty…fine. You're a good man, and you've been around long enough for me to know that, without any doubt. I trust you. That's not the problem."

"No?" I said, cocking my head. "Then what the fuck is?"

We locked eyes. Must've stared into each other's souls for a solid minute, her not saying shit, but her eyes giving me enough hints.

She wouldn't tell me outright. I watched as she broke the gaze first, shuffling to the other side of the bed, laying my gun and knife down on the nightstand next to her. I listened to wet, slippery clothes coming off skin.

Damn if my cock didn't throb each time I heard something hit the floor. I hated having to make that fuckin' promise not to touch her, knowing I'd catch seven kinds of hell if I ever broke my word, inside and out.

No, I knew what was eating her. She wanted it as bad as I did, but for some reason, the girl was too afraid to admit it.

"You can turn around now," she said.

I did, and saw her in bed, the sheet bundled tightly around her. A second later, I crashed down next to her, ready to focus all my attention on shutting up the lust churning in my veins.

"I don't mean to lead you on, Dust. You know as well

as I do what could happen if we get too friendly, go too far...wouldn't be good for either one of us, much less your club." She spoke softly in the darkness, almost a whisper, like she was afraid to finally hammer down the truth.

She swallowed something hard and bitter caught in her throat. "Please don't hate me. I really do appreciate the ride home, and stopping here tonight, just for me. After Huck, I think you're the best man I know wearing that patch, though all of you are pretty great. I –"

"Darlin' – hush." Reaching across the bed, I put my finger gently against her lips. "We've got nothing else to talk about 'til mornin'. You just get your beauty sleep, and I'll stroke myself off for being the biggest, baddest looking guardian angel you ever met."

That got a laugh outta her. Fuck, her sounds were so sweet, so innocent, so good they touched my heart for a micro-second instead of just that hard-on I pushed into the mattress, trying to stamp it out.

"Goodnight, Dusty," she said.

"'Night, babe. I've got an alarm set to wake us up by eleven to check out."

A little while later, I laid there wide awake in the darkness, listening to her softly breathing in her sleep.

Couldn't shake the truth she said because it was the same thing I knew deep down inside. Hannah Davis was too damned good for any man in this club.

I knew it, she knew it, and so did her big brother. If she ever crossed a line she shouldn't, or anybody else did, my Enforcer would be ready to jerk their spine outta their skin, even if that person outranked him.

Exactly what he ought to do as her big brother. No, fuck, I had to keep it in my pants with her. Didn't need the drama or the trouble with war on the horizon in a few more months.

Wouldn't be long 'til I came back through these parts, my club at my back, riding against the wind and into the bloodbath ahead. We'd take out the Deads, win ourselves a trade route with Blackjack's Grizzlies or Throttle's Devils, or we'd all die trying.

The club's problems were a nice distraction from fucking the beauty sprawled out next to me. I focused on them harder when she rolled in her sleep, moving toward me. Shit, now her half-naked skin pressed against mine, with nothing but a sheet between us.

I'd been tortured a few times on runs that went bad, and they weren't half as rough as this. Had to think of anything that wasn't Hannah's fuck-worthy ass wedged dangerously close to my dick, and I had to do it fast.

Sometime before sunup, I heard my old man's voice. Early always came to me in my dreams, day or night, whenever I didn't shut his evil ass down with Doctor Jack or Jim.

I can't believe this shit. You always were an indecisive fuckin' pussy, Danny.

Sleeping with this fine bitch – just fuckin' sleeping with her – proves I was right. Hard to believe I left my club in the hands of a boy who don't even know how to use his dick like a man.

Rage coursed through me. Wanted to walk up to the

corner where I saw his shadow talking to me, grab him by the throat, and spit in his big, bearded face.

Next time I looked over, he was gone. The fuck always disappeared before I could tell him how wrong he was, or how I was sick and tired of hearing his twisted shit.

I didn't run this club into the ground, old man.

I didn't get brothers killed for nothin'.

I didn't shit on Ma and leave her heart in a million pieces just for strange pussy.

All those truth bombs and more lodged in my throat.

Worst of all, I knew it wasn't really Early, coming up from his grave to taunt me like a ghost. It was my own brain, pulling make believe demons out of nowhere, mining them in my subconscious.

Deep down, some evil, screwed up part of my soul fought the rest of it, trying to tell me I wasn't good enough to bring my boys everything they deserved.

Good fuckin' luck.

I'd keep fighting, damn it. And one of these days, I'd spread the legs of the angel laying next to me, when she wanted it so bad I'd feel her little teeth digging into my skin.

She belonged on my cock, one way or another. I belonged in her, teaching her sweet young ass the dirty, addicting things a woman oughta know at least once in her life.

Wanted it. Needed it. Imagined it, right down to how her face would look when I took what was mine.

Opening her up, tasting her, fucking her with everything I had. Wasn't a question of if, but when.

Whenever that day came, I had a feeling it'd be the same day this club smiled on me for leading it to glory, bringing every brother a woman, a bottle of whiskey, and enough peace to enjoy it.

V: The Good Fight (Hannah)

It was early morning, and I fought the good fight.

Despite my worries, Dust was a total gentleman the whole night through. At some point, his arm strayed over to my side. I woke up with it wrapped around my waist, the tattoos inked in his skin shining beneath the sun.

Why didn't I push it away, or wriggle out of his grasp? Deep down, I already knew.

He made me crave his lips again, even when I just laid there and looked at them, studying the rough contours and tiny scars in his strong face.

He made me wet like nobody else ever had. Sure, I had a weakness for men with loud bikes and ferocious tattoos. Went with the territory in the dirty, dangerous place I'd grown up in, especially after Firefly found his place among their ranks.

Dusty made me think about taking my V-card and burning it in the worst way, and that wasn't going to change. Not when we finally got up and went about our day, or when I inevitably thought about him again the next time I wandered through my phone's contacts.

My nerves tingled in the best ways. Lust, fear, adrenaline, and disbelief all clashed in my blood, raging louder than the tremendous storms that swept over us last night, landing us in the same bed.

It wouldn't take much to give away everything now, if I wanted.

My instinct was raw, hungry, urging me over and over to pull the covers down, climb on top of him, and start to lick every sweet inch of his gorgeous skin.

Obviously, I had bigger problems to deal with once he brought me home. I'd need a whole new build for my app to cover everything, including the bastards telling me I'd die if I didn't cover their asses, too.

Thinking about what Dusty thought in his dreams each time he groaned should've been the least of my worries. But the biggest, baddest, most beautiful problem I'd ever seen was sprawled out next to me, his hand pulling at my hip a little more each time his face twitched in his sleep.

If only I could've given into him for a single second. Just reached out, touched him, slid one hand down the delicious stubble covering his cheek. Maybe it would've wrecked my worries for the rest of the day, cast Dom and his devils into the dark and dirty part of my head where they belonged.

My fingers stiffened. Slowly, my hand came up, moving toward Dust's face.

One little stroke, I told myself, just enough to feel his skin. I was nearly to his cheek when his eyelids opened, so suddenly I gasped.

Two bright, fearless grey eyes stared into mine, beaming

with total control. If he was surprised, he didn't show it.

"I-I'm sorry," I stammered. "I was trying to get the change you threw on your nightstand. Just wanted to get a drink from the vending machine, maybe see if they had a little coffee. I would've paid you back, obviously."

The boy had talent.

How the hell did he tie my tongue in knots and make my heart beat a hundred miles an hour over nothing? *Damn.*

Those steel grey eyes piercing into my soul narrowed, and the ghost of a smile tugged at his lips. "Looked more like you were thirsty for somethin' else, darlin'. You want some of that, be my guest any time. Funny, I always thought you'd at least say good mornin' first before moving straight to fuckin'."

"That's *not* what I was after," I lied, turning around in the sheets and pulling them tight, dragging myself out of his grip. "I told you already, I was thirsty."

"Mm-hmm," he said, rolling on his back, barely suppressing a smug smile. "Soda machine's down the hall. You take whatever you need off my nightstand, or below my belt line. Your choice, Hannah."

I stood, keeping the sheet around me. It wasn't like he was blind to my body, seeing how I'd stripped down to my bra and panties. Still, I'd lose it if he had a second look with *that* expression on his face.

"Actually, I think I need a shower. Why don't you go find us something to help wake ourselves up? I could really use a snack, too. Haven't eaten since the crappy salad they served on the plane last night."

"Whatever you say, babe. I'll take care of all your needs."

God! Is there anything he won't say that isn't loaded with innuendo?

I seriously had to stop and wonder how much was Dusty screwing with me, and how much was in my head, making it worse.

My nose wrinkled, unsure whether I was more annoyed with him or myself for getting wetter the longer he stared at me, the more he teased.

I couldn't even fire back. Sauntering past him, I held my sheet tighter, grabbing my little suitcase for a fresh change of clothes.

The long, cool shower helped. I took my time, hoping to God he'd be dressed and looking normal by the time I stepped out.

We'd started the day on a bad note. I wasn't going to deal with his biker bastard flirting the whole way back to Knoxville, even if it was only a short stretch home.

A couple hours on his bike might be an eternity with this kind of tension hanging in the balance.

No, we had to go on. Which meant touching his stupidly huge, hard, arrogant body, feeling him bristle with joy whenever my hands moved a little too low on his abs for their own good.

I hated this ridiculous dance, wilder than the pheromones that must've swirled around us every time we shared the same room. Hated it straight down to my core, which ached like a fiend for Dusty's hands, his lips, his savage, sexy threats smoldering in my ear.

Hated it.

Hated myself.

Hated him and his defiantly gorgeous looks, his testosterone incarnate, his ability to put every woman under a spell that made her want to drop panties and slide down on his stereotypically huge cock.

By the time I stepped out of the shower, dried myself off, and changed my clothes, I pressed my ear against the door, listening intently for him outside. The TV was on low, a morning weather report or something droning in the background.

Had he gone out to get us food and coffee? At least it meant he was up and about, which hopefully meant dressed, too.

Of course, I had to turn my head and catch a glimpse of myself in the mirror. There I was, bent over with my ear cocked against the door, worried I couldn't handle a naked man in the next room when I'd just walked away from the latest round of death threats.

Ridiculous. I jerked up, blushing, annoyed with myself for trying to spy on him like an anxious little schoolgirl.

I'd only known him half my adult life, after all. He was a fixture in the distance since the time Huck started wearing his prospect patch, bringing us spare food, giving rides, and doing everything to support a family down on its luck like a good brother in the MC should.

Club life fascinated me. Maybe my more sensible side had done everything in its power to run from the past, forget I ever lived in a trailer with meth addicts down the block, and had to fight to learn everything I knew because the defeated teachers at the run down school we went to stopped caring a long time ago.

I rose above all that. Made myself better. I'd been on track for riches, fame, stability, maybe a good man in a button down shirt and tie with a graduate degree…and then I took that fucking loan from a bloodthirsty shark, and blew my life to pieces.

It always came back to where it started, didn't it? Dust was practically family. My big brother's friend and boss since I'd been old enough to understand what those patches meant, and why that space between my legs began to burn every time I looked at him long enough.

The issue between us – the reason why we'd never be friends or one night stands or even more than that – didn't have anything to do with me being 'too good for him.' The drama it would create in the club with Firefly and everybody else didn't even matter either.

None of it did. I had to keep my distance, screw my head on, and pretend we didn't want to rip each other's clothes off for one simple reason.

He was everything I ran away from.

Just a big, handsome anchor threatening to yank me back to my roots, and that scared the ever loving crap out of me.

"Hey." His fist banged gently on the door, practically making me jump out of my skin. "Your coffee's getting cold, darlin'. Everything okay in there?"

I held my breath and grabbed the doorknob, tugging it open. My eyebrows went up as soon as I saw him, two mugs in one hand, and dressed…mostly.

"What the hell happened to your shirt?" I said, grudgingly taking the coffee and raising it to my lips.

"Still soaked from last night. I ain't wearing a cloth with holes in it sprouting mildew the whole way home. Having this cut slung over my shoulders will have to do."

Great. Not only did I have to hang onto him while we took the twists and turns through the mountains, I needed to cling to his *naked* abs underneath the open leather vest.

"Brought you some biscuits and gravy from the place up the street. Firefly always said you two loved 'em growing up."

Whatever else I felt, my stomach growled, reminding me that none of this craziness was worth passing up my favorite breakfast.

We sat down on our bed, tucking into our food. This town had to be tiny, judging by the lack of infrastructure and stores glowing through the rain, but somebody here knew how to cook.

"Wow. These just might be the best I've ever had since grandma's." Remembering her brought a smile to my lips.

"Yeah?" Dust asked, taking another huge bite of his own. "Never knew your granny could still cook when she was around. Firefly said her arthritis got real bad before she passed. Damned fine lady, I met her a couple times before I went into the Navy."

"Oh, no, she could barely hold her hands steady enough

to measure flour by the end. But nobody could stop that woman from fixing her Sunday breakfasts. I think she would've walked over hot coals and broken glass to do it. Best square meal of the week Huck and me had, really, especially after mama couldn't work anymore."

He nodded. "Here's to breakfast. We might have a reason to see this little town again someday."

"We?" I asked, taking another big sip of coffee, eyeing him over my cup.

"Sure." Dust smiled, realizing his mistake, running one hand through the salt and pepper stubble on his chin. "I don't close the door on nothing, darlin'. Maybe that's part of getting older and wiser, who the fuck knows. Truth is, I'm certain I'll be coming through these parts again with my boys when we decide to take a nice slice of Georgia for the club. Always a chance I might come back on my own someday, too, maybe with a lady at my side."

"Won't be me. Don't get your hopes up, Dusty." I turned my face to my food, cheeks warming, hating myself for sounding like such a bitch.

"You sure love hiding how you really feel, don't you, darlin'? Far as I'm concerned, we had ourselves a great time on this little getaway, even if I didn't find out what's underneath those bright purple panties you wore to bed."

More wicked heat rushed straight to my face, licking my cheeks bright red. His hand cupped my shoulder, gradually winding its way down my arm, leaving me covered in goosebumps.

"Don't ever think we don't have an understanding. I

know you want it just as bad as I do, but we've both got a hundred reasons it won't happen. It can't. Last time I'm teasing, Hannah. Let's finish up our grub and check the fuck outta here."

Ugh. Why did I seem so disappointed that this might be the last time today, or ever?

We finished our breakfast in peace, and then I got my stuff together, following him outside. It only took a few minutes to check out before we headed to the parking lot.

It was as warm day for early summer. The humidity in the air started adding an extra curl to my naturally wavy hair in just a few seconds. One more thing I didn't need as I tucked as much as I could into my helmet, slid down on the back seat, and curled my hands around his waist.

"You good?" he asked, just before starting up the engine.

"Yeah, Dusty. For real."

Like hell I am. I lied through my teeth for about the tenth time since we'd gotten together last night, but it wasn't like I had another option.

We took off into the high mid-day sun, relishing the shade from the trees along the winding roads. Didn't even stop for gas the whole way to the Smokies, his engine purring a reassuring white noise that nearly put me in a trance.

Honestly, I welcomed it. Needed something to forget about his warm skin against my fingertips, slabs of rock hard muscle more built than most men half his age. With a few more years on him, he could've been my father, or at least a solid stand in for my big brother.

Didn't matter whatsoever. My heart craved what it liked, and that desire sizzled every time we took the winding exits or climbed the elevation home, pushing my hands just a little more firmly into his immaculate flesh.

He was a bastard, a killer, a beast from a world I only understood because Dom dragged me into it. None of it stopped me from wanting him, and that steady, constant attraction turned me into a sticky summer mess by the time we were on Knoxville's streets.

We took the long way through town, heading for the outskirts, where I had my big, beautiful home just past the gate. Funny to think Huck and Cora shared it not so long ago, back when they were in trouble, enjoying more passion there than I ever had.

Dust pulled up to the gate before he helped me off, his engine still rumbling, making words difficult. At least, the kind of words I wanted to say, whispers about how fucking hard it was to step away without so much as a goodbye kiss.

"Take care of yourself, darlin'. We'll see each other at the clubhouse or some shit soon enough. If you're ever in a bind again, you've got my number." He smiled, all southern gentleman behind his smug lips and savage exterior.

"Dusty…" For a second, we stopped and stared, as soon as I said his name.

There was only one way to tell him what I'd wanted to say the last fifty miles home. *Fuck it.*

I leaned forward, dragging my fingernails through his short, dark hair, catching the tightest hold I could while I brought my mouth to his.

Forget the lightning when we'd kissed before. *This* was a hurricane, straight plasma hitting my system and igniting every single nerve. Probably the pent up want, the need coursing through me, the insane, unworkable desires I'd fought like hell to suppress.

It was the knowledge that this couldn't work, however badly we wanted it to. It was our bodies in full on mutiny with our hearts and our heads.

If he'd picked me up, thrown me back on his bike, and driven us to some secluded place, I wouldn't have stopped him.

But he pulled away, a familiar glint fading in his grey eyes like embers dying in burnt charcoal. "Darlin', you need to go. Now. Kiss me like that again, and I'm following you inside."

We exchanged one last smile before I turned my back, heading through the gate.

If we couldn't do what we really wanted, then at least I could thank him for the ride. I'd given him a real kiss goodbye.

I must've held my breath the whole way through my gate, across the long driveway leading to my home, and didn't let it out until I was inside. Then I collapsed against the wall, my chest rising and falling in shallow waves, rapid as my heartbeat.

We'd just had our last real kiss as a couple never meant to be. It gave me a shred of relief, sure, but it also tangled up my stomach into pure grief now that I was finally alone.

I'd see him again, no doubt about it. But we would

never, ever lock lips like that.

It ended today.

I had to let this go, for my good and his. Didn't mean it wouldn't sting like an utter bitch. Worse than the hot, bitter tears sliding down my cheeks, whenever I finally let everything I'd been holding for several hundred miles come pouring out.

* * * *

Four Weeks Later

My phone rang and I picked it up. Whenever I saw *Unavailable* on the screen, every hair on my body stood on end. I was probably the only person in the world praying for a telemarketer.

"Hello?" I answered, drawing in a breath.

The man was quiet for the first thirty seconds, before he slowly, angrily cleared his throat. "You got our shit loaded yet, or what?"

"Dom." Just saying his name turned my blood cold. "I'm not in front of my screen right now. If you want all the technicals, I can take a look. I –"

"Nah, peach, you know I fuckin' don't. I pass all that along to Brandon, who understands what the fuck you're saying when you talk about algorithms and structures. I want you to tell me it's done, and nothing about it's gonna be a problem."

I bit my tongue to stop everything I wanted to say from coming out. "You know I asked for more guidance when I sent you that text last week. I said there might be a security loophole that's a little beyond my means to figure out. You want this rushed, without giving me the right time and resources? Then I'm telling you mistakes will happen that could put us all at risk."

"Excuse me, bitch. Are you trying to tell me I'm wrong?"

Obviously, you stupid fucking jackass, I thought, seizing every fiber of willpower I had to keep from mouthing off to a monster.

"No," I said quietly. "I'm saying I need you to run this by your own technical team, see if maybe they can fix the vulnerability I don't have a good answer about how to approach it. I'm stumbling around in the dark."

"You're putting me on." Dom paused.

About two tense seconds ticked by before the explosion hit me in the ear, so loud and sudden I had to hold my phone away.

"After everything we've done, you're putting me the fuck on! Probably setting me up for a goddamned fucking sting, thinking I'm a chump!"

My heart went wild, banging against my ribs. I peaked around the corner, pressing the phone to my ear, wondering if he already had his men outside. They could've been waiting for the faintest signal to come crashing through the window and slash my throat.

"Dom, that's a little paranoid, don't you think?" I asked, trying to sound sweet instead of petrified. "What reason would I possibly have for going to the police? I'd lose out on my money, my house, probably wind up in a jail cell right next to you. Besides, my brother's in the Deadly Pistols, and working with cops isn't really in our makeup."

"Shut up," he snapped. "Shut up, you lying fucking cunt. I'll have my boys run a check on every fucking file you've sent, every text, every voice mail over the past couple months. If I see anything suspicious – anything at all – you're coming cross country for another face-to-face. Don't bother flying, we'll send somebody for you, and it'll be a one way trip."

"Go ahead, do it, if it'll make you feel better," I whispered, like a woman trying to tame a lion preparing to pounce. "I've got nothing to hide. If anything, I'm trying to work with you, figure out how we can hide the routing junk in the app so neither of us gets busted."

"That's your goddamned problem," he growled. "You think we loaned you several mil just so you could drop the fucking ball when you got your pretty little head into some coding quagmire you couldn't handle? You oughta be working your little fingers to the bone instead of jerking off those biker fucks you call family. If you don't, every single one of them is dead, and you'll wish you were by the time we get done with you."

I stood like stone, desperately searching for my happy place. Anything to send my psyche somewhere else before he reduced me to a sobbing, whimpering mess.

"Stop fucking crying. Tell me you'll fix this, peach. Tell me you know exactly what we're doing, and that we didn't make a big mistake wasting all this time, thinking you'd pay us back. If we're not getting our money, we'd might as well settle this shit now, the hard way."

"I'm on it, Dom. I promise. Whatever it takes. Just...please. Have your team look things over. If they have a better fix than I do, you know I'll put it in. I'll get it right. I'll keep anybody who shouldn't be looking off both our asses, just like we agreed."

"Yeah, Hannah. Just like that. You've got three days, and not an hour more."

By the time I realize he killed the call, I'd dropped to my knees. I hovered over the floor, tears splashing the handcrafted tile, lovingly installed to complete my home after I hit my first quarter million week in revenue.

No denying it anymore. I hated this house, this fucking prison, a fancy cell I'd built for myself with the finest materials.

That little trailer Huck and me grew up in didn't seem half bad compared to this. The neighborhood meth creeps never fucked with our place as long as we flew the Pistols flag. And I never needed to install several locks on my bedroom door, a tiny deterrent that still wouldn't be enough to stop them from killing me in my sleep if they really wanted to.

Hell, I'd probably count myself lucky if they did. Dom's style was never quiet. I doubted he understood, much less respected, the fact that I was trying to save both of us from somebody with an eye for app development and an ear to the Feds from noticing a whole lot of damning transactions.

How many weeks had I worked on the fix? It had to be a solid month, except for four days where I wiped my eyes to go to a computer conference in Florida.

Now, I was back in my jail, wishing I could throw my trusty laptop on the counter straight off the deck and into the gardens below.

Knowing I had a few days wasn't going to make me feel better. I couldn't work with so much venom in my system. Fear, hate, and disappointment turned me into a fucking zombie, not a genius.

Wiping my red, angry eyes on my sleeve, I bent down and looked at my phone. I rolled through my contacts, debating whether or not I wanted to bother Huck or Cora. Talking about the baby on the way added a smile to my stressed-to-hell face.

No, not today. They didn't need to hear me breakdown when they told me about a beautiful little niece I might never live to see.

There was another number on my contacts, staring me in the face. Maybe it was finally time to take Dusty up on what he'd said the last time we'd spoken, when he let me off here after that unbelievably tense night in Georgia.

If you're ever in a bind again...

His words stuck in my head, one of the few promises any man had ever made me, that I knew wouldn't be broken.

A simple bind didn't begin to describe this slavery. I wasn't even sure if I wanted to tip him off just yet because it would put the club in serious peril.

Still, if that man did nothing else, he'd make me feel better. And right now, feeling like I wasn't about to die counted a whole hell of a lot.

* * * *

"Hannah? It's been awhile," he growled, as soon as the phone connected. "Too fuckin' long, darlin'."

"Yeah." So long I had to stop myself from spilling my soul through the phone. "Come over," I told him.

"The fuck? Are you in trouble, woman? Tell me."

"Nothing you need to worry about, Dusty." I sighed after a long, tense pause. Another lie. "I want to catch up. I need you."

"Give me ten." All he said before the phone clicked dead.

I waited on the ivory painted bench outside my front door, looking across the fireflies dancing in the evening darkness. It wasn't even ten minutes when I heard a motorcycle rumbling just past the front gate.

I punched the code next to my front door to let him in, standing in the doorway while he approached, bringing his Harley and his gorgeous self to my doorstep like it was the most natural thing in the world.

"Darlin'…what's going on?" he growled, sweeping me up into his powerful embrace.

In his embrace? Nothing. I was safe there.

His inked, muscular arms had a terrible way of making everything all right. Fire and brimstone could've been raining down around us, and it wouldn't have mattered.

Whatever power Dom and his minions had over me, it was gone like ash, stubbed out in the night the second I had Dusty here. Had him in all his growling, intense, mysteriously masculine glory.

"Just a lot on my plate lately," I lied. "I'm lonely, Dust."

"Lonely?" He pulled back, giving me a long, hard look.

I worried my eyes would betray me. If he stared into them long enough, would he see the turmoil, the man with the literal gun to my head?

Worse, he might've seen *my* mistakes. That stupid, ignorant little girl I'd been last year, snapping up a loan shark's bait because the bastard saw her shades of grey, and used them to put her in the fanciest handcuffs this side of the mountains.

"Just come in," I said, reluctantly leaving his arms. "I'll fix us some drinks."

Dust trailed me, whistling a little when we stepped into the gourmet kitchen, a massive room with artisan finishes and more appliances than I knew how to use. "Damn, girl. A boy could really fix himself some breakfast in here. Firefly said this place was fine, but I had no fuckin' clue."

I smiled, reaching for whiskey and a couple glasses. Tried to ignore the bittersweet aftershocks his words left in my system.

"I'll take mine straight," he growled, when he saw me throwing my cocktail together.

"Always so simple," I said, smiling a little wider while I poured whiskey in his shot glass, and passed it to him. "You should really broaden your horizons one of these days."

"Maybe I will, soon as I know why the hell you called me outta the blue, and wanted me over." He paused. "Spending time alone raises the risk of something happening that shouldn't. I ain't a fool, Hannah. You're up to something if you're after me."

Damn. He wasn't going to let it go, was he? I took a huge sip from my cocktail, and walked over, taking a seat next to him at the breakfast bar.

"You're so dramatic," I said, rolling my eyes. "It's just work stuff. I wanted some company. There's no bigger conspiracy than that. It's nice to see you sometimes, Dusty, believe it or not. Even nicer when you aren't looking at me like a piece of meat."

He smiled, downing his generous shot in a single gulp. "Darlin', you'd be the finest sirloin any boy ever had. If life's got you down, then that makes two of us."

The way he clinked his empty glass on the counter surprised me. My eyes went wide, staring into his strong grey eyes, wondering.

"What's going on?" I asked, laying a hand tenderly on his shoulder. "Is it the club? Firefly cut me off pretty fast when we talked last week. I thought it was just the stress from Cora and the baby, but now I'm wondering if it's something else."

"Joker," he growled. "My damned Veep's been going straight off the rails lately. All because he's got some girl chasing his tail, and he's too big a fool to let her. Don't need that kinda shit with war coming."

"War?" I repeated, watching him tense up. I realized how deadly serious this was getting, and he knew he'd said too much.

"We're settling our shit with the Deads soon once and

for all. Gonna give my club the future it deserves, every single man and woman who's part of my family, including your brother. Also gonna make good on a promise I made a long time ago to my Veep and his kin."

"Yeah? What kind of promise?"

He pushed his glass to the center of the counter. "I ain't letting that slip so easy. Pour me another drink."

I didn't even argue. Just got up, took down the bottle, and this time left it there. He took another heavy shot before he looked at me again, grey eyes burning.

"Deads killed Joker's twin brother, Piece, a few years back. Put their Grandpa in a fuckin' nursing home from the stress. Dropped my poor Veep straight into hell and back, living with the grief every damned day, going crazy for it. And that's not the worst."

"What do you mean? There's…more?"

"You said you wanted the whole story, right? I shouldn't be saying a damned thing about club biz, Hannah, but you…you've always been around. More level headed than anybody else attached to the MC. Smart enough to bootstrap your way outta the muck. In case you hadn't figured it out, I respect the fuck outta you."

He reached into his pocket, bringing out his pipe and a thick steel lighter with the club's skull and smoking pistols carved in it. "It cool to have a nip in here? It's tobacco. Never been much for anything else."

"Go ahead," I told him, walking across the kitchen to open the nearest window.

"Yeah," he said, a numb look rocking his face while he

let the tobacco hit his bloodstream. "Worst fuckin' part about all this is, I lied to my own damned club. Nobody except Joker knows what really happened to Piece, and that's the way it's gotta stay 'til I can make revenge happen on my terms. If I'd told those boys years ago, they would've gone off like loose cannons, would've gotten themselves *all* killed. The Deads are a fuck of a lot bigger than us, and when we hit 'em, it has to be like lightning. We're only getting one chance at this. It's my job to hold down the ship just a little while longer, 'til we do."

"Wow." My heart dropped into my lower belly.

If there was next to no chance before of dropping my hostage situation in his lap, then there was absolute zero now.

I couldn't stand adding one more worry to his plate. And I wouldn't put my brother through it either, who'd jump at the chance to help Dust save me, if it ever slipped out what sort of danger I'd gotten myself into.

"Enough talk, beautiful. Firefly said you've got yourself a hell of a sound system here. Let's play some rock and roll. Forget all our bullshit for a few hours."

Exactly what we needed. He was good at cheering people up, even his own big, fearsome self. I reached into my pocket for my phone, opened the app, and flicked on the radio.

Guitar chords and drums beat their way through half the house, piping through the high definition speakers I'd had put in everywhere.

"Gotta love Zeppelin, yeah?"

"They're all right, but I'm more of a country girl," I said haughtily, flicking my hair across my shoulder. "This'll do for now. Whatever makes you happy, Dusty. You're my guest."

Snorting, he stood up, pouring more whiskey into his glass and mine. He passed mine, reaching behind my back with one arm, and pulling me close.

Before I realized what was happening, we were swaying in the middle of my kitchen. Whatever I imagined might come down today when I called him up, I never thought it would lead to me *dancing* with the club's biggest badass.

"Okay, Miss Country. Now that I'd told you the big secret, what's yours? Why am I really here?" Dust's whispered burned hot in my ear. "Can't just be because you're lonely, unless you really want this cock."

I laughed, pushed roughly against his chest, until he steadied me.

"My client," I said, trying to whimper when his hands ran down my back. "He's being a real dick lately, to be honest. Expecting me to work miracles without the time or resources to do it. I'm good, Dusty, but I'm not a genius."

"No? Sounds like bullshit to me," he growled, turning us around in a slow, controlled loop. "The fact that we're standing here in this place, soaking our asses on good Johnnie, dancing to the best damned beats I've heard outside the clubhouse tells me something different. Give yourself your dues, darlin'. You've done well, and you should enjoy it."

Yeah, enjoy it, I thought. If only it were that simple.

If only I could loosen up, tell him what kind of trouble I was really in, without making anyone else suffer for my stupid debts. I brought my glass to my lips and drained the contents, wishing the fire would hurry up, turn everything in my head to sweet numbness.

"I'll try," I said, another lie. "You know, there's something missing in my life. Everybody comes over here with their jaws hanging, but they don't see what's behind the scenes, what I'd really like to own someday. I guess that bothers me."

"Yeah?" he asked, bringing his hand up my side, until it cupped my cheek in his rough palm. "Woman like you is awful close to having the whole world. What's she missing?"

Sanity. Safety. Both words I would've said if I could've been open and honest.

But that wasn't an option here, not if I wanted to keep this *grin and bear it* charade to myself.

"A good man. A family," I said, thinking, dropping more truth I should've kept bottled up. "This place is huge, Dusty, and it's lonely. I want a man I can count on someday, with dinner around the table at six o'clock sharp, and the two-point-five kids I'm entitled to."

"Aw, hell," he said, smiling and shaking his head. "Thought you were after something that'd be hard as fuck to reach. What's the deal, darlin'? It's like you haven't noticed you're damned near perfect. With your brains, your looks, your success, and that sharp little mouth, you're gonna get your pick between billionaires and princes one fine day. No fuckin' ifs, ands, or buts about it."

He leaned into me, breathing in my scent. A movement like another shot of whiskey sent straight to my stomach, except this tingled in *all* the wrong places.

God, I wanted him. Just as badly as I yearned to throw down my worries, my fears, and the mountain of work I had waiting to save my life.

"What if rich guys and royalty aren't my type?" I whispered, rubbing uncontrollably against his chest.

"You mean you've got yourself a type?"

Obviously. And right now, the type of man who turned my blood to fire was up close and personal. So close it wouldn't take much effort to surrender totally.

No more talk. Words wouldn't tell him anything I hadn't already said.

I leaned in, grabbing at his cut for support, inhaling his natural cologne of leather, oil, and pure testosterone. We made the same move simultaneously, too much pent up hunger pouring out in waves.

Our lips crashed together, two starving fiends given a feast. We kissed, we bit, we passed so much tongue back and forth I could barely breathe.

Or maybe it was just the excitement from crashing through this taboo named Dusty yet again. We'd fought the good fight, trying to stay friends bound by the club.

We'd lost horribly.

Every dirty passion I'd wanted on my lips since that first night he'd given it to me exploded. Dragging us forward, he pinned me against the counter, tangling his fingers through my hair and tilting my face to his.

Then he leaned down, taking what he'd wanted for the last few months, everything I'd secretly wanted to give.

Dust growled into my mouth. My nipples rolled against his chest like stones through our clothes. He pushed between my legs and dry humped me, giving me every hard inch beneath his jeans. I wouldn't be able to take this for long before I started tearing off clothes, begging him to take me upstairs.

Every sense I had went into overdrive. The whole world beyond my kitchen suddenly seemed brighter, louder, given new life by the storm howling in my blood. My heart banged harder, a brute, rising tempo so true even my rational side could't ignore it.

This was everything I wanted. Escape, fantasy, and mad desire rolling into one.

Raw. Animal. Real.

"Oh, God!" My breath hitched. He'd moved his head down, stamping more fiery kisses against my throat.

Dust reached for my breast, cupped it like he owned it, and began to squeeze.

"Fuck, darlin'. *Fuck.*" He barely came up from my cleavage for words.

My pussy turned into an aching mess between my legs. Paralyzed with such need I could barely twist and moan under him.

Was I going to fuck a man for the first time on my kitchen floor, or the marble counter? Definitely a good possibility.

Then a door slammed shut deep in the house, and

everything came to a dead stop. Dust spun around, one hand on his gun, the other still meshed in my hair.

"What the fuck, Hannah? I called you like five times before coming –"

Firefly froze. He looked at us like he'd just walked in on a murder scene.

Hell, at some point, he probably had. This was much worse.

"Huck! What're you doing here?" I said, about to fall over.

I stood up, unlatching myself from Dust's strong grip. The Deadly Pistols' Prez took his hand off his gun and straightened up. All three of us tried to wipe the disbelief and horror off our faces.

The most awkward time of my life had officially arrived.

Firefly never answered my question. In two more seconds, he flew forward, getting in Dust's face, grabbing on his cut and snarling like a wild animal.

"After all that fuckin' shit you gave me about keeping my hands off Cora, you fuck around with my own goddamned sister?!"

I yelped, backing up, trying to keep away from the two-man tornado about to blow my fancy kitchen to smithereens. Firefly's hand pressed deeper into Dusty's neck, but the older, wiser man leashed his anger, and made his move several seconds later.

His knee went straight into my brother's guts with a loud *whump!*

Firefly hit the floor, banging his knees, swearing silently.

He'd lost the oxygen in his lungs, totally winded by the blow.

"When you catch your breath, pick yourself up and get the fuck outta here, brother. I don't want to hurt you again." Dust's voice seemed eerily calm behind the rage written on his face.

"Huck, I'm sorry, this wasn't supposed to happen…" I crouched down next to him, both hands on his shoulders, flashing Dusty a quick look. "Guys, no more fighting."

Dust nodded, a growl stuck in his throat. I leaned closer to Huck, whispering in his ear. "Do you need anything?"

Shaking his head angrily, he stood up, almost doubling over again. He swore softly, leaned on my big stainless steel fridge for a minute, and then walked out.

I wanted to chase after him, but he was surprisingly quick for a man who'd just been sucker punched. Before I could take another step, the front door banged shut, and his bike rumbled in the distance.

"Let him go." Dust laid a stern hand on my shoulder. "Fucking shit. Looks like we've both got ourselves a few more things to worry about, darlin'."

I turned to him sadly, cold water thrown on my lust. "I'm sorry, Dusty. Don't know what came over me. We never should've started up like that, and my fucking brother really never should've seen anything."

"Enough, babe. What's done is done," he said, pushing his forehead against mine. "We're both stressed to hell and back. Nobody needs to apologize for a damned thing. Here's what'll happen – we're both sitting down with some water, listening to a little more music, and then I'm taking off."

My heart sank. A thousand things ran through my mind at once, but one word was louder than the rest, needling me between the eyes.

Stay.

Stay, Dusty.

Please, for the love of everything good and holy, stay with me tonight.

Of course, I knew how stupid it would be to give those thoughts any voice. I turned my back, humming along to the music while I got us some water, and tried to pretend my world hadn't just gotten wrecked.

Dusty took his glass and sipped slowly, watching while I did the same.

"Do you really think it's going to be okay with Huck?" I tried my damnedest not to tremble or cry when I said it. Yeah, I was coming apart.

He narrowed his eyes. "Darlin', I know it'll be. Don't you worry about anything."

"This is what we were afraid of, though. The whole reason we couldn't be together before. I can't stand it if he's going to get pissed, drive a wedge with you and the club, especially when we haven't even –"

I stopped myself before I said *fucked.*

Jesus, I wished we had.

"Haven't what, babe? Done something we really shouldn't for plenty of other reasons?" He raised his eyebrows, sweeping me up in those stormy eyes of his again.

"If he hadn't walked in, honest to God, I would've been balls deep in you, Hannah. I know it would've been good. Might've been the best fuck of our lives, but it would've been something else, too."

My eyes went wide with wonder, and I leaned in, waiting for him to finish.

"A huge fuckin' mistake."

I wrinkled my nose, turning my face away from him. *Asshole.*

Even if he was right, I didn't need to hear it right now. Didn't want to think it would be anything short of amazing.

"Darlin'..." He reached out to me, laying a possessive hand on my shoulder.

"Are you sober yet?" I snapped. "Because I really think you should go."

"Sober enough," he said coldly, standing up and smoothing his leather cut. "Let's not have any bad blood over this, sweetness. You'll always be like family to me, and so will your brother, even when he's planning to slip a knife in my spine over what he just saw."

Refusing to speak, I sat there in killing silence, breathing each time I heard his heavy footsteps down the hall. Each one took him further away from my hidden, deeply personal hell. The monstrous situation I had to suffer, and suffer alone, without getting anybody else in the club stung over it.

Except, now that Huck had seen me coming undone with his Prez, something bad was bound to happen anyway.

I stood and crept up to the door, just quickly enough to

see his motorcycle roar out through the open gate. Punching the key to lock myself in, I released the bitter sigh I'd been holding since he said his last words.

"Goodbye, Dusty. Try not to kill yourself or Huck over me. We could've had something real special, in another world." Lonesome whispering only encouraged the tears stinging my eyes.

Another world. Easily something I'd never see as long as I lived, because I'd fallen too deep into a world that held nothing except darkness, greed, and soulless disappointment.

VI: Lies and Damned Lies (Dust)

Everybody sharing my patch had it in for my ass the next morning at church. I held the gavel in my fingers, letting Firefly's latest evil eye roll off me.

Knew I'd stepped into a shitshow before I walked in. Heard 'em all yammering about it inside through the meeting room door, their whispers becoming yells. Stood there with my ear pressed against it, Joker's big dog, Bingo, laying next to my boots.

Firefly and Skin were trying to calm each other down. Joker, stabbing his knife into the table, telling them both to shut the fuck up when he'd had enough. Sixty, Crawl, Lion, Tin, and three new prospects, minding their own business at the end of the table, or else keeping their cards close 'til they had to lay down.

I walked in and took my place at the head of the table, pretending the room wasn't a powder keg, ready to blow my face clean off.

Drama aside, we had business. I ran through the deal I'd struck this morning with Blackjack, Prez of the massive Grizzlies MC West of the Dakotas, and his allies a little further east, the Prairie Devils. Our reckoning with the Deads was coming damned soon, and when it did, the club would be making a whole lot more on the gun trade.

When I finally came to Firefly, I had one question.

"How soon can we be ready?" I growled, refusing to let yesterday come between me and my Enforcer. "Blackjack said he can get some men out here by next week. They'll be ready as soon as they're in, itching for action after the cartel wars ended out west. I want everything square in five days. Earlier, if we can swing it."

"Five days," he said, looking at me with payback on his mind for the blow to the guts. "Doesn't leave much time to train any of the brothers on the heavier shit. We've been getting more of it in and our range ain't great for this stuff."

"Fuck the big guns," I said. "We'll have manpower on our side. The Grizzlies are bringing a few of their newer toys, too. It'll balance out."

"Before we do this, there's something else," Joker interrupted us, sitting up in my chair. "That girl, Summer, who some of you boys saw the other day. She's got news on the Deads…"

Everybody's ears perked up. We all listened, wondering what kind of intel he'd gotten from that little stray who kept showing up at the clubhouse, needling him when he wanted nothing to do with her.

Then the motherfucker dropped the biggest bomb on our heads in months. That girl who'd been screwing around with him, Summer, she wasn't just a crush after the craziest bastard wearing our ink.

She was his old flame. His baby mama. Worse, she was in deep shit.

Christ. As if this fuckery wasn't complicated enough.

When Joker was done with his confession, Sixty made his usual smartass wise cracks, and we hashed out the details. Took a vote on how we'd move against the Deads, kill their leader, Hatch, and protect the woman and son nobody knew Joker had 'til five minutes ago.

I watched the Ayes roll in, one brother at a time. Unanimous.

At least the club could still agree on something. When I slammed my gavel down, everybody filed out, except for the Veep, who I grabbed, and kept hanging back with me.

When the room was clear, I gave him a stern talking to. Told his crazy ass he'd better keep a lid on it just a little while longer, even though the stakes had just gotten as high for him as they could for any man after revenge, who'd suddenly had a family dumped in his lap.

I watched him walk out shaken, his dead brother heavy on his mind, along with the new family he had a responsibility to protect. *Fuck.*

I'd asked him about Firefly, too. He told me the obvious. This thing with me and Hannah – this thing that hadn't gotten fuckin' started – wasn't gonna die. Not unless him and I had a face-to-face sit down to hash it out.

Didn't help that the entire club believed we were fucking by now. I walked into my office, poured myself a shot, and fiddled with my great great granddaddy's antique pistol in the drawer.

I needed the alone time. Had to sit there so I could hear myself think. Wondered how the hell I'd bought myself so much grief without really getting any pussy outta it.

The stakes kept going up, too. One wrong move could ignite this thing in the middle of our war with the Deads, and blow everybody to kingdom come several times over.

Several shots in, I saw somebody else standing in the room with me. My old man, Early, back to taunt me again.

Should've stayed outta the Navy, boy. If you'd done your job at my side growing up, learned to keep your fool mouth shut, and kept my fuckin' drug trade going, we wouldn't be in this mess.

"Fuck you," I growled, knowing I'd gone crazy. "I'm putting this club back on track. There's gonna be a lot of chop along the way, but we'll all come out better for it."

Better? He snorted. *Come the fuck on. Tell me you don't really believe that shit.*

I did. Believed it so fuckin' badly I pointed the antique revolver at the ghost in front of me, and fired.

Unloaded, thank fuck. The loud, jarring snap of metal was enough to shake my stupor.

So was the loud knock at the door.

Standing up, I shuffled over, realizing how drunk I'd gotten when I could barely grip the doorknob. Skin busted in, sliding past me, kicking the door shut and catching my the shoulders with both hands.

"What the fuck's going on in here, Prez? You look awful."

"Nothing, Skinny boy," I said. "Ain't none of your concern."

The brother wasn't stupid. His eyes flicked past me, saw the half-drained bottle of Jack on my desk, and inhaled the chemical stink on my breath.

"No, Prez, I think it's my concern if the man who's supposed to be leading us winds up so blitzed he can't hold the gavel. Come on, let's get you outta here."

I grumbled and gave him a half-assed shove. He had a better grip, holding me steady with one arm, leading me out to the garages, passing our bikes.

Next thing I knew, he had me in his truck. We rolled through the clubhouse's gate, leaving my poor abandoned bottle and family heirloom behind with my bastard father's ghost.

"Where you taking me?" I growled, staring across the sunset slipping behind the Smokies.

"Ruby Heel so you can sober the fuck up. You said you'd be by the place soon anyway to see how biz is running. I think it's time we took care of that."

I stared out the window like a damned kid on a field trip to the math museum – fuck, did they even have those? Now, I knew something was really wrong, when going to inspect the finest pussy this club had felt like a chore.

What had Hannah done to me? I thought about yesterday, remembering how close we'd been to driving it home.

I was almost in her. Still wanted to be.

Still tasted her on my lips, hot and eager, calling my cock to stir every time I thought about her little tongue moving on mine.

Thirty more seconds. All I would've needed if that fuck, Firefly, hadn't barged in at the worst time. I would've had her coming in her pants from my lips alone, and then it would've been a cakewalk getting everything off and slamming her down on the nearest surface, ready for my cock.

My head bobbed like a fishing lure by the time we pulled into the Heel. New sign looked nice, a glowing ruby slipper shining neon red hung above every entrance.

Skin and I walked inside, heading through the throngs of horny, loud drunks who'd gathered for another evening to forget their woes. A few months ago, I might've joined them, happy to plant myself in front of the stage with a drink and watch the night's prime tits and ass shake themselves a little richer.

We found Meg hanging out in her office, perched over a magazine, her PROPERTY OF SKIN cut constantly draped over her shoulders. When she saw me with her man, she looked up, startled, slamming the flimsy tabloid shut.

"Oh, Dust! I didn't know you were coming by tonight," she said, flashing Skin a *why didn't you tell me* look.

Next to me, Skinny boy signaled it wasn't nothing serious. I was too fucked up to care they were talking about me underneath my nose in goddamned signs.

"Relax. I'm just here to check in, see how things are running, have you and Skin break down the cash flow." I looked at my Treasurer, and saw his expression sour.

If he wanted to drag me out of my own fuckin' clubhouse for business, then we'd sit the hell down and talk business for real.

Something about the bright, flashy purple cover of that tabloid laying on her desk caught my eye. I reached over, picked it up, and held it up to take a look.

"King Silas – playboy to papa! Europe's biggest rogue tells the world he's never been happier, and more in love with his wife, with royal baby nearing." I finished reading the headline and slammed that shit down. "Really, babe? Is this the shit you girls read when the boys ain't looking? Or are you trying to tell Skinny here something about a new bundle of joy?"

Meg flushed siren red beneath her soft blonde locks. Skin went a little white, clenching his teeth, probably regretting the fact that he hadn't let Firefly go for my throat at church today.

"It's just a little harmless gossip," she said. "Should I print off the reports now so you can look them over?"

"Please." I grinned, reaching for Skin's arm and pulling him down into the seat next to me. I'd had my fill of busting his balls for now.

I sat still for the next half hour, listening to their briefing on the club's financials. Business was looking good. Far better than what we'd had with a couple beat up garages under my old man.

We'd turned the Heel into one of the most popular places around, even though we had to keep kickbacks to the city and the county going to avoid any bullshit.

When we were done, Cora came in for Meg, her belly bump growing by the day. The two old ladies disappeared to check in with the dancers for the evening acts. We'd kept our noses as clean as we could since day one – no whoring, no druggies, and no two timing bitches.

"Prez, just tell me one thing," Skin said after awhile. "Are you and Hannah *really* fucking?"

Fuck no, I wanted to say. *That's the real tragedy.*

I'd already landed the club in a world of shit for no good reason, so what was one more lie? Smiling, I put my hands on the desk and leaned in.

"Just between you and me, yeah, we are. Firefly's got every reason in the world to be pissed because she's the first one in a year I had more than once. Every fuckin' night, Skinny boy. Every damned morning. I'd take that woman on a silver platter, and I don't just mean cause she's rich. Hannah's goddamned *fine*. Brains, beauty, sass, and legs that go the whole nine yards. Shame she's gotta share blood with a brother, and my Enforcer, no less."

"Don't need the gritty details. I just wanted to hear it from the source to clear things up. Fuck." He buried his face in his hands, smoothing them back through his short hair, that scar along his cheek glistening as his lip curled. "Be careful, brother. We can't let these tensions chew us the fuck up when we're about to hit the Deads."

"Tell me something I don't know, boy. Ain't just my habits screwing us up, though mine are in the spotlight."

"I know. I'm worried about Joker, Prez. The last thing that crazy sonofabitch needed was a girl and a kid to worry about. He hasn't been the same since his brother bit it in that accident. This might push his sorry ass over the edge."

Accident? Fuck me.

I tried not to snort. Sometimes, I forgot the big lie I'd laid on the club, and had to catch myself.

If only they knew the truth. Joker's brother, Piece, had been hacked to pieces and burned. Everything except his head, propped up in their grandaddy's house, ready to look lifelessly at his twin brother the second Joker walked in.

Tore my fuckin' heart out, doing what was best for the club. One thing was for sure – he was right about Joker coming dangerously close to the edge.

If he ever leapt off it, and took my ass with him, exposing my dirty lie…it'd probably mean my gavel. Maybe my own fuckin' patch.

"You're worrying too much, Skin," I growled, grabbing him by the wrist and giving it a squeeze. "Let me take care of this shit. That's my job, long as I'm wearing this thing." I thumped my chest with one fist, just over my PRESIDENT patch.

Long as I kept wearing it, which wouldn't be forever if shit really spun away from me.

"You're right, Dust. Ain't the first time we've had our issues in this MC. Firefly's a fucking hot head, but he'll see reason soon enough. Long as you don't leave his sis' heart in shambles, we'll get through this, and back to everything we really ought to focus on."

"That's what I want to hear, Skinny boy," I said, standing up and lighting my pipe for a quick puff. "Get your ass out of here at a decent time tonight, and bring Meg's, too. Your wedding's coming up in a few more weeks, and you both need the rest. Don't fight me on it."

"Okay," he said, smiling, his dark eyes warming. "Should I round up a prospect for your ride home?"

"I'll do that myself. You relax." Telling him to take a load off wasn't much consolation, since I'd just lied several times over.

I stood behind the clubhouse, waiting for my ride. By the time we got back, I'd be sober enough to ride. Good thing, too, because I'd gotten sick and fuckin' tired of all these lies.

When a man bullshits enough, it sticks in his throat, rots his heart from the inside-out like a slow moving cancer.

My teeth clenched, and I practically heard my wicked old man whispering in my ear. *Everybody's gonna find out sooner or later, Dusty. Least when you're thrown out of your own club like the lying fuckin' prick you are, we'll have something in common.*

We'll both be dead to everybody who ever mattered.

I shook my head, wondering how much more I'd have to drink tonight to make him shut the fuck up. Goddamn, this stress. Made me almost as psycho as Joker, one evil day at a time.

Early lied to me and plenty of other brothers during the old days in the club. He'd skimmed extra money for himself, and bullshitted every man who'd been Treasurer before Skin about new money coming into the coffers. He'd gone to his grave, knowing we were running dry, and entire MC would be up shit creek soon.

Fuck him, and fuck this.

My lie was meant to save their lives. Wasn't just there to

keep things easy, or keep my free supply of perfect pussy flowing.

That meant something, didn't it?

Who the hell knew anymore. When the prospect motioned me over to his truck, a new guy named Barb, I got in and didn't say a word.

No more booze tonight. It'd only leave me with a hangover, and wouldn't repel my old man's pissed off ghost forever. Never had, and I should've figured it out a long time ago.

Luckily, I had something better in mind to steal a little truth. I'd make one of the lies I told real, or I'd lose my balls trying.

VII: Down Time (Hannah)

I sat at the counter with my laptop and a thermos of sweet tea, ready to pour it across the keyboard and then chuck the fucking thing out the window.

My latest attempt at patching the app wasn't working. Of course, that meant the Sicilian's had their dicks hanging out. Ready for anyone with too much curiosity and a computer science degree to stumble upon. And if Dom and his bastards had their pants down, then so did I, in more ways than one.

Closing my eyes, I pressed my face into my hands, trying to stop the raw headache banging my temples numb. I'd barely processed what a complete disaster the last twenty-four hours had been.

So, when the doorbell rang, patching me through to the intercom at the gate, I nearly screamed into it. If it was some door-to-door marketer, I swore I'd…

"Hannah? Let me in." No, Dusty's voice told me a simple marketer would've been far too easy.

"What do you want?" I asked, punching the button for the kitchen intercom. "Can't believe you're here after what went down yesterday."

"Believe it, darlin'. I want to talk."

I looked over my shoulder, staring sadly at the work I didn't know how to finish. My rebellious fingers hit the gate's button, letting him in. I walked outside just in time to hear his loud, familiar engine rumbling toward me.

Dusty never failed to make a good impression. Even when he was the last person I wanted to see, save Dom, the bastard looked magnificent. He switched off his bike, jerking his helmet away, throwing one leg over the Harley to come meet me.

I let myself take a good, long look – the last pleasure I was bound to have before he dropped more problems in my lap.

Mister Bad Boy Give-No-Fucks incarnate.

The man I'd nearly given up my V-card to yesterday, and still wanted at some strange primal level. The beauty, the beast, the gray eyed devil who painted my skin bright red whenever he got too close, or drilled his gaze into mine.

I leaned on the door frame, squeezing my legs together. "You'd better tell me what's up, Dust. I'm not in the mood for any games."

"Ain't just Firefly who found out about us yesterday," he growled. His hand flew up above mine and slapped the wall, his huge body towering over me, eclipsing us in his shadow. "The whole club thinks we're fuckin', Hannah."

The whole club?

Sweet baby Jesus. My heart nosedived into my belly, scattering the butterflies he'd summoned as soon as his bike pulled up.

"God. Are they angry like Firefly? I tried to call, late last night, but he wouldn't answer. Cora told me his phone was shut off, and he'd need some time to cool down."

"That's exactly what I'm giving everybody. Time. Me and him, we'll settle soon, face-to-fuckin'-face. As for everybody else, no, nobody gives a damn. Trouble is, this thing between us, whatever the fuck it is...just caused me to lie to my boys. If there's one thing I've been doing lately that turns my stomach, it's that."

I shook my head, trying to follow him. "And so...what? You want me to lie to them too? Put on one of those PROPERTY OF DUST jackets like all the old ladies wear for their men, and pretend we're something we aren't?"

His face tensed, as if he was actually pondering it. That scared me more than anything else.

"Dusty!" I gently slapped his chest, bringing my hand back, wondering how hitting a human being could feel so much like driving my palm into a smooth, warm, immovable wall.

"I'm fuckin' with you, darlin'." Taking me by the hand I'd just slapped him with, he led me inside, and we both sat down on the little love seat in the front room. "I'll be straight with you so we both know why I'm here, even though it's nuts."

Great. More crazy.

I tilted my head, looking at him uncertainly, one eyebrow raised. "Just tell me. Enough with this drama. I know it tears you up, lying to your brothers. You don't need to do that with me."

"I'm tired of mincing words, Hannah. Tired of sputtering around 'cause I've got no rudder. Shit, after everything we've been through the past couple months, it's probably more than just the club who thinks we're something else. I'm done lying to the world, bullshitting my brothers, and I think you are too."

"Then…what? You're sitting here, asking me for a favor…aren't you?" I asked, flicking my tongue nervously over my lips.

The tiny spark in his cool grey eyes looked hungrier than ever. His voice growled every word, edgier than when he was just mad or frustrated. This was on a new level, more than Dusty the tease, or the Deadly Pistols President.

No, he'd cut himself open, spilling out his heart.

"Yeah, darlin', I'm asking for honesty. Something I should've done that night I picked you up in Atlanta, and we shared that beat up little bed. Took me all fuckin' night to get to sleep with my cock straining in my pants. Had to lay on my own hands, just so they wouldn't drag you into me, take those tits in my palms, and start ripping away everything you wore to bed. Practically had to knock my ass out so I didn't stick my dick where it really belongs. Favor? Fuck that. I'm asking for what we've both been too scared to admit for too long."

"Dusty…" I said his name softly, completely locked in his gaze. "Why didn't you tell me before? I didn't know you felt so strongly about —"

He never gave me a chance to finish. Strong, angry hands jerked me onto his lap, moving through my hair, exploring me like we'd only started yesterday.

I didn't think his lips could taste sweeter and burn with more lightning than the night before. But I hadn't kissed him when he'd lost his mind until now.

Dusty gave me everything. Held absolutely nothing back.

His lust, his need, his rage and confusion at everything he knew blowing out of control – they were there in every movement. His lips crashed over mine again and again, before he sucked my bottom lip, binding it to him with his teeth.

And I gave back.

I kissed him with my horror, my fear, my ache for everything he offered that went way past his lips. My teeth dug into his lips too, scratching my chin on his rough stubble. I let everything we'd suppressed for too fucking long possess me.

Push. Pull.

Teeth. Tongue.

Lips. Flesh. Sex.

His kisses came faster, harder. His cock ballooned beneath me, making me moan into his mouth. My hips rocked instinctively into his hard-on, seeing how long I could tease him before he threw me to the floor, tore off my skirt, and bent me over.

We didn't need to slow anything down. My virgin insecurities shattered, swept away in the blinding chaos of his kiss, his hand moving between my legs.

His fingers moved down, igniting about a thousand

nerves along the way. He moved them straight up between my thighs, grunting while he pulled them apart, shoving my panties aside with his fingers.

"So fuckin' wet for me…so fuckin' sweet…I'm going to make you sit on my face, darlin'. Then I'm going to lick you into a damned coma." Dust rubbed his fingers up and down my slick folds, giving me a fraction of everything he'd just promised.

Holy shit. I never said anything, and he didn't need me to.

My world shifted. I was in his arms a second later, thrown across his shoulder like a woman ready to be carried off and defiled.

God, I wanted to be.

He was right about one thing – this crazy, stupid dance between us had gone on for far too long.

He never asked where the bedroom was. He just took me upstairs, slowly carrying me, bringing the same stiff fingers he'd used in my pussy a few seconds ago to his mouth.

Tasting me because he couldn't even wait. There was no hiding the fact that I'd be devoured, and no, I couldn't wait.

Upstairs, he threw me down on the bed, crashing on top of me, pinning both my hands with one of his. The other, he placed on my breast, teasing me more as we kissed, losing ourselves in the slow boiling bliss.

"Stand up, woman," he ordered, pulling me up when he'd had enough from my lips.

I complied, my knees shaking as I did. His arms

wrapped around me, drawing me in closer, his hands going down my back until they landed on my ass. He took my cheeks in his hand and squeezed, growling his desire.

"Fuck, you feel good, inside and out."

"You've barely tried the inside part yet," I said, wondering if I'd wind up getting spanked on top of everything else. Maybe I secretly wanted it.

"Believe me, darlin', I'm way past ready to own every fuckin' inch of you." Those words were his last before he started tearing at my clothes.

And I meant *destroying* them. If it wasn't for the huge wardrobe I'd accumulated since my intern days in Seattle, I might've been pissed. But anger wasn't anywhere on the agenda, not when Dusty's freaking hands ripped through my skirt and shredded my blouse, sending stray buttons everywhere.

I stepped out of the mess, almost naked before him. He kissed down my shoulder, taking me in his arms again, his fingers gliding toward my waistband. One jerk of his hands sent my panties halfway down my legs, and my bra came with it, the strap breaking with a loud snap from his savage pull.

"Don't be scared, darlin'. I want you so fuckin' bad it hurts, but I'm gonna make you feel better than any man ever has."

"Any man?" I whispered.

Yeah. About that virgin thing...

Approaching that subject with the huge, overbearing biker I'd crushed on since forever didn't seem like a realistic possibility.

But Dusty stopped, pushing my hair over my ear, tilting my face until we looked at each other. "What the fuck you mean, beautiful? You must've done this a thousand times before, same as me."

I shook my head. Could a woman faint from too much blood going straight to her cheeks?

"Bull. Fuckin'. Shit," he growled, fisting my hair slowly, his gaze on me tightening. "We can fuck in the open, Hannah. You don't have to put me on. I ain't standing here and believing you're a damned..."

His eyes widened and his lips twitched. Two distinct, awe struck signs he couldn't believe what he wanted to say.

"Virgin?" I said, somehow finding my ability to speak. "Yes, Dusty. I am."

His fist in my hair tightened. Pulling, stretching, tangling everything around his fingers until it burned in the roots. He studied me closely, searching for any sign I'd lied to his face.

"Fuck, it's true, ain't it?" he growled, shaking his head, closing his crazed grey eyes for a lengthy second. "You're sure you wanna give this up to me, darlin'? Whatever the hell happens between us after tonight, you'll remember this forever, being your *first*."

"Yes," I whispered harshly, pushing my fingertips into his wild, inked chest. His muscles flexed beneath his shirt, calling for my nails, urging me to mark him the same way he'd surely do to me. "I want you. You're the first man in a long time I've even thought about going to bed with. Take me. Fuck me. Anything and everything you want, just for tonight. And after it...we'll see."

His eyes narrowed, and he brought his lips to mine in a slower, fierier kiss. "I'm the luckiest motherfucker in the world to hear you say that, darlin'. Not just because you've got a special way of making my dick throb like mad. Couldn't walk away from this if I tried."

Pausing, he buried me in another kiss, his hand edging down my naked body. His fingers plunged down, stopped at my inner thigh, and then worked their way up. He cupped my pussy rough, and squeezed, pressing his thumb into my clit.

Moaning wasn't optional. It came pouring out, a breathless sizzle, like he was the only man in the world who knew where to find the switch that turned me on and took me away from hell.

"Fuck, I need you, baby girl. Need to suck you. Need to fuck you. Need to bury this dick to the hilt, every fuckin' inch, and shoot everything I've got into you 'til I'm empty and screaming for more."

"Dusty, yes!" I whispered, squirming against his hand again.

Wait, not squirming.

Flat out fucking his fingers, my hips grinding into him, begging for the sweet release only he could give me just then.

Dusty didn't wait. He picked me up, slammed us both on the bed, shifting positions until I straddled his massive body. Those steel colored gems in his head locked onto my eyes, hotter than twin suns.

I wriggled self-consciously, that space between my legs almost on his face. So vulnerable, so horny, and so fucking wet for anything he offered.

"Keep still. If I gotta force your legs apart when I go to town, don't you doubt for a fuckin' second I will, darlin'."

There wasn't any doubting his promise. Dust's fingers sank into my thighs, holding me open, his eyes never leaving mine as he moved his face into me.

One lick. One beautiful, searing, suffocating stroke of his tongue.

My pussy tingled. My brain spun in an endless loop of desire, caving in on itself, surrendering to the promise that I'd be coming on his rugged face.

His first licks were slow, teasing me when I wish he'd bring it home. He knew what he was doing, though, and the warm up paid off about a minute later.

The fireball in my belly was going to explode, ripping me in two.

Lust conquered my veins one lick at a time, electrifying my blood, a raging wave that touched every part of me.

Dusty growled between my legs, licking harder, tongue-fucking me a little deeper each time. Then his focus moved to my clit. I started to shake, screaming as he brought me over the edge.

"Dusty, Dusty…oh, fuck. Yes!" I cried out, wrapping my hands around his head, every muscle in my legs quaking as my orgasm burst free.

Coming!

I pinched my eyes shut, letting them roll in the mad

white ecstasy he'd thrown me into. When my legs strained, trying to flutter shut, he growled louder, held my seizing muscles in his hands.

This greedy, wonderful bastard was determined to milk every last ounce of pleasure from me.

And I gave it to him, I gave it all, coming harder than I ever had.

"Don't ever stop screaming my name," he said, after I'd finally stopped coming. "I want to hear it on your lips every time we're fuckin', darlin'. Tell the whole world who's making your pussy cream. You tell 'em, babe, and never, ever *ever* stop."

He lifted himself up, pressing his forehead to mine. Those stony grey eyes I'd lost my panties for bored into mine, offering a thousand more possibilities he wanted to do to me tonight.

Hell, maybe several nights. More nights than I ever imagined, if I kept my shield down, and gave up what was his whenever he wanted.

Growling, Dusty took me by the throat, his gentle fingers pressing into my neckline. "A virgin...an honest to God fuckin' virgin...you're like an empty canvass, Hannah. And I'm gonna paint it beautiful. Gonna give it to you slow and hard, make you explode and see stars. All the sweet colors a woman ought to learn."

I nodded, my skin moving softly against his grip. Slowly, I eased my legs open again, unable to stop my hips from rocking gently back and forth.

This want went full primal. He drew in a deep breath,

smelling the sex and pheromones swirling around the room. He stood up, lifting off the end of the bed, and began pulling off his clothes.

I watched in stunned silence.

First, his cut, then the t-shirt underneath stamped with the Deadly Pistols logo, rolling over his head. The fearsome ink underneath on his big, bare chest put the shirt to shame, works of art I'd admired before when he'd been shirtless, but hadn't had the audacity to touch until tonight.

I sat up, placing one hand against his chest while he worked his belt, letting my fingers freely trace his rock hard edges and ripples for the first time.

His abs were all muscle, but they'd been carved rough. Not in some gym like most men chasing the Hercules physique, but by a hard life of work, danger, and yes, sex.

Every powerful square inch of flesh attached to his bones was made riding, running, fucking, fighting, maybe even killing.

Dusty's belt dropped to the floor as he opened his fly, pushing his jeans down to the pile of boots at his feet. I'd never seen beneath his boxers before, but I'd felt the insane cock bulging there many times.

Licking my lips, I pushed my hand to the magnificent bulge throbbing between his legs, only concealed by a thin layer of fabric. I looked up, and his eyes met mine, brighter than ever before.

"Need to see my cock in your sassy little mouth, darlin'," he growled, running one hand through my hair. "Take it out. Stroke it. Suck it. Show me everything you've wanted to do to a man since you were old enough to wonder."

His open invitation caused me to stiffen, close my eyes for a split second, and let the shudder of excitement run through me. *Sweet fuck.*

My fingers tightened, molding to the huge, angry shape underneath his boxers. I put my other hand against his waistband, and slowly began to pull.

I barely moved his boxers several inches down his thighs before his full, raging hardness sprang out, hot and alive in my hand. I'd seen my share of dicks online, and this one was *huge.* Not just long, perfect for stroking deep, but thick.

He must've been half as wide as my fist, a crude reality that painted my cheeks red before I started trying to rolling my hand down his wild, tempting length. Dust growled, pushing his boxers down further, closing his fingers around mine.

"Just like that, babe. Stroke it hard. Get rough. Put your fuckin' tongue against my balls." His orders made me hot, wet, and everything in between.

I had to focus. Fighting the lust storm in my blood, I looked at him one last time before I stroked down to his base, and moved my lips down to kiss his most sacred part.

Starting low, I worked my way up, allowing him to take away his hand while I dragged my mouth up his cock, starting with his balls. He tasted like earth and masculinity distilled, his scent filling my lungs. I breathed pure Dusty, the gorgeous bastard who'd officially driven me out of my mind.

When I reached the crown of his cock, I pulled my lips

apart, dragging my tongue around the edges.

"Fuck! Yeah, yeah, yeah, baby girl, just like that. Be creative." He stiffened, and his whole body rumbled from the thrill.

When I moved my lips over his swollen, pulsing head, that tremble in his throat became constant thunder. He went full animal, pushing his hand gently behind my head, slowly guiding my movements. Somehow, he kept his composure, his control, held back on the need I knew he had to ram my face down on his cock in quicker, angrier waves.

And I'd changed, too. One taste of that hot, sticky, pearly liquid flowing across my tongue from his tip, and the craving I'd had before became ten times stronger.

I wanted to make him lose it. Wanted to push him over the edge like he'd done to me, gliding my hungry, plump lips up and down in a frenzy, until he shuddered, shattered, and erupted.

I had to taste his come. Needed it to come out in a rush, thick and fiery, flooding my mouth and spilling out all over me.

It couldn't get crazier than this.

There I was at the edge of the bed, sucking off my big brother's boss and his best friend, moving my free hand between my legs. When Dusty looked out from his bliss and saw me playing with my clit while I took him in my mouth, his eyes went wide.

"Fuck me senseless. You're that insatiable, darlin'?"

He had no idea. I tried not to smile, pushing my face

down harder, making him forget all about anything I was doing except trying to suck every last drop from his balls.

"Shit!" Dust stiffened again, his hand in my hair pulling tighter on my locks. "I'm gonna fuck you like I never fucked any pussy after this. Gonna bend you over, beautiful. Slap your sweet ass raw, beat my balls against your greedy little clit 'til your cunt drains every drop. Fuck you like you've been craving for years, Hannah."

Yes, yes, yes, and please. My hand moved faster, and I moaned on his cock, moving my lips faster.

His dirty words were driving us both over the edge. I hadn't even given up my cherry yet, and it *scared* me to think about how good it might feel when this cock left my mouth and found its way between my legs.

"Goddamn, you're a natural," he growled, putting his other hand against my shoulder, pushing his fingers deep into my skin. "Don't fuckin' stop, Hannah. Not for *anything.*"

Anything, huh? That was what I'd give him with my mouth, my breasts, my aching, creaming, virgin pussy, about to go into convulsions as I fucked my fingers again.

He was going over the cliff, and I'd surely follow. Both of us blown over, just as soon as he let go, and –

"Good goddamn, woman, here we fuckin' go! *Coming.*"

His cock swelled to nearly twice its size. I tried to focus, prepare myself for the hot, seething flood about to pour into me, but it all went to pieces when that fire I'd been kindling between my legs exploded.

We came together.

Loud. Grunting. Moaning. Messy.

Somehow, I kept bobbing my lips up and down his cock, driving my tongue into that little spot below his cock's crown that made him jerk and thrash like a bull in rut. He filled me, shooting his essence into my mouth.

It was hot, salty, and so divine I came unraveled again and again. My pussy burned against my fingers, each twitch deep inside me turning my blood to lava.

Dusty's come spilled out, streaming down both sides of my lips, then flowing lower. When the frenzy finally ended and I took him out of my mouth, I was wearing a warm, sexual necklace above my breasts that threatened to get me wet all over again.

"Down," he growled, taking me by the shoulders and pinning me to the bed. "I ain't done yet. You're a lucky woman."

"Why's that?" I asked softly, smiling when his stubble grazed my cheek. "Seems to me you're the lucky one, Dusty, coming like a bandit all over me."

"Yeah, and you're fuckin' beautiful, wearing my seed. 'Bout half as pretty as you'll look when I've pumped my load inside you, and watched it pour out that greedy little pussy." He paused, running two fingers against my folds, still slick and ready for him. "You really wanna know? You're lucky because I don't even need a minute's rest to fuck you into outer space. You've got me hard as a goddamned rock after comin' in your sweet little mouth, darlin', and that's really somethin'."

New tingles ran through my pussy, crawling into my

legs, which slowly opened for his huge, powerful body. "I don't know about this luck, Dusty. I think you'd better show me so I understand. I'm a virgin, after all."

I smiled sweetly. It was either play the part with a grin plastered to my hot, red face, or else let the nerves and awkwardness consume me.

Was that even possible with him, though? This all felt natural. So good, so right, so powerful, it unsettled me deep down inside.

But I didn't have long to dwell on his when he began kissing my throat. Dust's lips ran low, down to my nipples, growling the whole way. He sucked them slowly, needling them with his teeth and fingers, taking his time to warm me up before I realized I was moaning, grinding my pussy into his knee.

"Beg," he said, one simple word when he finally came up.

"What?"

"You heard me, darlin'." He smiled, quickly reaching behind my head and fisting my hair, leaning back so I could see his swollen cock pulsing, dangerously close to my pussy, eager to deflower me. Metal crinkled in his hand, a condom leaving its packet, before rolling over his relentless hard-on.

"I ain't taking this pussy 'til I hear the magic word. That was part of the deal we made, the one that said this beautiful thing won't go all the way 'til you tell me you're ready."

Unbelievable. I didn't know how he could stand it, remembering that stupid, flirtatious dance between us that seemed like a million years ago.

If my lust didn't have my pride on my leash like a dog, I would've balked. Instead, I grabbed his big arm with both hands, digging my fingernails in. I ran my legs up and down on his, loving how his hard muscle and tiny, manly hairs prickled my skin.

"Fuck me, Dusty. Please."

"Pretty please?" he offered, that wicked smirk on his lips growing wider. "No, I think 'please, sir,' has an awful nice ring to it."

He was teasing me now. Angrily, I quickened my strokes, tempting him to ravage every inch of me, wondering if there was any other way to make him lose control.

"You're…you're insane," I sputtered, the heat raging in my veins making it hard to form new words. "Do you know how bad I've wanted this? How long? How much I *still* wanted it, even after my fucking brother burst in and saw us tangled up? Dusty, I want every inch of you inside me, taking what's been yours for longer than I care to admit. So, *pretty fucking please* with a bright red cherry on top. Please, Dusty, *please*. Fuck me."

Heat braised my cheeks, nexus points for the frustration, desire, and filthy words shaming the sheltered little girl inside me. She was what I tried my hardest to bury tonight. The side of me that didn't fit anymore.

Not with this beautiful man, or the devils I ran away from.

Tonight, I wanted to be woman, and nothing else. Just the bride, the whore, the mistress who took the world's boot on her ass, and then gave it back harder.

I wanted to fuck this man so hard I forgot everything.

Fuck him with all the love and hate and confusion building up inside me. Make him fuck me until we could both pretend we were safe, happy, and completely care free, even if the illusion would fade as quick as the moon once morning came.

Dusty took a good, long look at me. Tempting me for the thousandth time with his hard grey eyes.

"You're better than most pros at sucking cock, and you beg like a woman who's about to have her cherry taken should. Almost makes me wanna slide off this bed, get my clothes, and walk the fuck away."

What? He had to be joking. My eyes narrowed, staring into his, totally ready to send my fists flying if he was fucking serious.

"You can't," I said, locking my calves around his, wishing I were ten times stronger to force him into me.

His gaze deepened. Bringing one hand down to his cock, he fisted it, rolling the thick head against my entrance. He held it there in a delicious torment, a physical symbol of the line we were both afraid to cross.

"Don't worry, darlin'. Condom's on. If I walked away now, I'd drive my fuckin' bike into the nearest ravine once I realized what sweet, tight, fuckable pussy I'd passed up. I ain't going nowhere," he growled, tangling his fingers deeper into my hair, leaning over me, ready for a kiss. "I'm done teasing. I'm taking what's mine because I can't leave this life 'til I find out what your sweet cunt feels like when it's coming wrapped around me. Find out how much louder you can scream my name. I wanted to walk the fuck away because part of me wishes I could keep you like this forever, darlin'. Forever pure, hungry, ready to give it up. Thankfully for both of us, there's a much, much bigger part of me that's ready to make sure my dick's the first and last you'll ever have."

First *and* last? He said it, and there wasn't a spare second to think what that meant once he sunk into me.

Dusty thrust hard, but sudden. He went slowly, grunting as his cock worked in, making me grind my hips through the curious blend of pleasure and pain brandishing every nerve I had with fire.

"Oh, darlin', you're tight," he said, stopping for a second when he'd finally pushed in as far as he could. "Why'd it take me so long to realize you've been hiding a fuckin' thief between your thighs?"

I smiled, pushing through the burn, bending my hips into him. He growled again, this time an octave lower, rougher and primal.

"Your cunt's gonna rob me blind, baby girl. Not before I steal all the pleasure I can by fuckin' you breathless."

He was as good as his promise. His hips started pumping slowly, pulling back and crashing into mine, each time a little harder. I rode the storm, biting my lower lip a little harder between his kisses, the only thing I could do to steel myself against the explosion he primed in my womb.

Hurricane Dusty tossed me around the bed until my expensive, imported mattress creaked and rocked beneath us like a cheap cot. He was wind and lightning, and I surrendered to the beautiful chaos formed by his muscles, his thunder, his take-no-fucks tattoos scrawled over every spare inch of his skin.

His cock gave, and I took everything it offered. I let it sink into me, tear through the faint remnant of womanhood I'd kept up as a wall against any man for twenty-three years, and plunge to places I'd always reserved for my prince.

Had I found him in this panting, groaning, growling mess we'd become together? Was Dusty the man I'd waited for most of my adult life, the one I told myself I deserved after I dragged myself up from that dark, dirty place where I was born and raised?

Tonight, he was. I didn't think this could last, not with a man as hard and experienced as him who lived freedom like a daily prayer.

Maybe it would end the second he decided he had his fill. After he'd finished tearing at my hair, stamping his furious lips against my throat, manhandling my breasts, and snarling his filthy, sexy pleasure into my ear.

None of it mattered when he was balls deep. I'd found my prince tonight, the greatest fuck of my life. My heart didn't need magic because his dick was enough.

Dusty pressed his teeth against my ear, breathing heavy as he fucked me harder. "Give it the fuck up, beautiful. I know you're fighting it. Fighting through the pain of my dick stretching you to fit. Fighting me because you're afraid I'll think you're something less if you explode on my balls so hard you soak the fuckin' sheets."

"Dusty..." I moaned into his palm, suddenly gripping my face, forcing me to look into his eyes. "I want to, I want to –"

"Fuck, yeah, you do. And you're gonna let your pussy do what it does best. Come for me, Hannah. Come so fuckin' hard the only thing left on your mind is when this dick's bringing you off again."

Holy shit. He'd gotten a little rougher with every stroke, a little more controlling. That meant a whole lot sexier in some strange, twisted sense I'd only started understanding.

Whatever he was, it seized my body like mad. I arched my back, threw my full weight into him, and rode his cock, taking his thrusts without holding back, even when they shook me down to the bone.

Dusty reared up, fucking me faster, harder, grinding his pubic bone into my clit. He lifted my ass with his free hand, tangling my hair in one fist with the other, throwing his full weight into it.

He railed my whole body, and I loved it.

Loved it so fucking much I couldn't hold back. Dom and his demons died with the ones inside me when the spine-tingling pleasure surged, overloading me, bringing every sense I had to ruin, save one.

Coming? No, this was more.

This was a full body, brain shattering supernova, a climax so intense it sent shades of red searing through me. I never understood how he held on, fucking me straight through it, slamming his cock in faster and harder while my pussy convulsed around every inch of him.

Dusty did, though. He brought me home. Carried me deep into myself and back to him again, down the places where life and death intertwined, and only our bodies could speak in a language that made any sense.

Our flesh must've written an entire volume in the next hour. My first climax blurred into the next, when he flipped me over, spread my legs, and mounted me from behind.

His muscles bulged, his breathing grew more ragged with every stroke. He wanted to give it up, but he wouldn't yet, not until he'd owned every inch of me several times over.

And every part of me cried out for more, a complete slave to his body for the night, hopefully the first of many.

"You're so fuckin' beautiful when you let go, darlin," he growled softly, reaching around my thigh for my clit. "I don't want to miss you going off again when I give you my come."

"Do it!" The words came out in a savage, breathless plea that almost seemed like they were spoken by someone else. "Please, Dusty. Please."

"Fuck, Hannah." His thrusts quickened, slamming his full weight against my ass as he went deep, his balls swinging up to slap my skin softly each time he did. "What the fuck you doing to me, woman? You're driving me outta my goddamned mind.. Like nobody ever has."

He'd let the frenzy overwhelm him. I shouldn't have let myself read anything into those mad, sweet words spoken in the blinding place before he exploded.

But I did. Damn it, I let myself believe him, let my heart

swing happily in my chest behind my breasts, rocking like mad. His fist in my hair jerked me up, and his hand came down on my ass, a single fiery clap sending me over the edge again.

My pussy came on his cock so hard I screamed, the best way I'd ever lost my voice. This time, it was enough to bring him with it.

Grunting, growling, thrusting like an engine designed to fuck me into oblivion, Dusty added his pleasure to mine. He came, his cock swelling deep inside me, slamming to a halt just short of my womb as his pleasure ripped through him.

"Fuckin' shit, babe, I'm –"

"Coming!" I finished for him.

Just a split second before we finished together, losing ourselves speechless in the hot, bright parade sweeping over us. Flesh, blood, and lightning gave us better words than any we could say for the next several minutes.

We let our bodies speak the secrets our hearts still weren't ready to give up.

* * * *

"You're going on the pill or whatever works best, darlin'. Next time we fuck, I want everything going in you, soaking the sheets when we're done. Only way it should be." Dust laid next to me, his big arms wrapped around me, resting my head on his wide chest.

"So there's going to be a next time?" I mused, slowly running my fingers down his body. Just like admiring a statue, some fine piece of art that had somehow tumbled into my bed and come to life.

Dusty's face tensed, as if he knew he'd said too much. "You're breaking all the damned rules. You know that, babe?"

"I expect it," I said, smiling at the stern, sexy confusion clouding his face. "Don't worry. The club doesn't have to know about any of this. Nothing beyond what Huck already thinks he knows, I mean."

"Shit, what's the point in hiding? I came down tonight because they had a good idea what's been going on between us. Only thing is, we finally made it real."

"We did," I said, running my hand up his strong neck, tracing his jawline, fingertips grazing his stubble. I couldn't get enough of it scratching my skin when he worked his way up, down, or sideways. "You worry too much, Dusty. My brother isn't the type to hold grudges. He'll get used to the idea, and then he'll get over it, sooner or later."

"Gotta be sooner for the club's sake. All hell's about to break loose when we hit the Deads, or if Joker decides he ain't playing by the rules no more."

"You can't control any of that." Easy for me to say when I had my own very big, angry dragon breathing down my neck, who'd murder me without a second thought because I had absolutely no control over it.

Jesus. I knew sex could change a lot, but I didn't know it could do the unthinkable – make me stop worrying.

"That's where you're wrong, darlin'. My whole damned life's been leading up to this point. I ain't missing my chance to clean house for good." He stared at me, his eyes determined. "My boys deserve to be happy. Shit, everybody wearing the patch keeps getting hitched and popping out kids lately. A man looses his taste for blood when he's got a family to chase after. My job's making sure my brothers never have to worry about catching a bullet, or coming home to their kin in pieces."

I smiled. Underneath the endless badass bluster and 'fuck all' armor, there was a heart underneath, a selfless one.

"What about *your* future, Dusty?" I asked, running my fingers over his brow. "Don't you ever think about what it'll take to make you happy? Maybe someday you'll find something that makes you want to settle down with more than just your business and bikes."

"Plenty of time left to sort that out," he said, his eyes growing distant and cold for a moment, before they snapped back to mine, warmer than ever. "Tonight, I've got all I need to put the devil himself at ease. I'm looking at her."

Could a woman swoon laying down?

Who knows, but his lips were suddenly irresistible, and not just because he had a knack for being kissable. By the time our mouths connected, his hand crawled down my spine, reaching for my ass.

Coding promised to be double hell tomorrow, after the fun was over and I watched him drive through my gate, returning me to loneliness. Didn't even matter.

I'd work my fingers hard, until they were just as tired as the space between my legs, and my own worn heart. I had to do everything I could to settle my evil debts and save my life.

Because for the first time in a long time, I had a future that wasn't a complete shit show staring at me.

So close I could taste it, touch it, let it pick me up and carry me away. And that's exactly what he did, over and over, deep into the night.

We enjoyed each other for hours, collapsing in a satisfied purr when our bodies refused to let us have any more. Heaven met my bed, and it was beautiful.

We kissed, we caressed, and we drifted away with our hearts in a single rhythm. And we were almost asleep when we heard the banging I thought would end the world.

*****

Dust bolted up, reaching for his gun, stumbling to get dressed. I just sat with the sheet pulled around me, my eyes filled with terror.

It couldn't be Dom or his men…could it? I chewed my lips, wondering if I should break down and soil our bit of heaven, confess everything I'd kept hidden for so long.

"Dusty? Where are you –"

He was already in the door frame, fully dressed, and spun around with a look that said *don't ask*. I nodded, the last glance we shared before he slipped out, slowly racing downstairs to meet whoever the hell was banging at the door at this ungodly hour.

I clenched my phone so hard I swore it would break in my fingers. Just listening, staring into the darkness, waiting for the gunshots that would make me scream into the night.

They never came.

I counted to one hundred before I stood, slipped on my robe, and stepped out very carefully, taking the stairs down a floor slowly, like I feared they'd send me tumbling down with a single misstep.

"Shit. Fuck! We gotta get that kid back, dammit." Dust stood in the entryway red faced, growling to a prospect, one hand on his forehead.

I'd been around Huck long enough to know that when a biker looked like this, it didn't mean things had just gone to hell. Something *awful* was happening.

"Prez, you want me to start rounding up the brothers? I came here first, soon as I heard. I'll hit the road, go by everybody's house, bang on their fucking windows 'til they're heading for the clubhouse."

"Do it, and I'll meet you there. Call Firefly and tell him to get *all* our assets on lockdown. Can't have anybody local fuckin' with us while we're ass deep in emergency."

The prospect nodded, and took off like a rabbit, running out the open door. My screen was about to slam shut when Dusty mashed his hand against it, heading for his bike.

"Dust!" I called after him.

He stopped, stared, and spun around like a whirlwind. He gave me about three seconds to catch up to him. I could tell he was counting in his head, wondering how much time slipped by.

"What's going on? You look terrible. Please tell me you aren't about to ride into danger without even a kiss goodbye." It sounded selfish, but I meant it.

He looked me up and down, his steely eyes traveling over me, as if for the last time. That scared me worse than anything.

"Some sick bastards got their hands on Joker's kid. I ain't promising you shit, Hannah, because I fuckin' can't. Not now."

"Jesus! Not the little boy…" My heart skipped a beat at the thought, and then again when I imagined what crazy, rabid Joker would do to get him back.

"Yeah, now you know. Darlin', listen. I'll do everything I can to drag my ass home in one piece, same as everybody else. You're too close to the club between your brother and me. You oughta be on lockdown with everybody else, walled off at the clubhouse."

No. I couldn't let that happen when I still had a mountain of coding to do, plus a madman with a gun to my head.

"Nobody knows about me, Dusty. I need to stay here for work. I'm not some defenseless little girl who needs the club's protection. Lord knows I've let Firefly post guards around here often enough." I gave Dust a reassuring look, but he wasn't softening.

"If you're staying here, then I'm pulling a couple prospects away from the clubhouse. They'll stand outside your gate like this is Buckingham fuckin' Palace."

"Dust…" I reached out, gently laying a hand on his stiff, angry shoulder. "I'll rent a bodyguard if it'll make you feel better. There are enough mercenaries around these parts to go around with all the bad juju that's been happening lately."

That was an understatement. I heard rumors about the assassins and creeps the Torches sent here over Cora, not to mention the dirty pimp and Deadhands bikers who'd nearly kept Skin from Meg.

"Fine. You've got one chance to get your fuckin' bodyguard, and text me exactly who he is by noon so I can do a background check. If he ain't clean or I find out you dropped the ball, I'm coming back here, darlin'. I won't be happy. Sure as I'm standing here, I'll *drag* your sweet ass back to my clubhouse naked, if that's what it takes to keep you safe."

He talked like he owned me, his to do as he pleased. *Infuriating.*

Or, at least, it should've been, being treated like his property, but a bizarre tingle ran through my blood. Possessive meant he cared in this twisted, gruff biker context, and I appreciated it.

"Dusty, I'm *not* your old lady. I know a thing or two about how to save myself. I'll be fine on my own. I've dealt with plenty of hired guns between Huck and Sterner Corp security."

"You know where I'm coming from, darlin', and you'll listen just this once. I get boundaries, but they're not worth a damn when your life's on the line. Don't make me shove a ring on your finger, stamp my name in your skin, and start calling you *mine*. Because believe me, Hannah, if that's what it takes to make you listen, I *will* fuckin' do it."

He'd never looked at me quite like this. Sure, I recognized the fearsome MC Prez barking orders, but it was more, too. I saw a man laying his claim. It shocked me so hard I had to put my hand against the wall for support.

"You'll hear from me by noon," I promised, slowly walking up to him. "Give them hell, Dusty. Whoever t*hey* are. Bring Joker's little boy home."

"I will, Hannah," he growled, grabbing me by the neck and pulling me to his lips for a rough, uneven kiss. "Then I'm coming back so we can finish everything we started here last night."

I stood in the doorframe with my heart in my throat, watching him climb on his bike, and roar out into the night. The stakes just got higher in the dangerous game I'd been playing – if Dom and his assholes found out I'd hired a bodyguard, they'd bring so much hell even the Pistols might not be able to handle it.

I had to take the chance. Lifting my fingers to my lips, I touched the numb, hot impression he'd left with his mouth, his teeth, his stubble.

His kiss promised he was worth the risk, and hinted at so much more. Whatever else I had to deal with before I could live something resembling a normal life, it took a backseat to finding out what else he'd promised.

VIII: Thanks for Nothing (Dust)

The worst week of my life in twenty years started the second I peeled away from Hannah's mansion.

Joker spilled the beans by the damned truckload. He told the brothers about Piece, the dirty, murderous secret we'd kept from everyone, and said point blank he wasn't waiting for revenge. He was gonna go and take it.

Then he took off alone. I got my dick nailed to the wall by my boys, who held off on a vote for my gavel 'til we settled with the Deads.

When we finally caught up to the Veep and came crashing into their lair, with a little help from our friends in the Grizzlies MC, we found a shit show.

They'd beat the shit outta Joker. Laid him up for weeks.

We killed every last miserable bastard wearing their patch over it, including their sick fuck leader, Hatch. It was a pleasure to carve the blood stained patches off his cut and bring 'em home for Joker and his grandpa to savor. Old man Taylor had been waiting a long time in that fuckin' nursing home to see his grandson avenged, and see the other one whole. He could finally die in peace, whenever the time came.

The club had new business, now that the Deads were in disarray and we had a route from sea to shining sea wide open for the gun trade. Blackjack and Throttle promised plenty of trade flowing down from their MCs. All three of our clubs had a beautiful corridor stretching across the country.

As for me fuckin' everybody over by holding onto secrets for too long, well, we settled that, too.

I sat through the entire agonizing vote for my gavel. Half the boys voted against me, hoping for a new Prez, and I didn't blame 'em one bit.

When it came down to that single swing vote, I thought I'd be fucked, considering it was in Firefly's hands. But the big, beautiful sonofabitch looked me coldly in the eyes, voting to keep me in charge.

Never expected that. Never thought he'd put the club's own good over the personal shit stirring him up with me and Hannah, but he did.

The man who had more reason than most to be caving my skull in gave me a second chance to lead, and I'd never forget it.

If shit seemed to be whirling by in a blur before, then it went twice as fast after all the deadly drama ended.

Everything changed. Before I knew it, we had two weddings on our hands. Meg and Skin were due to be hitched at the same time as Joker and Summer, making their love official once and for all.

I barely had a second to slip away to see Hannah with the whole damned world going to shit. But I managed, climbing over her gate before she opened it half the time, taking what was mine again and again like a maniac after another hit of the finest pussy on the face of the Earth.

One cool fall evening, several days before the double wedding, I walked into her palace and came face-to-face with a sight that almost pulled my dick straight through my pants.

Hannah waiting for me next to her fireplace, a bottle of wine on the mantle, and a roaring red glow crackling behind her. She wore her purple robe, pulled up too high for her own good, just enough to let me see the heels and stockings peaking out.

"Fuckin' hell, darlin'. Is that how you're gonna dress all winter? Because if that's the way it goes, bring on Jack Frost."

She laughed, reaching behind her for the bottle. The cork was already loose, and she pulled it out with her teeth, holding it in her mouth like some little creature tempting me to ravage her.

"No games. I need those lips *now*." I stepped up to her and plucked the cork from her teeth when I was close enough.

Our lips collided, fiery and restless. They always were when we got together, but lately it was only about once a week. Our bodies needed more than that – a whole lot more.

My hands wound their way into her robe, feeling that bare, hot skin I'd soon have under me. I was about to shred the velvety belt holding it shut when she batted at my wrist with both hands, giving me a push with all her strength.

"Not so fast. Are you spending the night? After last time, I'm putting my foot down and telling you, I ain't a wham-bam girl no matter how sexy and strong you look, Dusty." She narrowed her eyes.

Fuck. I thought back to last week, when I slipped out before dawn, pulled into a late night call with Blackjack. I knew I'd fucked up as soon as I left, putting business over her, especially when the crazy old bastard out west asked me why the fuck I was free at four in the morning, without a wife and kid to keep me busy.

"Darlin', I screwed up," I said. Never an easy thing for me to say. "I walked when I shouldn't have, when there wasn't any danger. I've learned my lesson. My ass belongs in your bed all night, unless there's life and death involved. Money can wait. We've both got ourselves plenty of coin. More will always be there tomorrow, but I can't say the same about another chance to get up inside you."

I slid my hands up her thighs, feeling those stockings, letting their sleek texture drive my dick mad. Hannah closed her eyes and purred, a soft smile on her lips, seemingly satisfied with the falling on my sword I'd done.

Right now, I would've told her she was the queen of damned England if it got her legs open. I wasn't just feeding her lies, though.

Meant every word I said. Every insane, unbelievable, alien word I thought I'd never say to any woman. She'd split me open, causing sheer madness to pour out my lips.

"I don't know," she said softly, grabbing my wrist with

one little hand. "Part of me wants to give you a second chance. The other part thinks you're just telling me everything I want to hear. You'll hop on your bike and ride off into the sunset like any other player wearing that patch after you've had your fill."

"You're calling me a liar?" I growled, running my hands over her more forcefully, winding its way to her ass. I cupped her cheek, gave it a hard squeeze. "I think I oughta find out what part of you believes I'm telling the truth. I'll fuck that part with my tongue half the night."

I move my fingers underneath her ass, gliding over her panties. She gasped, arching into the wall, and I suppressed another growl, sensing the wet spot swelling between her legs.

"And the rest of me?" she whimpered, trying to keep her eyes open, pretend she had the upper hand.

"The part that's calling me on bullshit, or thinks it is?" I took my fingers away from her pussy, bringing them back to her ass, but this time I lifted her robe, holding my palm over that sweetness, begging to be spanked. "I'll have to smack sense into that part, darlin'. No man, woman, or animal calls Daniel Grayson a liar."

My palm came down swiftly on her ass. Her eyes snapped open and she let out a little yelp, exactly like the kind she made most nights before I sent her into ecstasy.

"Oh! I was wondering when I'd hear your real name. Not that Dusty doesn't have a nice ring to it." She smiled sweetly, walking fully into my embrace, wine bottle gripped in her hand.

She brought it to her lips and took a big, teasing swig that could've put a sailor to shame. Seeing it glide down her throat didn't do anything to suppress the hard-on raging in my jeans.

"Consider yourself something real special, darlin'. Hearing my name at all means you can forget about ever thinking I'd lie to you," I said, taking the wine from her hand, and bringing it to my lips.

Normally, I preferred whiskey or beer, but this shit would do the job tonight. It went down smooth, landed in my stomach, and exploded in a fireball, adding its heat to everything lust kept fanning in my system.

"That's too bad," she said, licking her lips. "I was really looking forward to more spanking."

My eyes locked on her baby blues. Fuck, I wanted to make them roll. Wanted to *destroy* her tonight, and watch those eyes lose their shine to pure pleasure.

"Not half as much as I've been looking forward to what we're planning tonight, darlin'. Ain't nothing in this world like skin-on-skin. We're gonna fuck so much tonight, you'll be leaking me for days."

My words turned her cheeks rosy red, just how I liked them. I meant every single one, too, knowing this was the first night I'd be taking her sweet cunt with nothing in the way.

"Upstairs?" she asked, raising an eyebrow.

"Later. Why should we rush off to bed when we've got a perfectly good fire going here, plus a bottle of wine to suck down in between the next round of fireworks?"

I didn't give her any time to think about it. One arm locked around her, and my other hand tore at her robe, dropping that soft, purple cover straight to the floor.

Underneath it, she had her dark black stockings, her panties, and nothing else. Just the way I liked it.

She squealed and laughed when I grabbed her, pulled her down to the floor with me, and laid her out on the cool rug underneath us.

I laid into her lips like I hadn't had any for weeks.

How this woman managed to make me feel like I was getting my dick wet for the first time, every time, I still hadn't figured out. The woman was either magic, or something beautiful that went beyond tits and ass.

Something I thought I'd never have, much less crave the more I had it.

Every spare minute I wasn't dealing with the club's shit, I wanted Hannah Davis.

Her, not just her pussy.

Obviously, I wanted to be all up inside that, practically twenty-four seven, but we were going deeper than sex. I craved her in ways that weren't just about getting my dick soaked anymore.

We'd grown closer every kiss. Tangled ourselves up in each other a little more every time our lips connected and our bodies swapped sweat. Closer every time she laughed at my crap, and I buried her sass in another smoldering touch causing her to moan.

Hannah touched the man behind Dust. She lured Daniel to the surface, caused him to push her down into her pretty gardens out back, and left him craving more, even after he'd brought her upstairs.

She blue balled me, straight to my messed up soul. Left my head spinning a little more, and my heart more bitter, every wicked moment I had to walk away and go about my business, the other world that wasn't Hannah's lips, her laugh, her bed.

Deep down, I knew a man only came out of this freaky ass spell one of two ways: he came out whole, hitched, and seeing his woman every day of his life, or he went completely fuckin' *loco*.

I kissed her again, stroking my tongue on hers, tasting the sweetness I wanted to be mine, mine, and only mine.

Mine today, tomorrow, and next year.

She moaned into my mouth, slurring my name underneath her wine flavored flesh, turning my dick to granite.

Dusty. I couldn't get enough of that, hearing her recite my name with a passion and a hunger I'd never cared about on any woman's lips before.

A lot of assholes out there laugh about chemistry, insta-love, that caveman urge to claim a mate and keep fuckin' claiming her every time he gets his dick inside his girl. I used to be one of those assholes, thinking it'd never happen to me.

Technically, it hadn't happened yet.

Wasn't like I'd put my brand on her, or started calling her my old lady. But all that weighed on my brain heavier every day, creating a prickly fog I knew wouldn't lift 'til we had it all. I jerked off a little harder when I couldn't be with her, thinking about the day we'd be sharing a bed permanently, and I'd never have to waste a hard cock in my hands ever again.

My teeth grazed her throat. Hannah squirmed under me, tangling her legs around mine, begging me to bring it home.

Fortunately and unfortunately for her, it wasn't time for that yet.

I had standards. Didn't sink my dick in 'til I'd soaked her pussy good and hard. My tongue needed her taste, every sugary molecule of sweat sizzling on her flesh. I licked my way down good and slow, stopping to take each of her nipples between my teeth, pulling rough and lashing them with my tongue.

She practically came just from that. So sweet, so pure, so damned responsive to everything I did to her.

My cock jerked for the hundredth time in my jeans, leaking pre-come everywhere. Every voice inside me howled to rip her panties off and beast fuck her, but I told myself the same thing I told her body.

Not yet.

Not fuckin' yet.

She ain't coming on every inch 'til she's had my tongue, my fingers, and I've sucked her cream to my heart's content. If a day goes by when she forgets who makes that little nub between her legs burn, then I haven't done my damned job.

I wouldn't forget what she needed tonight. Wouldn't miss it for anything.

"Move with me, darlin," I said, grabbing her ass and lifting her high.

We rolled, repositioned, and soon her ass was in my face. My fingers dipped below the waistband hugging her hips. They came down in one quick jerk, so fast it caused her to whimper.

I left her panties around her knees while I grabbed her hips, shoved them against my face, and slipped my tongue into her.

"Oh…fuck!" she cried out, digging her nails into my leg for support. "Yeah, Dusty. *Yeah!*"

Hot blood frolicked in my veins, urging me on. I licked her high and low, shallow and deep, faster and faster, then so motherfuckin' fast she pinched her eyes shut, bucked her hips into my face, and tensed.

Too much pleasure, too soon. She tried to pull away, and I wasn't having it. I growled against her pussy, hugging her ass to me, pinning her where she belonged while my mouth owned everything.

Didn't take her long to find the rhythm. Each time my tongue plunged deep, she rubbed her pussy a little harder into my face, begging me to bring her off.

This was her lucky day because I was hellbent on doing it. My licks moved up, focusing on her clit. Took that little bead in my mouth and sucked it hard, dashing mad circles, reaching between her legs with two stiff fingers to fuck her while she took my tongue.

Make me hear my fuckin' name, I thought, whirling licks around her tender flesh 'til I was at my limit. *Say it, beautiful. Say it, scream it, give it the fuck up.*

We connected on a crazy, primal level I couldn't even fathom. Ten more seconds in, she seized up, her hips bending in to brace for the lightning ripping through them.

"Dusty...Dusty...Dusty!" Pure staccato pleasure erupted from her lips.

Her pussy convulsed on my face. I held her down, pulling her into me to keep on stroking her the whole way through her orgasm.

I brought her off hard. Licked up every sweet splash of cream gushing near my mouth, her pussy melting for me, coming completely undone.

No, fuck, just *coming*. And I'd make it happen about a dozen more times tonight before we were through.

I needed this woman. Needed to fuck her, own her, and pump my seed deep. Needed to mark her with my teeth, my come, my ink.

Just when she started coming down from it, her clit still humming against my tongue, I slapped her ass hard. She came a little more, a spankaholic if I ever saw one.

It was a miracle my dick hadn't torn through my jeans yet. But it came damned close when I felt her tense up, listened to how fuckin' much she enjoyed my hand impacting her sweet skin.

Lucky for both of us, she had plenty of sass to go around. I'd be bending her over my knee good and proper one of these days, and see how red I'd paint her ass before she came.

"Ease up, babe," I told her, as soon as the frenzy

weakened. "Turn the fuck around."

She did slowly, shifting on her knees. I watched her ass ripple, one hand on my dick. Our eyes locked and I took in the beautiful mess I'd created.

Hannah was still biting her lip when she looked at me. Her eyes were big, glossy, maybe slightly bloodshot from coming as hard as she did on my mouth. A hot, crimson flush spread around her tits like a sunburn, making me see a different kind of red.

It taunted me to fuck her more. I couldn't take waiting one more second to have her bare.

"Lose the panties, darlin', and pull down my jeans."

She did, blushing a little as she finished shimmying them down her legs, throwing them behind her. I'd loosened my belt and I lifted my ass, kicking off everything I could, holding myself in a crunch to get my cut and shirt off.

My eyes hit the bottle next to the fireplace for a second, and I wanted to laugh. Way things were going, we might not touch the wine for at least a few more hours.

That was just fine.

Hell, what she had between her legs, calling to my cock…no, fuck fine.

This pussy was pink perfection, and I was about to make it mine like no man ever had, or ever would as long as I had two fists and a gun to my name.

"I think we're ready for this," she said, sucking at her bottom lip. "I need you, Dusty."

"Thinking ain't good enough. Darlin', I'm *sure* you're

ready to take every inch I've got in that tight little cunt. Ready to come on my cock with nothing in the way. Ready to feel everything that's burning in my balls up in you."

"Yes!" She laid her hands on my chest, slowly guiding her pussy over my cock, hesitating for one more unbearable moment.

My hands went to her ass, pinching her cheeks in my fingers. "That's it, Hannah. Ride me like you've always wanted. You don't get off this dick 'til we're nothing but a grunting, steaming, twitching mess. Whatever's in your head right now, forget it if it's got nothing to do with fuckin'."

My hands moved, pulling her down in one stroke. Her lips opened wider than her eyes when that pussy engulfed me for the first time. I clenched my jaw, growling out my pleasure, wondering how I'd lived so long without ever having a woman this hot, this tight, this wickedly amazing.

It took us both a full minute to remember how to fuck. I moved my hips first. She slowly matched my rhythm, getting into it, her gorgeous blue eyes fluttering shut while nature took over.

"You feel so fuckin' good, darlin'. Better than anyone I ever had." I shouldn't have said that shit, but it came out anyway.

She smiled, but it melted just as fast by my dick driving into her again, replaced with a face that put soft and happy to shame. Pleasure contorted her lips, her eyes, pulled her nipples into peaks, softening the hard little stones they'd been a minute ago.

Christ, she was beautiful. Gorgeous through and through. From the tips of those sweat-dabbed brunette locks flowing down her back, to the ends of her toes, curling against my legs while I thrust into her faster.

Hannah taught me a whole new dictionary filled with words I never understood in forty fuckin' years.

Delectable. Corruptible. True.

And most important, *mine*.

That last word, I felt in every stroke, pushing harder through the hot, wet bliss clenching around me. She gripped my shoulders now, rocking her hips into mine like a demon, ready to go off any second.

I pushed back, taking as much pleasure as I gave, marking her from the inside out with the power, the force, the heartache chained up in my soul.

Fuckin' her gave me everything I never had. I saw it in every swing of her hips, every time her mouth opened, and she let out another little sound threatening to spill my load before I meant to.

My fist reached into her hair when she started panting. I fisted those locks, pulled them tight, 'til I saw her pretty eyes open, staring into mine.

"Come for me, baby girl. One more time, before I fill you straight to your womb. Come for me. Come with me. Come your sweet fuckin' brains out."

She'd been on the edge, and that pushed her right the fuck over. Hannah's fingers scratched my skin, raked raw, burning grooves into me. Gentle pain only added to the fire.

I pistoned even wilder into her, pumped her so hard I

wasn't sure how I didn't knock her off me, slamming my hips into hers so rough I gave her every inch, had her whole pussy wrapped around me.

"Oh, yes. Oh, fuck. Dusty!" My name left her mouth one more time before she lost it.

Her pussy pinched my dick like a vice, and I joined her in the maelstrom. My balls erupted, lit my spine on fire, turned me into a fuck machine made for throwing my come into her.

"Hannah!" I roared her name right back when I came, my dick swelling inside her, releasing its flood.

We came together. Our pulses matched beat-for-beat, becoming one.

Something ferocious and new I'd never had with the dozens of sluts I'd fucked over the years. Some were honest-to-God wildcats, the kind who'd shriek through the walls and leave scratches on your back the next morning.

But damn, the dirtiest, wildest, most shameless whores had nothing on the girl I emptied my balls into now.

Hellfire bathed my brain, sending its inferno through my body. Shit, even into hers. This fuck made us *one*, just a big, unbroken chain of flesh, fused in our pleasure. Rocking, sweating, and grinding out ecstasy, her pussy sucking in every thick rope wrung from my cock.

She winded me. Honest to God.

I gasped for air right alongside her when my dick finished jerking, spent like an empty clip. Incredible, really, because sex *never* winded me before.

What the holy fuck was happening here?

When she opened those ocean blue eyes, I had a good idea. My hand cradled her face, and I moved my lips to hers, taking one more taste of what I'd conquered while I was still hard inside her.

"Do you think it'll always be this good?" she asked, staring at me like I'd just handed her the moon.

I smiled. "Darlin', it only fades because people let it get boring. We've had ourselves another first tonight, but I've got about a hundred more in mind before we start getting really fuckin' kinky."

"Damn. And here I wanted to skip right to the bright pink ponytail buttplugs and nipple clamps!"

Grinning, I rested my forehead on hers, taking another taste of her lips before I said anything. No hiding how my cock twitched inside her when I thought about a couple clamps swinging from those sweet tits.

"Don't tell me you've been reading those dirty books like Meg and Cora. Always catch them reading some shit on their screens about guys hung like mammoths, or how Prince What-the-fuck exposed his dick for the millionth time, when they don't think anybody's looking."

"Sorry," she teased, cocking her head. "I like my men hard, tattooed, and alpha to the core. Rugged, dirty talking men with good hearts underneath. It's easy for a girl to settle with book boyfriends when there ain't very many like that around in real life."

Book boyfriends? I snorted. Was she trying to make steam shoot out my fuckin' ears?

Jealousy shocked my system too easy with her, even

when the assholes after her were fictional.

Before, there was only about a ten percent chance I'd lose my hard-on and have to wait before she fed me those words. Now, it was effectively zero.

"Guess it's your lucky day then," I said, running my fingers through her soft hair, holding her eyes in mine. "You've met your hero."

"Yeah? Lucky me." She tried to sound sarcastic, but her eyes betrayed hope.

"Believe it," I promised, beginning to pump my cock in her again, screwing through the mess we'd made. "Because you've been fuckin' him for about a month, and he's about to give you every inch he's got again."

She moaned, wrapping her hands around my neck, giving into the best sex of our lives. We barely had a drop of wine that night before we passed out. Exhausted, entangled, and wondering how the hell something so good kept happening.

* * * *

"Come to the wedding with me," I told her the next morning, chewing on the breakfast I'd cooked up for us in her fancy kitchen. "It's coming up fast. Just a few more days away now."

I turned, just in time to see her hesitate, taking a long pull from the coffee. We both took it extra strong to pry our eyes open after the naked gymnastics we'd done well past midnight.

"There a problem?" I asked, knowing damned well there

was when she took too long to answer.

"No…I want to, I mean. It's just that I'm so behind on my work," she said sadly. "I know this club stuff means a lot to you. Means a lot to Huck, too. We're about to be one big happy family, and I should really try to be more involved. Maybe it would help iron out the tensions in the group if they saw us as a couple."

"Fuck the tensions. Our family's about to get a whole lot bigger with your niece on the way. Won't be long before Skin puts a baby in Meg's belly, too."

My Treasurer and me had two things in common. We both went after rich, fiery chicks who oughta be outside our grasp in any sane world. I'd also heard his shit going into Meg's ear when he thought nobody else was around about putting a kid in her sooner, rather than later, possibly as a wedding present.

The old Dust would've winced, wondering what man begged for a pile of responsibility dropping in his lap. Didn't think much like that anymore.

For the first time in my life, thinking about knocking a woman up caused my dick to stand on end, instead of deflate.

"Come on, Hannah," I said, smiling, throwing more bacon onto her plate. "You can step away from the keyboard for one evening. Don't just do it for me. Do it for the club. They'll love to see you there, and so will I."

I reached for her hand. She took my fingers, but it wasn't like she wanted to. Gave me a grip like a person holding something back, hiding a secret chewing her up inside.

"I'll think about it, Dusty. Really. I wish I could just say yes." She rolled her eyes, sighing. "This project…it's endless. I can't wait to be done with it for good."

"So, say it," I said, trying not to lose my patience. "Look, I know running your business and tending to that matchmaker app is real serious. I respect how you've clawed your way up and made yourself something."

Her eyes signaled mine, shy and sad. Holding onto something I wanted to pry out of her, find out what the fuck made her pretend she couldn't go due to 'work.'

Business, I could buy that anytime. But the tension in her face gave away extra, mirrored the look I'd seen on folks a hundred times when they had more than just money at stake.

"What's going on, darlin'? If it's more than just coding, I need to know. Tell me." It came out like a demand. I realized I was squeezing her hand so hard it might hurt her, so I eased off.

For a second, that little glint her eye sharpened, like she'd drop everything in an avalanche. Instead, she sat up straighter, slowly spreading her palms on the counter with another heavy sigh.

"It's…really just work. Nothing else. It's stress, Dusty. There are millions on the line. *Millions.* Obviously, I've got plenty of that to go around in the bank, but I grew up with nothing. It's a scary numbers for someone like me. Ever heard of imposter syndrome? Some days, I still wake up, afraid this could all come crashing down if I slow down too much, if I take my foot off the pedal for a split second."

Tears sparkled in her eyes. Guilt tugged at my chest, hating how I strong armed her into spilling it like this.

Maybe she had the same syndrome I'd seen bring down too many others. Workaholism, one more sick fuckin' ism I'd love to see wiped from God's green Earth.

"Forget it, Hannah. I'll check in with you soon. We don't have to stay attached at the hip, for fuck's sake. If you can make it, fine. If not...well, I ain't busting your ass over it."

Might even ease any unexpected bullshit with Firefly if she doesn't show up, I thought, keeping that part to myself. My big Enforcer hadn't said much since he'd voted to save my gavel. We shared an icy peace, knowing it could go up in flames anytime. He hadn't accepted anything between his sis and me.

"I'm heading out," I told her, lifting my mug to knock down the rest of my coffee. "Too much work today, or I'd stay longer. Try to take a few breaks so your fingers don't fall off."

She smiled, tense and uneasy, nodding. I put my mug down and got halfway to the door before I heard her feet pounding the floor after me.

Hannah crashed into me from behind. I turned around, a thousand questions running through my mind, second guessing my own damned second guessing about what the hell was going on here.

Didn't want to upset her more. I helped her up, smoothing her hands over my leather cut, and kissed away the tears rolling down her cheeks.

"Please don't read anything into this, Dusty. I'm really, *really* close to a breakthrough with my work, and once it happens, I'll have all the time in the world for the things I want to be a part of." She grabbed my hand, pressed it against her cheek, stamping her lips on the back. "I'll be there if I can, I promise."

"I'm serious about keeping those fingers intact, darlin'. Plus every other beautiful part of you. You can work yourself to death, and the world won't wait. It just goes on with people livin' and dyin', popping out kids right and left, weddings and funerals all over the damned place."

"Jesus, don't you think I *know?*" She let go. More hot tears streamed down her cheeks.

Shit. I hadn't meant to set her off.

I grabbed her, held on for awhile, calmly stroking her hair, savoring this touch like it might be the last, even though I was certain it wouldn't be.

"Do what you need to, Hannah. No judgment. Love you anyway, whether you're there or not."

Double shit. I just let a loose grenade tumble out my mouth.

She looked at me, wide eyed and scared, when we both realized the crazy fuckin' L-word that fell out.

"Gotta go." I cut it short, doubling my speed out the door, taking the shortcut across her lawn with a quickness I only used in a gun fight.

I kept it together 'til I hit the road, riding home, and letting the screen door bang shut behind me. Then I sat down in the worn leather armchair, cupping my face in both hands, giving myself a second before I went for the bottle of Jack I had waiting under the counter.

You're coming undone, you stupid bastard. All over pussy, too.

I looked up, imagining my old man standing in the corner. Early shook his head, his big beard gnarled, a nasty sneer on his face. Kind he always wore before he cut me down over nothing, or told ma she was just imagining the other women.

"Fuck off!" I spat. "Ain't in the mood."

Whether I said it to him or myself, assuming they weren't one and the same, who knew.

Things were changing.

And that was a goddamned understatement. A couple more days, I'd watch two more of my boys tie the knot, happier than they ever thought they'd be a year ago back when the club was on its back.

Had to get a grip. *Had to.*

Hell, if I kept letting Hannah make me hallucinate the asshole I called dad, I'd take Joker's spot as the resident psycho wearing our patch. I stood up, staring angrily into the empty corner of my living room where I'd seen him a few seconds ago.

"Thanks for nothing, deadbeat asshole," I growled. "If you hadn't spent thirty years shittin' on me, maybe I'd know how to handle this girl. Maybe I'd throw my club together again, easy as pie, and get the brothers' knives away from their own throats. Maybe I'd have a wife and kid of my own, and I'd treat 'em right, better than you ever fuckin' treated me and mom."

I stopped. Talking to a dead man wasn't doing me any favors. Rambling to my own demons wouldn't do anybody a lick of good.

Only way to set this right was to get through this wedding, whether Hannah showed herself or not, and then find out what was really eating her.

If it was just work, I'd deal. And if it was something else…well, shit, I'd deal with that, too.

Deep down, I'd claimed her, and I wasn't letting go. Nothing would stop me from keeping her mine.

* * * *

Ma came by a few days later to meet me before the wedding. I sat at my kitchen counter, staring at my phone, wishing like hell Hannah would've changed her mind.

Having her there to watch Skin and Joker get hitched wasn't happening, and I'd have to live with it.

She sent the last text that morning. My eyes scanned over it, biting the end of my pipe hard while I drew in a long pull of fresh tobacco.

Dusty – I'm sorry. I need to get this database right, or I'm risking the entire infrastructure coming down. Give your boys my very best. We'll talk soon.

"Ah, I wondered what had you so uptight this morning," Ma said, standing over my shoulder. "When are you going to introduce us?"

I spun around, taking a good, long look at the wry smile on her face. *Never,* I wanted to say. Besides being a bald ass lie, it would've made me feel guilty as sin because maybe some part of me wanted to take Hannah to meet her.

"Whenever," I said, drawing my pipe out of my mouth, watching the smoke curl out the end. "Won't be today, Ma. She's a busy lady."

"Really? Busier than you?" She stared at me with way too much amusement on her face, one hand resting on her hip. "Daniel Stonewall Grayson – are you telling me you've met your match?"

"Fuck no," I said, standing up to get more coffee. Only decent option I had to take the edge off. "I'm saying we're taking it slow, Ma, but don't get any crazy ideas in your head. It ain't that serious."

Bullshit. The fact that I'd just watched my phone like a hawk since sunrise said things were more serious than they'd ever been with any woman.

"Oh, Danny, just when I thought today couldn't get any sweeter." Wearing that stupid smile, she shook her head, as if she couldn't believe what was rolling around inside it. "Looks like I'm going to see you married after all, one of these days. Take notes today. It'll be like a trial run for your own wedding. I'll bring the extra tissues."

"Ma!" I stamped my boot, sloshing coffee onto the floor. No woman survived life in this club without sass, but she brought it by the ton. "You're getting carried away."

I'd never seen her so happy since…shit, probably not since my old man died. Red faced, laughing, covering her old grey eyes, I left to her to the moment while I mopped the floor with a paper towel.

"If you're done cackling, we've got to get our butts in

gear and go. Preacher man's pretty damned punctual about when he starts these things."

"Sure, Dusty." She was still dabbing at her eyes when I came up, tossed the paper towel away, and quickly chugged the rest of my coffee. "Bet he's getting tired of doing so many weddings so close together. What's his story anyway?"

I thought about the turtle faced hell raiser we all called preacher man, who'd given the club its moral support for several years now. "Old friend of the club's. You know how it goes. He thinks we're guardian angels or something. Like we need a man of God keeping us on track, fulfilling our destiny, or some shit."

Ma nodded, thinking it over.

Truth was, preacher man prattled on about that crap plenty of times, but he had a better reason to help the club when duty called.

Early bailed his ass out back in the day, not long before he bit the bullet. The quiet, small town preacher went through a bad spell. Got himself mixed up in dope and crystal, and unknowingly opened the door for the bastards selling it use his church basement for storage and production.

Didn't last long. My old man killed every last one of those fuckers muscling in on his turf, burned the filth below his Sunday flock, and chained up preacher man 'til he stopped sweating like a pig and crying for his mama. I stood guard that night, when the junk he'd gotten hooked on was leaving his system, listening to him pray to the almighty like he never had in his life.

He cried like a baby when he realized what he'd done. Asked the Lord to take him then because he could've gotten people killed.

I stepped up and put my boot on his foot 'til he cried harder. Told him to shut up, turn himself around, and make amends for his God and for himself. I helped him up when he'd had his fill of pain, let him bawl in my arms like a little boy who'd gotten himself into something far too serious for his years.

Preacher man swore he'd do right. He'd serve his people. I told him I'd be checking in to make sure he did, and if he ever went off the track – well, he'd be fuckin' lucky to end up in a Tennessee prison cell.

Of course, my old man didn't give a shit about him getting clean, or the fact that the meth lab in the church might've blown several blocks to kingdom come. Early was pissed because the drug trade around here was *his*, and nobody muscled in on his territory with that cheap, inferior junk cooked up in test tubes.

Preacher man came out clean, and stayed that way. I kept an eye on his ass every other year, and occasionally had the prospects look through his windows when he wasn't around. They'd never seen him relapse, and he'd become a gospel sensation around town ever since, all because we'd made him a believer in everything he said.

Faith is a powerful thing, but sometimes it needs a helping hand.

Ma ran upstairs to change while I returned to the counter, stuffing my pipe in my pocket, wondering how I'd handle Firefly if he wanted to have it out over his sis at the big shindig about to go down.

Hopefully, he wouldn't be stupid. With any luck, we'd save settling our accounts for another day, since nobody wanted to put their personal shit in between another brothers' vows.

"Ready when you are, Dusty," she said, standing by the door, wearing a purple Sunday dress I hadn't seen in years.

"Fuck me sideways. Guess I know why you're nosing around my dating life, Ma," I said, hiding the smile pulling at my face. "Who the hell is he, and how hard do I have to kick his ass?"

She blushed, laughing, giving me a gentle push when I got next to her. "Please. You know just as well as I do I'm too old for any man except your father."

"Yeah," I said, the giddiness fading when I thought about my asshole old man. "I'll start the truck."

She'd sacrificed her whole damned life looking after me, and that asshole who'd given me half my DNA, plus a whole lot of grief.

Much as I teased about her meeting somebody knew, I had a feeling she never would. Too bad.

Part of her died the day they lowered Early in the ground, dressed in full patches, his dagger laid out across his chest. One day, she'd be buried with him, and I'd shed a few tears over this senseless fuckin' tragedy we called our lives.

Tragedy? That what you're calling the cozy life I left her with? My old man's nasty voice growled at me from the passenger seat. *Fuck you, kid. I gave your Ma more than you ever will, even though I took some privileges when she wasn't lookin'.*

I slapped the steering wheel and tightened my hands around it, soon as I climbed inside, before Ma joined me. *No, Early, fuck you.*

I wouldn't let his shit get to me today. Wouldn't even let Hannah's absence get me down. Ma was laughing, just like plenty more people would be soon. That meant a whole hell of a lot after everything the club went through lately.

I'd see my brothers hitched with a smile. Come heaven, hell, and everything in between. Even if I had to nail it to my fuckin' face.

* * * *

Men roared. Happy couples kissed. Bingo howled, thumping his big grey tail on the grass for hours, overwhelmed with excitement.

We held the big bash on the land I owned a little ways outside town. It was a serene, wild place with the Smokies towering over us. History roamed deep in this soil. It'd been a place where regiments drilled during the Civil War. Didn't have to look hard to find my share of old bullets and cavalry gear wedged in the dirt.

Meg and Skin were electric like always. They laid their lives on the line for each other when they said their piece, and kissed like they wanted to wake the dead.

But Joker and his girl, Summer? Crazy motherfucker stole the damned show.

Almost had to let my pipe spill hot ash on my skin to believe what I was seeing. The most twisted brother in the club suddenly had it all, and then some. One big happy family with the wife, the kid, and the dog who hardly ever calmed down.

Brothers, family friends, and club associates milled around, digging into barbecue and slugging down booze. I went light on the Jack and pork, and lighter still on my usual lectures I gave everybody about the history rooted in this land. Paid my respects to my Veep and his beautiful bride before they took off for their honeymoon, leaving the rest of the party to go deep into the night.

Fires were lit. The last holdout fireflies came appeared in the autumn night, burning bright as stars, before nature stamped them out for winter.

I sat by Ma, listening to her humming to herself, smoking my pipe. "Beautiful ceremony. Simply gorgeous," she said, turning to me.

"Yeah, Ma. It really was. Never thought I'd see Joker ride off so happy. Glad I was wrong."

"It'll be you someday, boy. Count on it."

I cocked my head and snorted like always. Wouldn't show it, but for some fucked up reason, her fantasy words hit me deeper than before. Up 'til recently, I hadn't realized I wanted any of this shit, the woman, the kid, or the wedding.

Would that happen with Hannah, if things got serious enough? Was I ready to give it all up to make sure it did?

Who the fuck knew. I sure didn't, when I walked into

the night, stepping away from Ma and the crowd to give myself some time to think.

When I found a quiet corner, I pulled out my phone, searching for any new texts. Nothing.

Shit, that bothered me. Worse, I hated that it did, wasting the minutes when I should've been celebrating pining after the chick who'd been the hardest lay of my life. No, more than just a lay.

If it wasn't for her, I would've told a prospect to drive Ma home because I'd be going back to my place with a fresh bottle and brand new pussy on my bike.

Ain't that sweet. Yearnin' after your carefree bulllshit days. I looked up and saw Early's ghost leaning against a tree, a pipe uncomfortably like mine tucked into his beard. *You know marriage don't have to change that shit, Dusty. You can have the wife, the kid, and all the pussy in the world on the side, long as you wear this patch like a man.*

"Shut up," I growled quietly, into the night, swiping my hand at a few fireflies blinking in my face.

Too bad preacher man didn't do exorcisms. Hell, maybe I needed a shrink.

'Course, I'd give up my gavel before I went there and confessed my sins to some quack.

I had blood on my hands, good and bad, just like my old man. We were too fuckin' similar, no matter how much I tried to do right by my brothers, right by Ma, right by the woman I was starting to call *mine.*

Every boy gets the good, the bad, and the ugly in droves from his father. Me, I'd gotten a world of shit, all of his strength, and a flashing red warning not to make his dumb mistakes.

Honestly, it wasn't just dad's women who made Ma suffer. Life in this club wasn't easy for any woman, and half the girls just hitched were only realizing what they'd gotten into. They bore the brunt of it like champs, sure.

Could Hannah? Fuck, did she even want to?

I didn't know, and the uncertainty chewed me apart, piece by bitter piece. I turned around angrily, just in time to see Ma coming toward me with a yawn.

"If you've had your fun…I'm ready to head out anytime," she said, smoothing out her purple dress, so different from the scrubs she wore for work, or the jeans and t-shirts she donned on weekends.

I waited 'til we were halfway to the parking lot before I dropped the bomb building in my brain. "I've got a question. When you were with dad, did you ever have any doubts after you took his brand? Ever stop and wonder what the fuck you were doing mixed up in all this – the club, the danger, the bullshit, I mean? I need to know."

We stepped several paces later. She looked at me intently through the night, a soft, reassuring smile on her lips.

"I'm only human. What do you think, Danny? You were there those nights I shut myself away and bawled my eyes out."

Of course. How the fuck could I forget? I never would. I'd never know peace from it either, all because I'd let my fuck of a father shuffle off his mortal coil before slipping on my brass knuckles and busting his jaw.

"Why'd you stay?" I forced the question through my teeth. "You could've taken off anytime. You're a smart woman, good career. Could've made a fresh start anywhere. Was this all worth it?"

"For me, Dusty, the answer will always be *yes.*" She grabbed my fist with both her hands, pressing it tightly between her fingers. "When a woman puts ink on her skin and wears that PROPERTY patch, she's locked in. It's a vow, no different from the oath you saw your brothers and their new wives take tonight."

"Contracts get voided. Half the shit he did to you qualifies," I said, staring down at her as she began the standard head shake whenever I told her what a bastard he'd been. "Look, I know you'll live out your days feeling differently about it than me. I'll respect it. But fuck, Ma, I ain't ever gonna get it."

"Love isn't easy, Danny. I had a higher tolerance than most for blood, grit, and toil. I opened my heart. I took my bruises to the heart. Kept hoping he'd change, when every day said he wouldn't. Hoped Early's bad habits would never rub off on you. So far, knock on wood, at least one of those wishes has come true."

My eyes went wide. "Ma, I've spent my life running away from his shit. Trying to bury it for myself, for you, for this club. Just put him behind us for good. You're a strong woman, living with your regrets, looking 'em dead in the eye. The brothers, you, and all the girls who gave up their other options to become old ladies in this MC…I get it, they're stuck, and they want to be. Trouble is, I don't know if I can bring somebody else into this insanity."

We both knew I was talking about Hannah. Probably sounded ridiculous, too, seeing how she'd grown up with one foot in the club as Firefly's little sis. But she'd gotten further away from this world than anybody raised into it, for fuck's sake. She wanted to leave this behind, and she'd practically succeeded.

Making her mine, making it official...wouldn't that be dragging her back?

Screwing her over? Leaving her with the same regrets Ma still hadn't come to terms with, regardless of what she said?

My stomach turned. Ma leaned in, gave me a peck on the cheek, and turned away before I could catch more than a glimpse of the tears beading in her old eyes.

"Why are you still here talking to me, son? Take me home, and then go see her. There's only one woman in the world who can help you sort this out, and she ain't me."

Blunt as hell. Never failed to respect it.

I swallowed the rage and confusion building in my throat, nodding.

We walked to my truck without saying another word. Kept it that way the whole way into town, listening to the radio to avoid the awkward silence.

I let Ma off and waved, waiting 'til she got inside before I revved my truck's engine, and peeled out of her driveway. My hands shook like a motherfucker as I held the wheel, sheer emotion tearing through me, a fuckin' lifetime of hell trying to work its way out before I flipped it on its ass.

Bringing Hannah closer upended everything. But fuck

if I'd get cold feet now, or let her slip away, all because the past kept me from making the moves I should.

No more half-assing it. No more regrets, just like Ma said. I'd march into her mansion, sweep her off her feet, and have her right by my side while we took the joys, the sorrows, and everything else a man and woman should. Long as they did it together.

"I'm coming, darlin'. This time for good," I whispered into the darkness. "Get ready. I ain't leaving 'til I see you wearing PROPERTY OF DUST with a smile on your face."

IX: Ashes to Ashes (Hannah)

Several Hours Earlier

Why I thought I could sit on my laptop doing this crap tonight, I'd never know. I already felt terrible lying to Dusty about my absence, the mountain of work I had that stopped me from going to the big club wedding tonight.

Well, at least the mountain part was right.

I hadn't made any headway whatsoever with the transactions problem. A fix didn't seem possible in the app's current infrastructure. I'd have to rip apart *everything*, probably take down the program for several hours, and lose a lot of business in the meantime.

I let out a sigh, angrily slamming my computer shut. Pulling out my phone, I stared at the screen, sadness shooting through me when I saw the last text I'd sent.

SORRY, D. CAN'T MAKE IT. DUTY CALLS.

He hadn't responded, but why should he? Dusty had a sixth sense for knowing something was wrong, and I had a feeling he knew lies when he heard them, too.

Sooner or later, if I didn't come clean, he'd confront me.

The same cruel dilemma stared me in the face, promising to get nastier, the longer I let it linger.

Was it worse to lose him over these lies, even if they might save his life? Or should I give up, admit I'd gotten in *way* over my head, and tell the club everything?

They'd try to help me, at least. Knowing they had my back, that they'd do everything they could to make sure Dom and his men disappeared forever, would make me feel better.

Until the first shots were fired in the war, and the first man wearing a Deadly Pistols patch came home in a coffin. They'd avoided casualties in their latest clashes. But everybody's luck ran out eventually, and the Sicilians came armed with unfair advantages.

If telling them got Dust, Firefly, or any other man killed…

Then I'd probably douse this fucking place in gasoline and light the match. Nothing else would do for appeasing the gods of greed I'd given my soul to before they killed my man or my brother, and taking more blood to quench their thirst.

I cracked. Hot, restless tears rolled down my cheeks. My temples pounded, a fresh headache stabbing at my brain, taunting me for the millionth time over the mess I'd gotten myself into.

Since I wasn't going to work anyway, I thought about calling Dusty, toying with the idea of telling him I'd be there soon. It would be too late for the ceremonies, but I could join the reception. Maybe wish the newlyweds well before they took off, and show Dust that I wasn't such a high strung whack job I'd put coding over him.

I balanced the phone in my hand, almost ready to dial. Before I could tap to make the call, someone took a hammer to my door. That's what the pounding sounded like.

I held my breath, knowing whatever it was, it couldn't be good.

Walking down the long hall to answer it, I had no fear. There was no guessing who might be banging away like that, climbing over my gate to smash their fist on my door, as if they had a better claim to this place than I did.

I halfway expected to see Dom himself standing on my porch when I cracked the door open.

"Let us the fuck in," Tony said, pushing the barrel of a gun through the door, right in my face. Another one of Dom's lieutenants, Franco, stood behind him. "Not gonna ask you again, peach."

Peach. They all used the same disgusting nickname. Like I was nothing more to them than a soft fruit meant to be sliced apart and devoured.

The gun in my face only left me one option. My fingers didn't even shake as I let them in, stepping back before they shoved their way in, banging the door angrily against the wall.

"I'll put on some coffee. It's going to be a long night, isn't it?" I asked, wondering if this eerie calm running in my veins would get me killed.

"No shit. So, you know why we're here?" Tony paused, eyeing the gun in his hands. He didn't give me time to answer. "You're late, bitch. Dom hasn't heard a fucking peep for days, and everybody knows that's a *big* problem."

"Yeah, I'm sorry. I had other things on my mind."

"Other things?" He looked at me, smoothing an angry hand through his thinning hair. "Franco, I want you to get this cunt against the wall, and help me pat her down. I think she's lost her fuckin' mind."

The other man smiled. I didn't resist as they threw me against it, lifting my hands high above my head, waiting to get this over with.

Hell, maybe they weren't too far off. I had to be crazy to go along with this without fear turning my blood cold, right?

I always thought a person under the gun just stopped caring in the mysteries and movies. If I'd reached that stage...then I'd might as well start digging my own grave.

Tony took his sweet time rubbing his hands up and down my body. Closing my eyes, I waited for the disgusting sideshow to pass, still leaning on the wall when their hands were finally off me.

"She's clean," Franco said reluctantly. "Think I should check upstairs? See if she's got a stash? We've seen these rich fucks lose it before. Usually because they're popping pills or sniffing powder."

"Fuck that. Can't be drugs with this one. She's too fucking smart for that, unless something's really changed." Tony grabbed me by my wrists and spun me around, throwing his weight in as he pinned me to the wall. "I'll tell ya what's gonna happen, peach. You're taking us to every goddamned computer in this house. You'll unlock them, help us find what we need, and sit with us while we take a good, long look at what the fuck you've been doing."

"But –"

"But nothing!" He shook me, spittle flying in my face. "You'll do everything I just said, or I'll get you on your knees right now and put a fucking bullet in your head. That's probably how it's gonna end anyway, but we're nice enough to give your pretty little face one more chance."

I wasn't out of it enough to argue. They'd find out about my total coder's block as soon as they opened my programs and saw exactly nothing over the past week. And that was assuming they'd understand any of it, and didn't just decide to kill me anyway in their confusion.

"Okay," I said, letting out a sigh.

Tony released me angrily, giving me a push with his hand. The gun replaced his fingers, pressed against my spine. They marched me into the kitchen like a proper prisoner, their eyes raging the entire time.

Men like this didn't just kill. If they decided to murder me, they'd probably take their pleasure first, making sure I suffered for going against the Brotherhood.

I wished I hadn't lied to Dusty about hiring the bodyguard after Joker's boy disappeared. I'd given him a name I knew in Sterner security, and the background check came out clean. I hadn't actually hired the man, knowing he'd be a goner when something like tonight finally happened, but at least I wouldn't be dying alone if I'd given him the job.

God, what am I saying? I wanted to kick myself for driving deeper into crazy town, but I was too busy opening my laptop, pulling up the files that would seal my doom.

Tony snatched the computer away from me, nearly breaking it when it banged on the counter's edge. "This it?"

"Yeah. It's the only thing I use. My old desktop crapped out a few months ago. You can send Franco down to check the hard drive if you don't believe me."

The two men shared a look. Tony clenched his teeth, taking a seat at the breakfast bar before he said anything.

"I don't trust anything this bitch says or does. Go find that fucking thing, pull it out, and we'll bring the data home with us." Tony grabbed my neck, pinching it tight while he worked the keyboard with one hand.

Franco took off, wandering into my office downstairs. Several minutes later, I heard things breaking, and knew he wasn't going to spare anything while he pried open my poor dead computer.

I stood awkwardly next to Tony, watching his frustration mount as he quickly opened and closed documents, comparing them to the program I used for working on the app. Or trying to, anyway.

"Explain this shit," he said, stuffing a greasy finger against a line of code I'd highlighted in red on the screen.

Small satisfaction they still needed me to figure any of this out. Maybe that would delay hot lead going through my skull, just for a little while.

"That's me thinking to myself, the part I've been trying to figure out. At first, I thought I might be able to cloak the transactions going to your accounts, just ghost them so they weren't part of anything visible at all. But as you can see from this line, it ain't so simple." I paused, pointing at the screen. "Reworking that will mess with the payment system where the paid subscriptions run each billing period. That means I have to take down the whole thing, give it a whole new framework, or we're going to have our asses hanging out for any competitor to stumble on the money laundering scheme. Trouble is, that also means building a new billing system for subscribers, and it won't run nearly as smooth with all this extra junk up in it."

Tony angrily scrolled through everything, pretending he understood it, for several more minutes. Then he slammed my laptop shut and pushed it away from him, sending it spinning across the counter.

"There's no fucking point to laundering more money if this thing comes down and causes a stink with its real customers. We can't lose business trying to cover our tracks."

"And we would," I snapped. "You don't know how addicted people get to these things. If my app isn't there anymore to play matchmaker, give them something to swipe left or right, they'll move onto the next big thing. And that means a lot less money for both of us. It's all momentum, Tony."

"Fuck you, bitch. I'm not stupid. It's your debt. Your goddamned job to figure this out!" He slammed his gun down on the counter, slicking back his thin dark hair one more time. "Christ. Dom said you were some kinda wonder kid with this technical bullshit. I can't believe he fucked up here, seeing more than just a *kid*."

Inwardly, I bristled. If only I kept the knife wrack on this side of the kitchen, I might've used my anger to pull my sharpest blade, slamming it into his throat before he knew what hit him.

But that wouldn't stop Franco downstairs. I'd never win a gun fight, considering I'd passed on the range like an idiot every time Huck offered to take me.

Another missed opportunity. One more gut-wrenching regret to twist my stomach in knots during what might've been the start of my life flashing before my eyes.

Franco came up a minute later, slamming my PC's guts on the counter, next to my battered laptop. "Should we gather up all this shit and her, take them both somewhere we can get some real answers?"

Tony looked at his henchman, frustration growing in his dark eyes. "Fuck, I don't know. I need to call Dom."

I sat like a stone while he made the call. Franco pulled a bottle of wine from my wrack and pulled the cork with his switchblade, taking a long drag straight from the bottle.

My stomach turned over. I remembered the last time I'd drunk wine straight from the bottle with Dusty, and now we might never get that chance again.

Christ, my last contact with him might be the lying text I sent that morning.

After I disappeared, he'd come for me. I imagined him breaking into this empty house by himself.

He'd realize I was missing if I didn't respond for several

days. He'd bring the club in on it, and they'd mount a full search. But they wouldn't find me in time if the two bastards occupying my kitchen had anything to say about it.

Plenty of girls in the club had wound up captured, and lived to tell the tale. Those were other biker gangs, though. The Sicilians were pros, never as sloppy as the Deadhands MC or the Atlanta Torches.

Odds were, I'd wind up a missing person. An empty question mark haunting everyone I'd ever cared about for the rest of their lives.

"Yeah...yeah, boss. You got it. Sure, I'll tell the fucking cunt." Tony nodded into the phone pressed against his ear. Franco gulped more wine loudly, the sickening smack of his lips bringing me back to earth. "Forget about it. We'll do what we can here, whatever we can fix, so you don't have to see her lazy ass again."

Tony clapped his burner phone shut. He turned around, eyeballing me and Franco. "Good news and bad news. Boss says we're supposed to keep this bitch here, and put her to work. Rough her up any way we need to until she figures shit out."

Franco grinned while my heart sank. "Best fucking news I heard all day, Tony. What's the bad?"

"We've got five hours."

"Five hours?" I cut in. "That isn't even enough time to pull down the site without major errors in backup, much less –"

"I *said,* five fucking hours!" Tony roared, running to me,

shoving the cold gun against my temple. "Five hours, bitch. Count 'em. If you're still blue balling us without any answers by two AM, you can forget about paying back your debts or taking your next breath. Dom says you're more trouble than you're worth, and the contract's terminated. We'll take down your fucking site, empty this place out, and dump your body off in the mountains."

That fear I'd sat on all evening caught up to me. I felt it in the gun's cold steel, his finger poised on the trigger, ready to end my life if I so much as sneezed at the wrong second.

It tugged at my throat, jerked me toward the black pit swallowing up my future, whispering in my ear.

Time to pay your debts for real, trailer trash. Did you really think you'd take off with your money, your man, your success?

People like you don't make it. They make bad moves and trip all over themselves when they try to claw their way up.

You're going to die alone with money that was never yours. Oh, and fuck your broken heart, too.

"What the fuck's the matter?" Tony whispered, tracing the gun along the tears I'd suppressed, spilling down my cheeks. "Easy, peach, before you get too upset. We're doing you a big goddamned favor, giving you this chance to sort things out. I think you oughta stop being so fucking selfish, and give us something back. Fix this, darling, and we won't have to end your life."

Darlin'. I heard Dust's voice in my head when I reached up and wiped my tears. Tony lowered the gun as I reached for my laptop, and opened the screen, praying the bastard hadn't cracked it while he'd tossed it around.

It was still in one piece. Lucky me.

Everything inside me, that's what was shattered, and it didn't matter worth a damn.

I didn't have a miracle on its way to save me. And I'd lied away the only hero who might.

This was up to me. I had to move my fingers, work my brain, and do everything I could to save myself.

I took a deep breath, and tried to focus. *Okay.*

Step one – pretending the problem staring me in the face wasn't a completely hopeless shortcut to my grave.

* * * *

I took a break near midnight. No closer to a solution than I'd been several hours ago, before they'd shown up and pointed a gun in my face.

They let me take a walk through the house for fresh air. Standing in front of my screen, I stared into the darkness, listening to the icy silence. Autumn meant a slow creeping decline for the bugs, the frogs, everything that reminded a person the world was still alive at night.

My heart clenched. I didn't really know why. Maybe because I thought I'd die without even nature's warmth to comfort me, much less anyone I ever cared about.

I *really* fucking regretted not going to the wedding now. At least if they'd burst in and killed me later, I would've had one last sweet memory to hold onto. One more round of laughter with my brother and his wife, a few more drinks with friends, a couple more fiery kisses from the man I'd never see again.

Or would I?

Something moved in the distance. When I saw the faint headlight switch off next to my gate, I reached up, rubbing my eyes.

Stop. You're hallucinating, I told myself.

I'd read about it before in a hundred true crime stories. When a person believes they're backed into a corner, they'll hang onto any hope, however crazy, wrong, or impossible.

Except it wasn't just my imagination this time. Something heavy dropped into the bushes off to the side a second later, far from the gate. My heart began racing.

It couldn't be Dusty. And Jesus, if it was him, and he hadn't seen their car...he had no clue what kind of mess he'd wandered into.

I gripped the door tightly, peeling it open a crack, straining my ears. I wished they'd tell me if this was real, or if I'd just fallen for the biggest case of wishful thinking ever.

"Hurry up. We need you back at the keyboard," Franco's nasty voice whispered behind me, making me jump. "Tony says you've had your break long enough."

Turning slowly to face him, I looked him dead in his evil eyes, wondering if my glance betrayed anything.

My shirt caught his blood when half his face exploded a second later, spattering me in sudden red mist.

Shock. Awe. Horror.

Franco stood for about two more seconds, as if his body hadn't realized he'd just taken a hole through the head, and then dropped swiftly at my feet.

"The fuck was that falling out there?" Tony yelled from the hallway.

I turned back to the door, my knees shaking, only catching a quick glimpse of the dark, shadowy figure outside before my knees went into overdrive. I hadn't run so hard since cross country senior year. Every muscle fiber in my body came alive, knew this was my last chance, knew I had to get the hell away from the dead man before his friend caught up.

"Sonofafuckingbitch!" Tony slurred one long curse through the screen, hurled it open behind me, and whipped out his gun.

"Roll!" Dusty's voice roared. He hit the ground, reaching for me several feet away, throwing his entire weight into his legs to crawl.

He tackled my knees, pushing me onto my butt, just in time to dodge before the gunshots exploded in a messy circle around us. Grass and dirt flew high into the air, raining down against my face.

Dust crouched on one knee, his gun drawn, holding my face against the earth with his other hand. Protecting me.

What happened next was in God's hands. I pressed my face deeper into the soft, cool grass, coiling into a fetal position, expecting to feel hot lead rip through my body any second. And that was if I didn't catch a bullet through my brain or heart first, making sure I wouldn't feel anything ever again.

Three more shots in loud succession. So fast, so angry, so deafening I couldn't tell who fired.

After the fourth shot, there was another sound. Something hit the ground, falling onto the bushes next to the door with a *whoosh*. Dusty's hand wasn't tangled in my hair anymore.

Slowly, I turned, halfway covering my eyes before I forced myself to look up. Dusty dashed several yards in seconds. He stood over the bushes, his lips peeled back in a hateful grin, gun aimed at the ground.

Tony's voice was faint, muffled. I couldn't understand anything.

"I ain't here to listen to you beg after you almost offed my girl, motherfucker. Shut up. Whine to Old Scratch when he meets you in the fuckin' fire." Dusty's words were clear and savage.

Tony screamed for half a second before the last loud shot silenced him forever. Dust climbed over his body, shaking one of the bushes. He had his phone in his hand before I even got up.

"Get every prospect on duty out here right now. I need backup. No, I ain't ruining Joker and Skin's honeymoon for this. Just some fuckin' trash for the night crew to pickup. You heard me, kid." He shoved his phone back into his pocket, staring angrily at the dead man in the bushes while he pulled out his pipe.

"Jesus, Dusty. It's a miracle. If you'd showed up a second later, I might not be –"

"Work," he snapped, cutting me off. The sparks centered in his grey eyes glowed like steel knives catching light. "You told me *work* was the reason you weren't at the wedding. Hannah, what kind of fuckin' work are you doing when I show up here, and have to kill two assholes before they kill you?"

I froze, my mouth hanging open.

Words wouldn't come. Being dead suddenly didn't seem half bad compared to being caught in this stupid, reckless lie.

"Dusty...Daniel...I fucked up." I closed my eyes, wondering if using his real name would soften him.

"Darlin', you don't know the half of it."

"No, I do. Let's go inside. I'll tell you everything."

He looked at me for a long second. I gasped when he reached out, snatching me by the wrist, jerking me to his chest.

"Better be the truth, the whole truth, and nothing but the bald fuckin' truth this time around. If I think you're hiding so much as what you ate for breakfast this morning, I *will* pull down your panties, throw you over my lap, and spank you 'til you scream. Got it?"

I did, shuddering. The time for denial ended. It would've be suicide to do anything else with this crazy, beautiful bastard who'd just killed two monsters, and saved my life. He still turned me on, too.

Whether it was just his crude promises or raw adrenaline humming in my system, my panties were soaked.

Amazing. Especially when I looked down at my collar, the same place he fixed his eyes, and I realized I was still wearing Franco's blood.

"Can I change first?" I asked, my eyes slowly meeting his. "Please, Dusty?"

"Do it fast. Put that fuckin' shirt in a bag, and hand it off to me when you're done. We can't leave any missing pieces around when my boys show up to clean this mess." Dust walked several steps past me. He ripped open the screen door, holding it and waiting while I walked past, into my home, now freed from its evil occupiers.

I ran upstairs for a quick change, careful to throw the bloody shirt into the bathroom trash, and then pull the whole thing out. I'd solved a lot of problems in my life, but I never thought I'd be dealing with *accessory to murder*, even if it was justified self-defense.

My eyes were red in the mirror. Too many tears, too much stress, and now they held a thousand questions.

Was there any coming back from something like this?

Sure, Dusty saved my life. I'd be grateful, no matter what happened. But he'd also picked me up and thrown me into uncharted waters.

Time to sink or swim. If I couldn't adapt, learn to forgive, and keep my head up, a lot more people were going to die.

Dom was still out there. He'd come for me when he found out what happened to his men, and he'd be after the club, too.

Face, meet palm. Everything I lied my ass off to protect was exposed.

* * * *

An hour later, we sat in my kitchen, listening to the noises down the hall. The prospects scrubbed things clean, disappearing every last trace of the Sicilians' DNA. Their bodies were already long gone.

I didn't ask where. It wasn't any of my business. Ironic, I guess, because my entire miserable life just became an open book for the handsome angel of death sitting across from me.

Dust had his hands on the table, staring me down like a lion. He'd refused the wine and whiskey I offered. Muttered something about how he never drank when shit went down. Not until it was over.

Nothing except the truth would calm him down. I only got a few words in before the tears came.

"I'm sorry...this is really hard for me to talk about," I sputtered.

He snatched my hand, squeezed it in his, and raised it to his lips. His lips landing on the back of my hand set me off all over again. Brutal anguish rolled out in waves, pure poison, fermented by the months I'd clung to my dirty, shameful secret.

"Take as long as you need to dry your eyes, darlin'. Then you fuckin' talk. I ain't backing down 'til you tell me what the hell's going on here."

He deserved that much. I had to collect myself for him. Make no mistake, it *hurt* to admit I'd done wrong.

Pain reached through me, hijacked my heart, and reminded me I'd done far worse than *wrong*. I'd almost screwed him over, and gotten myself killed, all in the same go.

"I lied to you. Lied to my brother, to the law, and to myself."

"Already figured that much," he said, his voice rough and low. "Why?"

"Huck and me grew up with practically nothing. You've heard his stories, I'm sure, the Christmases we were lucky to get marbles and chocolate bars. The gun momma kept underneath her pillow, all of us sleeping in the same room…it shapes a kid, and not for the better. We lived under siege, grew up closer than any family ought to be. She'd be near us if the meth heads down the street broke in, tried to rob us, or worse."

"Everybody's got a sob story, darlin'," he said roughly. "Believe me, my heart's bleedin' for you. But I'm not seeing how it's the least bit fuckin' relevant here."

I looked at him angrily. "I'm getting there. I thought maybe if you knew the background, you'd understand."

"You're missing the whole point to this, babe. Am I pissed you lied to me? Sure." His eyes narrowed, pulling me in a little deeper, into the endless storm raging in his grey irises. "Judging you for whatever the fuck you did or didn't do won't fix a damned thing. We can sort the rest of this out when you stop giving me your life story, and start telling me why the fuck I killed two assholes who wanted you dead."

I had to skip ahead. "Whatever. So, you know I did my interning with the Sterner Corp. I learned a lot, got a great education, thought I'd found my place up in the world. Just like how Huck became Firefly, and found his purpose in the club."

Dust nodded. I broke away, staring at the counter, the pain in my chest sharpening.

"A job in Seattle with a good starting salary wasn't good

enough after I interned. I wanted *more,* Dusty, and I jumped at the first person who gave me a chance. I had this idea for an app…the matchmaker software I've given my life to. Trouble is, it cost money, and I didn't want to do it the hard way, taking out loans, risking my credit, schmoozing angel investors. There was a man I met at a Sterner Corp party. He seemed legit. He got me drunk on champagne one night, got me to tell him all my big dreams about becoming a superstar." More tears came, wild and hot. How had I been so stupid?

"Everybody fucks up when they're young. Who was he?"

"Dominick Barone. Loud, pushy, able to make things happen like magic. I didn't realize it was thanks to his mafia ties until after he put his claws in me. Sicilian Brotherhood. I looked them up when I realized things weren't adding up."

"One of the worst," Dust growled. "Gonna be a pleasure to skin the motherfuckers alive."

I went on, trying to push the gruesome image out of my head. "I did the coding work in no time flat, and launched it with real marketing behind it. Bought and paid for by his generous investment. The thing earned millions in a few months. I was overwhelmed, ready to celebrate, and live it up a little. So, I bought myself this place while Dom shrugged off my questions about paying him back. He told me not to worry about it, said he'd come to collect when it was time."

Dusty's grip on my fingers grew hotter, angrier. "Motherfuckers. I've heard 'em going after the brilliant and gullible types before."

Ouch. Gullible hurt because it was true.

"I guess that's fair," I said, wiping my eyes. Yes, I deserved to feel like an ass in front of him, but it still stung viciously. "I was an idiot, Dusty. I took the bait, and I've been paying for it ever since. They made me set up a new account for their businesses, link it into my app's infrastructure. Money laundering, you know. They wanted more the longer this arrangement went on. Last time I met them in Seattle, they handed me a new project. I couldn't figure out how to hide the ridiculous things they wanted. It would've meant restructuring everything, and they wanted it done *now*. They expected me to work miracles…or they wanted me to die."

"That's why they were here tonight," he said, giving a satisfied nod. "Every puzzle fits together real neat when you've got the right pieces."

I nodded glumly. "They had a gun to my head. Told me I'd die if I didn't fix what they wanted tonight."

New anger crossed his face. Dusty clenched my hand harder, brought it to his chest, and wouldn't let go.

"I'd kill the motherfuckers again for that, if I could. How many more are there? Where are they based?"

"Honestly, I don't know." My stomach twisted as my worst nightmare came true, thinking about him and the club putting themselves in more danger just for me. "I usually met Dom out west, when I went back to Seattle for business. Please, don't do anything hasty. We need to figure out how we're going to keep everyone safe, first of all."

"Darlin'…" He stood up, came over to me, and cupped

my face in his big hand. "You've been through a fuck of a lot for a woman as smart and sexy as you, so I'm gonna give you one pass. Focus on resting up tonight, knowing you're safe. Stop worrying about the rest. I run my club, and I'll figure this out. Make sure those mafia cocksuckers never threaten anybody again."

Suicide. That's what he was proposing. I heard it over and over in my mind while I looked into his eyes. This raging, arrogant, gorgeous man wasn't going to stop until he'd solved my problem once and for all. Not even if it killed him first.

I sighed, shaking my head. "I lied to you because I didn't want to put *anyone* in danger. This is my problem, Dusty. I can't live with myself if it ends up hurting you, or Firefly, or any of the men."

"Wrong. Your problem turned into mine the second they started fuckin' with my girl. I'd be a sorry excuse for a Prez if I let any man rough up my woman, plus a brother's little sis. Far as I'm concerned, they fucked with club property. They fucked with what's *mine*. You ain't stupid, darlin'. You know how this goes. Whenever anybody fucks with the Pistols, we fuck back a hundred times harder. They're dead, first chance we get. How it happens, that's up to me. Not you, darlin'."

I nodded, more tears rolling down my cheeks, into his hand. He brushed them all away, clearing a path to kiss me.

His lips brought me back to life. They forgave me, warmed me just as much as his words, the ultimate reminder that somebody actually *cared*.

"Dusty..."

"Enough. Go clean up and sleep like I said. I'll post a prospect outside your room if you're too scared to sleep. Nobody's coming or going without me knowing about."

I shook my head. "No. I'm sure the men who died were the only ones here. And if they weren't, the Brotherhood won't be so stupid to come charging in a second time. I'll be fine."

"I'll crash next to you when I can," he said, pulling his hand away from me. "Too much work to do first. Gotta make sure this mess on your doorstep is finished before I do anything else."

No argument here. Before I left him alone, I threw my hands over his neck one last time, standing on my toes to reach his glorious lips.

"I'll never forget this, Dusty. Obviously, this night would've been a whole lot happier if I'd just gone to the wedding and told you what was going on. But I think it might be pretty special, anyway."

"Special?" He raised an eyebrow. "That what you call it when I pump a couple holes in the bastards who wanted you dead?"

"No, crazy." I pushed gently against his chest. "Special because you saved my life. No one's ever done that before."

And God willing, I hope they never have to again. I kept that thought to myself as I walked away, flashing him one more grateful look over my shoulder.

The most unlikely hero in the world stood there like a giant, ready to rip apart anything that got in his way. I smiled, letting the insanity of the night finally take over.

However fearsome, however stubborn, however insane…he was all mine.

After everything that happened, it meant the world.

X: Laying Claim (Dust)

A whole week went by since we wiped up their blood, dragged their bodies deep into the Smokies, and fixed Hannah's landscaping with our crew. I'd barely left her place to run the club.

Thank Christ half the brothers were away on their honeymoons. But it was only a matter of time before Skin and Joker came back to raise hell, assuming the others didn't start to first. I'd brushed off Sixty, Lion, and Tin when they called to check on me.

Firefly hadn't sent me shit. Long as he cleaned the guns and ran the patrols, he kept his distance, too pissed over me and Hannah to come knocking over me disappearing for a few days.

Maybe he wondered why I had so many prospects pulling double duty. They'd keep their mouths shut if they wanted to earn their bottom rockers. If even one person squawked about doing extra patrols this side of town, near his sis' place, there'd be hell to pay.

For her, I'd paid the devil's toll several times over. Wouldn't hesitate to do it again.

Once you killed for a woman, something primal went off inside, an urge to destroy every last motherfucker who came around threatening her life.

Hannah mostly stayed in her room, or worked on her computer, frantically messing with her software. She wanted to rip apart the money laundering scheme at the roots and get her app back on track as a legit one.

The Sicilians probably realized she'd broken her chain. That meant I had to hit them first, before they could get it together and come digging for their dead men.

Our attack goal came easy. Finding out where to hit them, and how…I'd rarely met as big a bitch as the problem staring us in the face.

Wasn't easy doing research, just Hannah and me, desperately seeking out a lead on where they called home. Six days in, I wanted to tear her fancy place apart, knowing it was only hers because she'd built it under the gun. Worse, we couldn't find the bastards who'd made it possible, and mortgaging her life on death threats.

"You look terrible, Dusty. Take a walk," she said, looking up at me over the computer, wearing her glasses. "I'll stay here and work. We'll run into something sooner or later. Nobody keeps a clean nose online. A little more detective work, just a little while longer, and we'll have them."

Easy for her to say. She knew a lot about proxy this and deep web that. More than I'd know about computers if I gave up riding tomorrow and spent every waking hour at the keyboard.

Right now, only thing I knew for certain, I wanted to take her to bed wearing nothing except those thick black frames around her eyes.

"Keep the candle burning, darlin'. I'm going for a ride," I told her. "I'll make sure the prospects hang out by the gate 'til I'm back. You stumble across a miracle that leads us to 'em on that thing, you let me know. I'll be back in thirty or forty."

Chances were, we wouldn't sniff out the Sicilians today. Too bad.

The longer they stayed hidden pushed everything back – briefing the club, dealing with the fallout, coming to make them pay in blood.

Patience, I told myself. Just a little while longer, like Hannah said.

Nobody hid forever. This club had tracked and slaughtered more bastards who deserved to die than anybody else in the state. Meanwhile, there was another problem I could solve today, one with a solution a whole lot clearer.

First, I headed home. Took me about twenty minutes to dig through the old tool crib in my garage. Besides the ratchets, hammers, and drills, I kept a few handguns locked up, plus several ghosts from the past.

Found the little ring box lurking underneath some old newspaper. It was wrapped up in the same faded articles Ma put around it last year when she gave it to me. She said I should keep it safe, in case 'something happened' – the phrase she used for worrying about her own mortality.

I'd snorted at her then, scoffed at the whole idea of holding onto my grandma's wedding ring. She told me to shut up and take it because she didn't have any use for it anymore. Because, one day, I'd find a girl worth giving it to.

Seemed impossible at the time. Now?

Fuck. I, Daniel Grayson, had officially fallen to his knees.

Went down hard. Foaming at the mouth to end forty odd years of bachelorhood. The man who'd always pushed cupid down like some yappy little dog had his arrow lodged deep, and that shit was poison.

I couldn't go on without seeing this old gold band on her finger. Couldn't breathe easy every day Hannah wasn't wearing my ink. Fuckin' her blew my brains out, but I wouldn't truly own her 'til I saw that ring against my dick every time she wrapped her fingers around me. Love wouldn't mean what it should 'til I bent her over, took her from behind, and saw PROPERTY OF DUST tattooed on her shoulder, her ass, wherever she damned well pleased, as long as she was *mine.*

Clenching the ring box against my palm, I nodded to myself. *Let's fuckin' do this.*

One more stop waited before I brought it to my woman.

I rolled up to preacher man's door on the other side of town. Walked up the broken steps and pounded on his door 'til he opened up, greeting me with a cup of coffee in his hand and a flannel shirt around his skinny shoulders.

"Dusty? Something I can do for you, son?"

"Yeah," I said, watching as the fear and respect flickered in his eyes. All these years later, he remembered how I'd saved his ass, and he owed me for the rest of his days. "Get dressed, climb in your truck, and follow me down the highway. I want a wedding, and I need it now."

His eyes bugged out, but he didn't argue. This guy knew when the club called, he answered, and gave us whatever the hell we wanted, without asking too many questions.

I went back to my bike, waiting for him to lock up before I started the engine. We pulled out of his driveway and hit the road together, his truck behind me, heading for Hannah's place.

We were home in no time. The prospects were gathered outside the fixed up bushes, pacing around leisurely as they had their smoke breaks. They looked at preacher man tailing me through the gate with more than a few questions in their eyes. I stopped in front of Apache, fresh meat wearing our prospect patch, just home from Afghanistan with no job in sight. We'd given him plenty to do in our garages.

"Prez? There a reason we're seeing the preacher again?"

"Stand guard in the house and find out. Pass that along to the rest of the boys," I said. "Gonna need a few extra witnesses for what's about to go down. Get everybody inside, quick as you can."

He nodded one more time as I blew past, rolling through the huge iron gate. I climbed off my bike, grabbed the ring box from my saddlebag, and told preacher man to wait with the prospects 'til I returned.

That little black box in my fist burned like a hot stone. I waited on Hannah's doorstep for about a minute before I shoved the door open and stepped inside.

Today, I had a date with destiny to win over my wife. I wasn't going anywhere else before I had a yes out of her.

* * * *

"Darlin', put that down, and come out back. We need to have a talk."

She looked up at me over her laptop, tucking a lose lock of soft, brunette hair behind her ear. "Now? I mean, I was just getting deep into the database. I'm digging into everything I can find about Dom in the Sterner Corp files. Mister Sterner graciously got my old access restored this morning."

"Now," I said, giving her a shallow nod. "You'll be back talking to billionaires and playing detective as soon as we're done. Right now, we've got business."

That wasn't totally true. If my proposal went off like I planned, I'd have her down the hall in the library within the hour, with preacher man hitching us then and there. And we'd be marking the occasion by going upstairs, hitting the bed, and taking our pleasure 'til she knew I hadn't lost my mind.

I'd show her this was real. Show her I meant for it to last *forever.*

I loved this woman, dammit. No more denying that, no more running, and no more lies.

I'd kiss her, hold her, and fuck her 'til she realized the truth.

I stepped out onto her balcony and waited. Waited for her hands to land on my shoulders softly before I turned, looked at her, and invited her into those fires burning in my eyes.

"What's wrong?" she asked, her eyes going wide.

"Wrong question, darlin'. We both know what's wrong, what's eating at us, what we need to do to get the Sicilians off our asses. We're working on it." I paused, grabbing her hand, pulling it close to my chest. "We're having a heart-to-heart because I want to put the mafia shit on hold for a second to remember what's right."

She titled her head, a curious smile tugging at her lips. "You're talking about us?"

I nodded. "You, me, and the next fifty years we're gonna have together on this Earth. I know it sounds crazy talking like that right now, and I damned well know it. Guess what?" I moved my arm around her, bringing her close, never breaking eye contact. "Doesn't fuckin' matter. Long as I've got you, and you're wearing a smile on your face, nothing else does. We'll settle with the Sicilians. Smooth things over with Firefly. Kill every asshole standing in the way of you, me, and the future we deserve. Leave the club biz to me. We got together in the first place because we both wanted to wind up in bed, darlin', but it's a whole lot more than that now. No denying it."

"Yeah…" She looked down and opened her lips, softly whispering. "You're right."

"I've walked through Heaven and Hell, Hannah. Watched brothers crash and burn, then pick themselves up to take another swing at life. I had to crawl out of the shadow left by my old man's sins, and hell, I'm still doing it." I waited for her eyes to meet mine again before I cupped her cheek, tilting her face to mine. "All those awful things made me wonder about a fuck of a lot. It's hard for a man to have much certainty when the ground keeps shifting under him. You, on the other hand...fuck, babe, you're my rock. Go ahead, tell me I'm crazy, or it's fuckin' soon to say it. Then ask me if I care. I'm telling you the God's truth, what I knew the first night we got together at your brother's wedding. I'm telling you I've had *enough*."

"Enough? Of what?" She looked like she was in a trance, hanging on my every word.

I smiled. "Enough of pretending this ain't going nowhere. Like it's just a fling, one more fire in the night due to burn out when we've had our fill. Enough of acting like we can't have a future, or we're only in this together because we've got history, or I'm just playing hero just to keep you alive."

"Dusty...this better not be a joke." Her big blue eyes flashed hot, telling me she'd slap me across the face if I messed with her now.

Thankfully for her, I was in so deep, so real, second guessing didn't have any place, and never, ever would. "Why you gotta doubt everything, darlin'? Think everything's a fuckin' prank?"

Her face softened, cheeks blushing red. "Maybe because I know who I'm dealing with. You're a strong man, Dusty, and you have a good heart. But you're also the oldest bachelor in the entire MC. You're telling me – no lies – that you're honestly planning to settle down? With *me?*"

She practically squeaked the last word. As if her own disbelief and fear reached up, caught her around the throat, and refused to let go.

"I'm done telling you anything with words, darlin'. Brought something better to do the talking for me today."

The sun came out behind the clouds just then, shining down on us. Like I needed another sign the time had come.

She watched me reach into my pocket, clench the little black box tight against my palm, and drop slowly to my knees. I grabbed her hands with mine, bringing them to my lips. I kissed each one before I said anything else, wondering why the fuck I had this bitter lump building my throat when I'd reached the happiest moment of my life.

"Marry me, Hannah Davis." My thumb popped the box open. I let that antique gold with the diamond in the middle shine on like a crazy star sent to earth. "Whatever else happens, I want you wearing my ring, calling me your man. I want you sharing my bed every damned night, on the back of my bike when I remind the Smokies who owns 'em. I want to see you smiling like that when you're carrying my kid. Want you to say 'I do,' darlin', and know it'll make me the happiest man in the world."

I watched her stand there for several seconds, too shocked for words. Didn't think we were in trouble 'til her knees began to buckle, and she came crashing down into my arms.

Fuck! So much for that yes I'd staked everything on.

Hannah couldn't tell me anything because she'd passed out cold.

* * * *

The prospects came running when they heard me swearing up a storm. I motioned them to stay behind the screen door, leaving me to hold her, press her tight against me, measuring her breathing.

It was shock. Nothing life threatening. She'd simply overloaded, and I needed a little time to bring her back.

"Darlin'...wake up. Open those sweet eyes, and tell me you'll be mine." I moved her face softly to mine, kissing her lips.

The old Dust would've rolled his eyes at this scene, like watching a twisted fuckin' fairy tale where the Prince wore leather and his damsel in distress wasn't even officially saved yet.

"Dusty?" Very slowly, Hannah's eyes fluttered open. It was my turn to hold my breath, anticipation strangling me by the throat.

Had she blinked out because she loved the idea of us getting hitched? Or did she want to head for the hills, screaming?

"Hannah, if you ain't feeling up to it, you don't have to answer me now. I think you oughta –"

"Kiss you?" she said, her energy returning, folding her hands tight around my neck. "I will, because that's the only thing I need right now. I want my fiance's lips on mine, and I don't want to wait."

Couldn't remember the last time I wore such a shit-eating grin before I took a woman's mouth with mine. Our lips collided like runaway trains. Crashing, rolling, fire in every movement, fueled by the happiest words I'd ever heard leaving anybody's mouth.

When I looked up, we both noticed the noise. The prospects stood behind us, roaring while they slapped the glass and the walls, ready to bang my fist as soon as I came through the door.

"Do we really need an audience?" she asked, flashing me a wink.

"Nah. They're for part two of my master plan."

"Part two?" I helped her up into my arms, making sure she was steady on her feet, before I said more. "When I asked you to marry me, darlin', I meant *today*. I've got the same man who married the rest of my brothers and their girls waiting out front. He's ready, if you are."

"You're insane," she said, laughter breaking through the huge smile on her face. "How did you know I wouldn't insist on having a huge ceremony with all our friends and family?"

"Because if you gave me a yes, it'd be because you want it as bad as I do, babe." I pulled her to my chest, planting another kiss on her hot, wanting lips. "When I make decisions, I don't fuck around. We'll have the reception later, once we're out of this mess, and the brothers are ready to come pay their respects to my wife. Today, I *need* that ring on your finger to mean what it says in gold and jewels."

I grabbed her hand, twined my fingers in hers, and

squeezed. I studied her, hoping she wasn't about to collapse again.

No, those big blue eyes in her pretty face were steady. True. Still smiling, she shook her head, giving her body a sweet, sexy ripple. My cock stood on end, ready to consummate our vows upstairs, soon as they were done.

"You're lucky you're so right about me, Danny." My real name slipped out, and it sounded damned good hanging on her lips. I led us inside, turning an ear to her as she whispered a little more. "Guess the fact that you know me so well means it's meant to be."

"Yeah, darlin', we are. I'll kiss fate's ass all day if it means kissing you every night," I thundered in her ear, moving a possessive arm around her waist while we headed for the huge library in her house, where I'd told preacher man to wait. Apache passed my orders to the prospects ahead of us, and they were waiting.

"Careful, Dusty. Poets aren't supposed to ride motorcycles," she warned, her sassy little tongue protruding through her teeth. "You can kiss the devil himself if it'll keep us like this forever, just as long as you clean your mouth first before coming to me."

We both laughed. I pulled her closer, stopping in the library once we'd arrived, while preacher man jerked up from a nap in the big office chair and walked to the desk, getting his shit together.

"Bullshit. You like it dirty, woman. And you ain't sharing me with anyone. I'm giving up all the pussy on the planet for you, darlin', and I'm dead serious about it."

She turned, subtly moving her hip against my cock, just enough for me to notice without anybody else seeing. The prospects stood near the walls, whispering among themselves, shocked to hell that they were about to see the Prez tie the knot.

"Hmm, such a sacrifice." She narrowed her eyes, sweet sarcasm dripping off her tongue. "Guess I'd better make sure I keep you happy and well fed. Because if you go rogue while I'm wearing this ring…"

She lifted one hand to her throat, flattened it, and made a swift cutting motion.

Smiling, I watched her eyes soften, the jealousy fading. The hunger in those beautiful blue gems of hers matched mine. I held in a louder, lust charged growl in my throat, tightening my grip on her hand, ready to lead us down to the preacher.

"Darlin', if I was that kind of fool, we wouldn't be doing this. I'll die before I hurt you. Now, come on. You can serve me another helping of that fine ass upstairs, as soon as we're done."

* * * *

"And do you, Daniel Grayson, take this woman to be your lawfully wedded wife? To love and to cherish, to have and to hold, in sickness and in health, until death do you part?" Preacher man looked at me, his spectacles as honest and questioning as the eyes of God.

"No question," I said, squeezing Hannah's fingers in mine. "I do. I will. I promise."

The prospects stirred in the seats behind us, their excitement getting to them. I knew if I spun around, I'd see four crazy smiles, big as the Tennessee sunset. Only regret I had about this was doing it without my brothers there, too, or my Ma.

She'd forgive me when she found out I'd taken a bride. If she didn't, then she'd damned sure get over it when the first grandbaby came along.

Preacher man didn't stop for anything. I took my eyes off him and looked straight into my woman's soul while he turned his attention to her, several thousand books lined up around us on the high shelves mirrored in his glasses.

"And do you, Hannah Davis, take this man to be your lawfully wedded husband? To have and to hold from this day forward, for better and for worse, for richer –"

"I do!" she shouted, her hands trembling in mine when the words burst out. "You don't need to finish. I don't need riches or perfect health, to convince me to marry this man. I just need Dusty because he's right, and because he's mine."

I quirked an eyebrow. She said that last word with such wild fuckin' vigor it nearly beat my own. I'd have to take her ten times harder tonight for that.

Preacher man paused and smiled. He looked up from his Bible, giving me the same look I'd seen him give my brothers when they'd gotten wed.

"Then by the power invested in me by the great state of Tennessee, and the trust given by the Deadly Pistols Motorcycle Club, I am honored to pronounce you husband and wife. Please, kiss the bride."

Like we needed any encouragement. The prospects whooped and hollered while our mouths connected, explored, and claimed each other the same way I hoped they'd do for the rest of our lives.

Hannah always tasted good. Up here, at this makeshift altar, she tasted like heaven itself crawled out of her, onto her lips.

Didn't want to take my mouth off hers, but I had to, just to say one more thing gnawing me deep down. "I love you, darlin'. Love you like I've never loved anything, and always will 'til the day I die. Nothing will ever, ever, *ever* fuckin' change that. I'm saying it today, in front of everyone, because I want to remember it when the times get rough. I want this love banging in my chest twenty-four seven, louder than my own heart."

"Dusty – I love you, too!" she purred, staring at me like she had a lot to say, too.

I never let her get that far.

Taking the ring, I shoved it on her finger, and smiled when I saw the perfect fit. Sometimes things are meant to be, and the world gives up a hundred signs confirming it.

This was one of those days. Perfectly imperfect.

Soon, my lips joined hers again, and this time they didn't stop. We were still kissing while I scooped her up in my arms, and headed for the stairs. We left behind preacher man and the prospects cheering us on. They were smart enough to have a few drinks and keep watch while we got some quality time.

Sweet, merciful fuck, we needed it, too. If anything

interrupted us before late morning tomorrow, dragging me away from my wife's beautiful body, I'd morph into the meanest, craziest motherfucker anybody ever had the misfortune of laying eyes on.

* * * *

"I meant what I said down there, Danny. I really do love you," she whispered, the soft glow flickering around us.

We stood next to that big bed of hers, completely naked, my hand stroking between her legs. She'd soaked herself for me before I laid a single finger on her.

My cock pressed against her little belly, rabid to seal the deal we'd just done the only way a man and woman should. We'd have a proper honeymoon after we dealt with Dom and his assholes. 'Til then, we'd have the most electrifying sex anybody ever had.

"I know you mean it, darlin'. We've fought this thing between us longer than we should've. Never been so glad to lose a battle in my life." I pulled her face to mine, taking another kiss, stroking my tongue on hers to taste Hannah's sweetness.

"Before today, I was afraid to let on how much I felt it," she said, slowly closing her eyes, moving her cheek against my hand. "Didn't know how much I meant to you, how much you meant to me. It's so sudden, but it's right."

"Fuck yeah, it is. We sorted out the right and wrong, as soon as I put that ring on your little finger." I took her hand, turning it over in the light, giving me a perfect view of my family's ring against her skin.

My cock twitched, hornier than ever. I'd marked her once with my wedding ring. We were only getting started.

Next, she'd get it from my teeth, my cock going off inside her, and the needle when she took my name on her skin. We'd skipped the unwed old lady stage and jumped straight to outlaw's bride. Fuck if it wasn't right, every single part of it.

"I want you so bad, Dusty. You don't even know." She stopped, moaned, and I moved my thumb against her clit.

"Think I've got some idea, darlin'. We've used our mouths to talk enough today. I'm more interested in using them for something else. Lay back, spread those legs, and let's speak another language."

She smiled as I eased her back, tumbling onto the bed. I crashed down on top of her, fisting her hair, pulling her head up to give me access to her sweet, pale throat. I kissed her there. *Hard.*

Stamped my lips on Hannah's skin in a slow, steady worship line down her body. Every few seconds, I'd stop and linger longer on the spots that made her jerk, moan, beg. I sucked her tit, rolling the other nipple between my fingers, dreaming about the day they'd be swollen and full from knocking her up.

I'd never wanted kids before. It'd be awhile before we went there, but I couldn't fuckin' deny it, this raging urge to knock her up building in my balls. My sperm were wild, yearning to be in her, even though we had all the protection in the world.

Her sweet cunt coated my cock in its cream as I rubbed

between her folds. *Up and down, up and down. Soak every fuckin' inch, down to my balls, darlin'.*

My swollen head pressed against her clit. She moaned louder, twisting her hips, still pleading with her movements when I dragged my dick away to continue the downward march of my lips.

There's a time for slow and sensual. Tonight wasn't fuckin' it.

Soon as I had my face between her thighs, I pushed it straight to her center. Bouncing, squealing, and gasping for air, I locked her legs around my shoulders, pushing them down tight. My tongue rode her pussy like mad.

Only eased off to make her work for it. When I pulled back too far, she whimpered, grinding her cunt into my face. I rewarded her, bringing her in closer, burying my lips, my tongue, my teeth in that pussy 'til it imploded on itself.

"Dusty!" She hissed it. My name struck my ears like music when she tensed up.

I licked her faster, harder, sucking her little clit between my teeth 'til she couldn't remember her own name, much less mine. I devoured my new wife like I hadn't before, and I loved it. Alive like my first time taking her while she twitched against me.

My tongue fucked her the whole way through, guiding the firestorm in her hips, owning her 'til she came for me.

With her legs still trembling, I came up for air, sucking the last of her cream off my lips. Let her rest for about a minute, holding my cock rigid against her entrance, leaning over her and stroking her hair.

"You're so gorgeous," I said, planting another kiss on her lips. "I held out forty goddamned years for the perfect package, darlin', and you're it. The wait was worth it. Beauty ain't enough, even though you've got that in droves. I wanted the brain and the heart, too. I'm one lucky SOB."

"You're right about that," she purred, smoothing her legs up and down mine. "Just for the record, I always wanted a man like you. The ones in suits who flinch when somebody gets in their face, they never had much appeal. Always had a crush on you, Dusty, even before I went off to college. You wouldn't look at me then because I was too young."

"Yeah, you were, darlin'. Never thought much about patience being a virtue before, but it damned sure was this time," I said, amazed how I'd watched her turn into a smart, sexy woman before my eyes. "We're gonna make this right, Hannah. Everything between you and me, Firefly, the club. It gets better from here, babe. Never been so sure about anything in my life."

"Why wait? Make it better now, Dusty," she said, brushing her lips over mine. "Fuck me."

What little power I had left to resist went out the door. I rolled my hips back, letting my cock angle down to her entrance. Watched her suck her bottom lip when she knew what was coming, and let her little moan slip into my ears when I sank down into her.

"Fuck!" I cursed, awed how she felt just as good as the first time.

Taking her hands in mine, I pinned them above her

head, more kisses smothering her lips while my dick fucked into her. I thrust every way I knew how, the start of owning her tonight from every beautiful fuckin' angle.

It wasn't just seeing that ring I put on her finger shake every time our hips crashed together. It was knowing I'd made her mine, inside and out, tonight and forever.

"Dusty, yes – oh, God!" she cried out again, just how I liked, when I fucked her over the edge a second time.

Her greedy pussy pulled at my cock, tried to bring me off, and I damned near lost it deep inside her. But I wasn't done yet.

Soon as her legs stopped shaking, wrapped around mine, I eased out and flipped her over. This time, I watched her sweet ass bouncing as I took her, pounding my balls against her clit while I fucked harder and faster than before.

My grandma's ring glittered while her hand tensed, clutching the sheets. A slow, feminine growl poured from her lips while we fucked. Each time I quickened my strokes, she matched me, moving her ass back to meet my thrusts.

My hands moved like demons. One snatched at her hair, giving it a pull, turning her gasps into grunts of ecstasy. My other hand straightened, came down on her ass several times, making her fuck me back faster.

I wanted to demolish her tonight, and build her up as mine. More beautiful, more sexy, more sweet than ever before. But my body wouldn't let me do it in one go. When her cunt clenched my dick again, I lost it.

"Fuck, darlin', I'm coming!" My cock ballooned while I snarled the words.

My balls slapped her one more time while I drove in, held it, and let the wave pour out of me, into my bride's womb. Hot, thick fire erupted in steady, wild jerks.

I came like a motherfucker deep inside my wife for the first time, and kept on doing it long after my seed slipped out the space between us, spilled onto the sheets, and carried us deeper into bliss. We fucked for a small eternity, grunting our pleasure, grinding our flesh, whispering each other's names through clenched teeth.

When it was finally done and I pulled out half-hard, I wondered if a man could get so hot he'd fuck right through his woman's birth control. If it happened...we'd figure it out.

I took her in my arms, stroking her brow, wiping away the sweat and breathing in the scent of sex. "You're gonna kill me in this bed one of these days, darlin'. Least I'll die happy."

"Sorry, no room for death anytime soon," she said, squeezing my hand, resting her head against my chest. "There's just you and me tonight, Dusty. No reapers allowed."

"Deal. No fuckin' reapers. I'm a helluva lot more interested in making a life for us than taking anybody else's."

She cooed her agreement into my muscle. I stroked her hair softly, imagining my old man standing in the corner, shaking his head in sick disapproval at what I'd just said.

He'd raised me to be a badass, a killer, his successor in Dixie's meanest MC. I'd lived half my life doing it, but I'd always let the good outweigh the blood.

Now, that went double. For the first time forever, his ghost didn't haunt me. I never gave it a second thought by the time she turned her face to me, begging to be kissed.

* * * *

Three Weeks Later

The mansion was just a distant memory. We didn't have the crew to guard it twenty-four seven, run all our biz, and keep tracking the Sicilians, so Hannah moved in with me. My house meant a smaller space to cover, and less chance anybody unexpected tracked her down without making their presence known in town first, asking for intel.

If sharing the same bed every night seemed like paradise, then having her there in my own place was nirvana.

We took things slowly at first. She worked hard on her machine when I wasn't around, always protected by a couple prospects. I showed up around the clubhouse again, taking club business by the horns. I made sure we kept our coin rolling in, despite the distractions.

Ma? She *screamed* when I finally introduced them, and explained what we'd done. Left out the part about the savage, relentless bastards we had to deal with. I told her we'd eloped, gone off and done our own thing, while we figured out how to break the news to the club and everybody else in our lives.

Ma gave me plenty of shit about that. Thankfully, it didn't last long. By the end of the evening, I saw the two favorite women in my life chattering away over chai tea lattes. Ma stopped to wipe tears from her old eyes when she thought nobody was looking.

The unthinkable had happened. Her son was married. Such a surprising, surreal, and beautiful happening it nearly brought a tear to my eyes, too.

As for the club…not so fuckin' easy.

I waited for all my boys to come home, get back to work for several days, before I decided to do church. We were three weeks in since we'd moved the wife none of them knew I had to my place.

Firefly took more time away with Cora's baby coming. When I gaveled the briefing open that day, I should've seen his blows coming, before they hit me in the face. A new baby puts stress on the strongest man, pressure I hoped I'd known personally one fine day, so he had good reason to be extra wound up.

"Boys, there's been a few developments while were you off having fun. I handled it myself 'til now because I wasn't gonna shit on anyone's honeymoon." I paused, searching their reactions, taking a long pull from the fresh tobacco in my pipe.

"Tell me it ain't the Deads." Joker's gaze shifted over. Having his revenge and gaining a family drained a lot of his venom, but something still lingered, a lifelong urge to destroy anybody wearing the Deadhands MC patch.

"Nah. Our friends down yonder in Georgia can barely even find what's left of 'em since we took down Hatch and his crew. This is something different."

Yeah, *different*. Good candidate for understatement of the year.

"Fuck it. There's no way to say it that's gonna please everybody, so I'm just laying it out," I growled, choosing my next words very carefully. "Hannah's in trouble."

Firefly nearly hit the fuckin' ceiling. He stood up, his big hands gripping the edge of the table. If there was ever a time to slam the gavel, calling for order, it was now.

Skin, Lion, Crawl, and Tin jumped up behind him, took him by the arms. I wondered if four burly men would be enough to stop him from turning the room upside down.

"She took a loan from the Sicilian Brotherhood." I said it coldly, listening to men shake their heads and hiss between their teeth. "It was an honest mistake. Something she did when she was young and dumb, before she made all her money, and now it's caught up with her. Me and the prospects were protecting her house when we took down two vicious motherfuckers there to kill her. We got them first, and dumped their bodies off in the usual places. Brothers, it's a clusterfuck, no bones about it. But she's asking for a favor, and I'm willing to answer. She needs our help, and she's going to get it."

"You two-faced weasel sonofabitch! First you fuck her, then you hide this?" Firefly roared, his spittle flying several feet through the air. He strained in the brothers' arms, trying to break away like a bull charging through a crowd.

"Shit, Firefly! Easy!" Skin growled, taking a rough elbow to the gut when my big Enforcer got some leverage.

"Fuck everybody, and fuck you, Prez! You wanna do her

a goddamned favor, you can stay the fuck outta her life. She's too good for this, damn it. Too fuckin' good."

"This is turning into a shit show," Joker said, leaning toward me, maintaining his icy calm. I looked at him and nodded.

Fuck's sake, I had to tread lightly. I'd narrowly saved my patch a couple months ago, after that dust up with the Deads. More horrific infighting in this club would do me in for good. Brothers at each other throats were easy targets for any outsiders looking to pick us off.

"I'll give you boys the rest of the details as soon as I can hear myself think." I waited, eyeballing Firefly, feeding the rage boiling over in his eyes.

His face was red. Every few seconds, his temples bulged, grinding his teeth like he wanted to chew me up and spit me out. If he ever regretted the swing vote that kept me at the head of the table, it was now.

"They roped her into a money laundering scheme through that matchmaker app of hers. She's torn up their infrastructure, cut them off, and thrown out their shit since we killed the two assholes. This file, here, contains everything we know about the *capo* after her, a man named Dom Barone." I pushed the manilla envelope in front of me toward Joker.

My Veep flipped through the flimsy pages, ignoring the chaos around us, giving me a quizzical look before passing it to Sixty next. "Hardly anything there."

"Yeah, that's our biggest problem at the moment," I said, drawing more smoke into my lungs, before I let it out in a good, long puff. "We need more intel. Need it fuckin' bad. I moved Hannah into my place because we're spread too thin to watch her mansion around the clock."

Firefly twisted in his brothers' arms, his eyes becoming pure death, fixed on me. Almost like he knew what was coming next before I even said it.

"She's living with me. It's no secret –"

"Motherfucker!" Firefly lost it, struggling with all his might, elbowing poor Skinny boy in the guts again. This time, Skin lost it, winded. Crawl took his place, grunting as he tried to hold the giant back. Took the rest of the boys in the room jumping up to hold him against the wall, howling like a maniac the whole damned time.

I stood up, putting out my pipe. "Brothers, I ain't the enemy, and neither is Firefly. We've got our disagreements, and I'm hoping one day, we'll put it all behind us. It's no secret me and her have had a thing for a long time. Half this club knew. So did the brother who's pinned down, trying to tear my head off."

Moving between my men, I stopped about three feet from Firefly, close enough for the fuming hulk to spit in my face if he wanted. He looked up, opening his lips. "You're a two-faced, cradle robbin' sack of shit, Dusty. You put a bigger fuckin' mark on her head than the Sicilians ever will."

Several men jeered. Others whispered among themselves. The brothers were getting pissed with his antics, and we'd have a full blown fight on our hands real soon if I didn't play lion tamer fast.

"Firefly, we've rode together, fought together, bled together, even fuckin' wept together. I can live with you wanting to reach down my throat and pull my balls out through my teeth," I said coldly, coming closer, 'til we were face-to-face. "One thing I ain't tolerating is you letting your anger spill over, fuckin' up the rest of this club when Hannah needs our support. She'll always be your little sis, yeah, everybody knows it. We get it. But she's more than that now. She's my old lady, brother. She's my wife. And I'll take a hundred kinds of death before I let your bullshit cause hers, or anybody else's wearing this patch."

"Wife?! The fuck?" Half a dozen identical cries went off, almost at once.

Firefly's eyes bugged out his head, and then pinched shut. For a second, I feared he was having a goddamned stroke. Several brothers probably wondered the same thing, holding him down, looking back over their shoulders at me for instruction.

"Leave him be," I said quietly, watching as big man finally overloaded himself, and slumped. Overwhelmed or giving up, who the fuck knew, but he'd lost his will to fight. "You all heard me the first time. Hannah and I got hitched about three weeks ago in a quick little ceremony in her library. Just a couple days after Skinny boy and Joker tied the knot. I couldn't wait a day longer, knowing the danger, and the fact she'd be facing this world like a defenseless fuckin' lamb if I didn't protect her with everything we had."

"She had that anyway, Prez," Skin said, the scar on his cheek rippling as he twisted his lips. "The girl's always been family, before you came along."

"Yeah, but she wasn't mine, and that had to change. I love her."

Nobody argued. Firefly opened his eyes. The lightning hot rage scorching through his body faded, but a deader hatred simmered on his face, focused on me.

"This club's doubled down on Hannah's life, brothers. Skin's right about us owing her a helping hand from day one, thanks to her blood, same as our very pissed off Enforcer here. Now, she's wrapped up in this patch even deeper, part of our hearts and souls." I thumped the skull with its smoking pistols on the back of Joker's cut, just above his bottom rocker. "I know this shit's getting real old. Seems like every month, we're chasing down some jackals, trying to keep them from eating us alive. This ain't no different from what we've done before. We're going after the Sicilians for love, for peace, for vengeance, for money, or maybe just because they're demon fucks who deserve to die."

Half the boys in the room nodded. Lion looked at me, taking one hand off Firefly to scratch his scruffy beard. His closest brother, Tinman, stood behind him, still trying to wrap his head around why this club oughta have more heart than a man needed to sink his dick into new whores begging for the patch. Crawl held onto Firefly's arm, his dark features making him look even more determined in the dull light.

"We've taken pure hell this last year," I said. "So much shit. We've had survived beatings, bullets, knives, rogue pimps, and two of the meanest fuckin' clubs who ever set up shop in Dixie. I'm asking ya'll to step up and stand strong one more time."

"Prez, you can stop right there," Joker said, a little bit of his trademark crazy returning to his hazel eyes. "We're with you. Whatever mistakes were made before with the Deads, they're ancient fuckin' history. We ain't leaving anybody's old lady to suffer alone, especially not yours."

"Old lady, wife, over my goddamned dead body…" Firefly snorted harshly under his breath, shaking his head.

"I couldn't ask for better friends and brothers. All of you," I said, bowing my head gratefully. "We'll hash out the details as soon as we know more. Skinny, I want you on the financials in that folder full time. See if you can use your sense for numbers to find out where the fuck those shell accounts go."

"You got it," he said, a slow smile pulling at his scarred face.

"I'm trusting every man in this room to do me the biggest solid of my life. I'm counting on you. Even the ones who want me dead right now…well, here's hoping we can't put that shit aside, and make sure Hannah lives out her days in one piece. We can settle what else that means with fists or words later."

I looked Firefly square in the face. He stared at me while I walked back to my seat, never saying a word.

"About half you boys got women and kids to worry about. Believe me, I'm starting to share your frustrations with the river of blood we're always trying to cross without drowning in this biz." Skin and Joker nodded.

"Everybody else, you're still deciding who you are. Maybe you'll be content to fuck bitches, make money, and ride with the wind for the rest of your days. That's your right, and there ain't nothing wrong with it." Sixty looked at me and grinned, his goatee twitching in a way that said he'd never give up the partying.

"We're all different, every man wearing this patch, but we took an oath to each other. If we don't live by it, and die by it if need be, we don't have shit. When I slam this gavel down, bringing church to a close, I want three brothers bringing Firefly to the bar. Give him as much as he needs to calm the fuck down." I paused, locking eyes with my big pissed off brother again, hating that he had the same baby blues as my Hannah. "Firefly, when you sober up, we'll sit down and talk. Whenever and wherever you want. Let's talk this out like men, unarmed, and make ourselves a deal we can both live with."

"I ain't making shit with you, Cap'n. You're a backstabbing son of a fuck who stuck your dick in the wrong fuckin' place. Fuck you. Fuck –"

Skinny boy cut him off with a quick, blunt punch to the gut. We'd all had enough.

"I'm closing this out for the day, boys. We'll all sit down and talk, soon as I've found us something work talkin' about."

I slammed the gavel down so hard the handle nearly snapped. Sitting back in my chair, I watched my brothers haul Firefly away, still spitting and cussing me out.

It'd take a lot of whiskey to soak his ass happy. And even then, some poor bastard might wind up with his fists in their face, taking punches I deserved.

Joker nodded, the last one leaving the room, giving me a brotherly slap on the shoulder. I lingered behind for a few minutes, staring at the relics lining the wall. Old photos, flags, and patches hung in frames like museum pieces, capturing a hundred good times, bad times, and dirty fuckin' times under my old man's rule.

I'd finish what I started, turning this club around. I fuckin' had to.

It wasn't all about Hannha, even if she'd taken centerstage. Every man who had my back deserved a happy ending. I'd put my ass on the line a hundred times over if I could bring it. I'd even see the day when Firefly got over his shit, hugged his sis, and sat next to me with a beer while we watched our kids playing at our feet.

XI: Fading (Hannah)

Seven Weeks Later

Three weeks after I started living in his modest house, it grew on me. I hadn't appreciated small spaces growing up. Probably because the mobile home Huck and me were raised in was dirty, desperate, and surrounded by crazies.

But this cozy little rambler on the other side of town…this was nice. I sat on his deck every evening, my laptop sprawled out around me, listening to the birds coming down from the Smokies to say hello.

It was already November, with Thanksgiving coming up fast. Soon it'd be too cold to sit out here, even in a jacket. I normally did the holidays with Huck, whenever I wasn't off traveling. This year should've been extra special with Cora and the baby.

Too bad my brother hadn't called me in weeks. Cora sent texts every so often, cautiously trying to make peace, but I could tell she was afraid to get in the middle of it. I wouldn't press her either, especially with her baby due anytime.

Limbo made the long, sad season even more melancholy. I pressed him all the time about the Sicilians, and he mostly cut me off after a point. Every time I heard *don't fuckin' worry, darlin'*, or *club business*, my fears pitched into overdrive.

They hadn't found a solid lead. Even stranger, Dom and his men hadn't tried to hit us yet.

I expected it every night, laying wide awake sometimes. Just waiting for a window to cave in, sending broken glass flying everywhere, about a second before evil men with guns were at the foot of our bed.

I wasn't the only one who was restless. Dusty slept fitfully, mumbling in his sleep. Sometimes, I'd catch him sitting up, staring into the darkness, one hand on his nightstand, just inches from the nine millimeter he kept for protection.

Other times, he'd fall into bed with me, hold me in his big, strong arms, and rock us both back to sleep until all our worries were a million miles away. I loved this man more by the day because he cared. I even appreciated his hurt because he couldn't finish things like he wanted.

One morning, about a week before Thanksgiving, I woke up sick. It must've been the late night burger, an order from a greasy spoon I'd shared with him before we passed out, exhausted from more late night detective work after I'd done my coding for the day, and he'd done his bossy biker businessman thing.

"We'll fuckin' find them, Hannah," he'd growled the night before, after sex. I laid against his chest. "Don't care how long it takes. Don't give a damn how many dead ends, loose ends, and worthless ends we keep running into. I ain't letting you down, darlin', not 'til we can sleep easy because every last one of those fucks is dead."

His words were reassuring, like always, on the surface. Deep down, they scared me. If his best intelligence and my brightest detective work online couldn't find a meaningful trace of these people, they could hit us anytime.

The mobsters knew who we were, where we were, and what we did. We were blind.

Washing up, I splashed cold water on my face, wishing it was the reason I shuddered. If only it weren't Dom, his threats still stalking me, every day he lurked out there, without being found, and dealt with.

I came downstairs, drank some water, and laid on the couch, letting the soft grey November light spill across me. Several prospects stood on the deck for a smoke, my permanent guard. There were constantly at least two outside when he'd left for the day.

The shitty morning turned around when the text came in.

BABY COMING, SIS. MEET US AT THE HOSPITAL IF YOU WANT TO MEET HER.

Firefly's number. I jumped up, ripped open the screen door, and shook off my weird sickness.

"Guys, I need to leave! Follow me to the hospital if you want. Cora's about to have her baby."

The prospects smiled. One of them, a big man named Apache, followed me in, got on his bike, and followed my car the whole way to the hospital.

I met Huck in the waiting room. God, it had been forever since we'd hung out. I remembered how much I missed him as soon as his big, brotherly arms enveloped me.

"Damned good to see you, sis. You've always got a place with us, whatever happens with *him.*"

I pulled away and looked into his eyes, sensing the smoldering anger when he referred to Dusty. "I'm here to meet my niece and support you guys. Wouldn't miss it for the world."

We both shared a smile. Good timing because about a second later, a nurse wearing scrubs tapped him on the shoulder.

"Mister Davis? You can come with me, if you're ready. It's almost time."

I squeezed my brother's hand one more time and watched him head for the delivery room. I found myself a chair, a sexy, suspenseful read for my phone, and settled into the waiting room.

There hadn't been enough good news since the wedding, but today was going to change that. Smiling to myself, I leaned back in my chair, content that I'd be meeting the brand new addition to my family in just a few hours.

* * * *

"Look at her. She's got Davis eyes." A very tired Cora passed me the baby, laying in her bed, smiling from the fierce labor she'd just gotten through.

Firefly smiled, hanging over my shoulder, watching as I snuggled the little bundle to my chest and saw her face for the first time.

Total darling.

"Oh, Lucy. Could you even be any more precious?" I whispered down to her, my heart fluttering a hundred beats a minute when the tiny baby opened her bright blue eyes, and gave me something like a smile.

More precious? Obviously not.

Firefly laid a tender hand on my shoulder, admiring his daughter, the same rich, manly scent Dusty wore rolling off him. "Wish like hell mama could've seen this," he said.

My eyes lingered on little Lucy for a few more seconds before I looked up, stared into my brother's eyes, and gave him a bittersweet nod. "She's looking down from a better place, Huck. I have a funny feeling she's never been prouder. You're going to give Lucy the best life a little girl could hope for."

"You got that right," he said, reaching for the baby and bringing her to his chest. "Already had plenty to fight for before today. Now? Shit, it's like I've got ten times as much."

Cora and I shared a look. We were both trying not to cry as Huck held up his daughter, cradling her tiny face to his. Those big biker hands folded around her like shields, two protective paws that would never, ever let her down. Not for anything.

Would being a father mellow him? Maybe when he got them home, and settled into his new life, he'd reconsider things with me and Dusty.

Seeing little Lucy gave me new hope that the bad blood would fade. Even faster if we could just track down the Sicilians, finish the job, and turn all our attention to our brand new lives together.

Whether it happened quickly or not, life didn't slow down. It went on, rich and vibrant and ever changing, quickening as the years went by. I looked at my brother and brand new niece again, smiling wider.

Whatever happened, I had a strange feeling it involved another baby, sooner than I imagined. Dusty talked more about a family every week, and the idea didn't scare me like it used to. With my husband, anything was possible, however scary or impossible it might've looked just a few short weeks ago.

I walked over to Firefly and Lucy one more time, stroking the baby's brow before I said goodbye. "I'll be back here tomorrow, guys. Looks like you both need some sleep and quality time with the new baby girl. I won't get in the way of that."

"Wait." Huck spoke sharply when I was halfway to the door, one hand reaching for the silver handle. "Give my best to the Prez when he gets home tonight. Him and I still ain't on good terms, but staring at each other like fuckin' tigers every day we're both at the clubhouse is getting old. I don't want to be his enemy, even if I think he's a rat bastard for marrying you under everybody's nose. I'm re-thinking some things, Hannah, and I want him to know it. Tell him. Please."

Just when I thought the day couldn't get any better...

My fingers tightened on the handle, and I nodded. "I will, Huck. You're a good man, and Cora's a lucky woman. You're going to be just as good a father as you are my big brother."

One more tender look before I stepped outside, and gently closed the door behind me. Thank God.

It was about all I could handle before I broke down, spilling more tears than little Lucy would as she tried to learn the baffling ins and outs of this world.

No, life wasn't perfect, not even close. But there were hints that it might be, sooner than I ever believed.

* * * *

YOU'VE GOT A PRESENT ON THE BED WHEN YOU GET HOME, DARLIN. YOU AIN'T THE ONLY ONE WHO CAN BUY FANCY LINGERIE.

Dusty's text made me stop near the door to the parking garage and giggle. I covered my mouth, standing against the wall, sending him a quick reply before I got *too* wet for the drive home.

All these weeks living together, newly married, and we hadn't slowed down. At the rate we were going, he'd need a new mattress next year.

Lately, he'd teased me a lot about several outfits I'd seen in a catalogue, plus some other items that still made me blush.

EASY, TIGER. WE HAVE A COUPLE THINGS TO TALK ABOUT BEFORE WE TURN IN EARLY TONIGHT. LOVE YOU.

I wasn't quite sure how to tell him what Firefly said. It was good news, at least. He'd probably welcome any chance to bury the hatchet with my brother to get the club back on track, and our little family, too.

The hospital parking was ridiculous. I had to walk down a long corridor to the elevator before I could get to the right floor. A long, spartan, dimly lit hallway no woman wanted to travel alone.

I moved as quickly as I could, breathing a sigh of relief when the elevator button lit up, bringing the lift down to my level.

If only I hadn't stopped to look at my phone again. I might've seen the hand coming when it reached through the doors, grabbed me by the throat, and flung me against the wall so hard my spine cracked.

I hit the metal lining the elevator with a resounding *thud*. The doors slid shut behind the silhouette who'd attacked me. A man I'd never seen before stepped into view, just as the fiery pain in my lower back hit my brain.

"You scream, you die, bitch," he snarled, pressing the flat edge of his switchblade against my throat. "You knew Franco? He was my fucking brother."

Shit.

Shit, shit, shit.

If only there was a string of curses in the world fit for this. He was tall, dressed in a neat Italian leather jacket, his face vaguely familiar because he shared the dead man's features.

"What do you want?" I whimpered, closing my eyes.

"Me? I want to put this fucking knife in your throat, and then keep going. Slice you clean open." My heart leapt into my throat while I heard him sigh angrily. "Real goddamned shame Dom's got other plans for you, peachy-pie. You're coming with me."

Like I had a choice.

He punched the elevator key again, never letting go of my throat. His knife pressed cool against my skin the whole time the elevator moved.

I quietly prayed the elevator wouldn't stop again. Unless it was the entire Deadly Pistols MC, nobody stood a chance of helping me. They'd only get themselves killed if they walked in on me and this monster.

His knife pulled away when the elevator dinged. Then the goon grabbed me by the wrist, jerking me forward, dragging me out the doors with him.

My happy dreams died with every step.

I eyed each corner, looking for any signs of cameras. Just my luck that security around here was so lax, there was nothing.

Even if there were…what good would it do?

It wouldn't make this mad man release me without anybody else getting hurt.

It wouldn't bring me back to Dusty, Firefly, Cora, or Lucy.

It wouldn't take me to the beautiful place I'd begun to call my home.

"Stoop down and get the fuck in," the goon commanded, giving my neck a rough push. We stopped in front of a black sedan.

He reached for the key fob, flicked the button, and I heard the doors unlock, heavy as a tomb rattling open. *Oh, God.*

Instinctively, I knew the second I got inside that car, I wouldn't be coming back. It would probably be the end of me. Dom's face flashed in my brain, evil and furious, ready to rip me apart with his switchblade with the same ruthless precision he used on pomegranate skin.

A heavy blow crashed across the back of my head. "Bitch! Do you know how to listen? I said *get in.*"

I'd waited too long. Hiding my tears, I reached for the handle, popping the door open. I dragged myself into the backseat and laid down.

"Honestly, I never thought we'd find you. Thought I'd go to my grave knowing the cunt who killed Franco got away with it. I don't care about the honor or the accolades. I'm after all the things Dom's gonna do to you when I get you home." He paused, his dark eyes staring back at me in the mirror. "I want to watch you suffer. When Dom says the word, I'm going to make damned sure I'm the guy holding the knife."

His vicious threats blurred by me as my mind detached. Adrenaline heightened my heartbeat, my nerves, my need to run for my life at the first chance. But it also numbed the sheer terror I should've felt.

I pushed my face into the leather seats in the back, still laying down, and breathed the strange, luxurious calming scent. This was the closest thing I'd find to Dusty's familiar leather smell, whenever he wore his cut.

The car moved. We roared through the parking garage quickly, down the ramp, and stopped for the ticket agent.

My captor laughed, muttering a few words as he paid the parking fees. "Real bad stomach bug for the wife. Yeah, she'll be all right. Just got to get her home, give her the old routine of soda and crackers..."

I dared to twist my face up then, just enough to see the monster's eyes staring back at me in the mirror. *Don't you fucking scream, bitch,* they said. *If I go down, you're coming with, and so is he. I'll gut this asshole in the booth in front of you.*

My hand drifted slowly down to my thigh. He'd torn my purse away from me when we were in the elevator. I managed to stuff my phone into my pocket before all hell broke lose, and he hadn't noticed in the commotion.

But the phone wasn't what I was after.

Ever since the fateful week we'd gotten married, when Dusty dispatched two of the same animals as easily as pulling up weeds, I hadn't taken anything for granted. He'd given me another wedding present, something the stupid, sick asshole at the steering wheel forgot to check for when he'd marched me out to his car.

My fingers slipped into my pocket when we were several miles from the hospital, heading for the highway. The switchblade's cold, steel handle rubbed my thumb, and I felt the groves outlining the Deadly Pistols MC logo.

Dusty told me it belonged to his father, once. Ironic, since I could tell he hated the man, even if he never went into a lot of detail. The old blade practically burned in my hand, as if it wanted to live again, kill again, and save my fucking life.

Deep breaths, I told myself. *Count to ten. Wait for the car to slow, just enough to give me a chance to survive the crash. That's when I'll do it.*

Once I knew I had a good grip, I sat up, rubbing my eyes to make him think I'd been too busy crying to worry about anything else.

"Fuck, you don't look so good." His cruel eyes flashed back at me. "Put your fucking seat belt on. Last thing I need is a state trooper giving us shit if I get pulled over. We're blowing through these mountains fast, all the way to Nashville. There's a private plane waiting for us there."

A plane meant there could be only one final destination in mind. I'd be back in Seattle if I let him take me, staring at Dom face-to-face. My odds of surviving this would go from about one percent down to zero.

He drove on a few more miles in total silence. I let the hate come into my eyes, taking a good look at the man I wanted to kill.

"Why the fuck you staring at me?" he snorted awhile later. "Don't tell me it's that PTSD shit setting in already. We haven't even started yet!"

My fingers tightened on the secret weapon in my pocket. I narrowed my gaze on him harder, sharper, never breaking for anything.

"You're one creepy little bitch," he spat, steering us slowly into a sudden bend around the mountain. "I shouldn't care what you look like, one way or another. How did Franco look when he died? Only fucking thing that matters!"

His voice trembled. Grief poured out his lips. The extra jerk in the steering wheel wasn't much, but it was noticeable.

I knew the roads around here, but not so well I could totally predict the sharp mountain turns. I'd wait for the next one before I took my chances. Fortunately, he wouldn't know either, so he'd be taking the entire pass slow.

I saw my opening.

"Now you're going back to sleep?" he asked, noticing my eyes were closed. "Okay, I get it. You just want to fuck with me. Well, fuck you, too."

"When you asked me about how your brother looked when he died...did you really want to know?" I said, slowly looking at him again.

His eyebrows went up, confusion setting in. "What kind of question is that? Seriously, how fucking stupid are you? I wasn't really asking, Miss Creepy Shit-for-Brains –"

I snapped my seat belt button and lunged forward, grabbing at his throat with one hand before he could finish. He stomped the brakes. I leaned forward with all my might, fighting the G forces trying to throw me backward.

Time to pray.

The next few seconds were critical, the last before he died, or we both went spiraling off the next curve, into the nearest ravine.

Mafia man howled, roaring his rage at my ambush, right before I plunged the blade into his neck. Spinning, the entire world turned upside down, flinging me back against the passenger seat while his blood went everywhere.

Wheels screeched. Vengeful goon gurgled blood. Glass exploded the next time the car jerked violently, whipping my neck around in a savage twist. There wasn't time to scream before the darkness hit me like someone throwing a pitch black blanket over my head.

* * * *

The first thing I heard when I woke was something dripping. The second was my phone pinging me awake.

I tried to sit up. Something stank, motor oil and death strewn together into a sick new odor I never wanted to smell again. My neck burned like something crawled inside it and bit me, but all my limbs were there.

I hoped.

The only way out was up. I looked through the hole where the passenger window had been, and reached for the door's handle where I expected it to be.

Gone. Thankfully, it didn't matter, because the lightest pressure moved the broken door up like a loose lid on an open can. One more quick shove and I climbed up, out of the wreck, toppling over the mess of broken metal, onto the pavement.

I scampered away, toward the abandoned truck stop in the distance before I let myself stop and survey the hideous damage behind me.

Miracles were real. Twisted metal became jagged teeth, stabbing into every passenger spot except the tiny space I'd been lodged in. Asshole's inhuman remains were crunched into what was left of his seat, one more grim reminder I shouldn't have survived.

And yet, I did. I'd lived without getting cut open by the car or murdered by a very pissed off mafia goon. It hadn't even started on fire or exploded like I'd expected after watching so many action flicks.

The wreck wouldn't go unnoticed long. Several headlights passed by, too dim to spot the damage without really slowing down, or maybe the drivers were just in such a hurry they didn't care.

The next couple hours were a complete and utter blur. When I should've dialed Dusty, Firefly, someone from the club to come and help me, I called the closet taxi service instead, only after I'd gotten about a half mile up the road.

Even more miraculously than surviving the wreck, I hadn't gotten torn up too bad. My neck ached like someone took a crowbar to it, but nothing seemed fractured. The driver asked me about my cuts and bruises, what little he could see in the dark.

I smiled, told him not to worry about it, and offered him a *really* nice tip if we could finish our trip in silence.

It took forever to get back to the hospital. I didn't think about what I was really doing or where I was going until I was in my car, outside Knoxville, and heading northwest.

Deep inside, I already knew. Tonight wasn't just a collection of freak events, happy little Lucy's birth and Firefly's olive branch blurring into the nightmare of ambush, death, and blood.

I'd murdered a man to save myself. Justified, maybe, but it wouldn't be the last time.

If I wanted to survive, I'd have to kill again. Or someone else would do it for me.

All my old fears about Dusty, Huck, or God forbid, innocent kids like my niece getting caught in the middle leapt up, riding me like demons.

Worse, it wouldn't be the end. Dom had a lot of dirty friends to come after me, if he didn't make the trip himself. The asshole who'd ambushed me at the hospital had to know I was there for a reason – and it wouldn't take much work to find out about Firefly, Cora, and the new baby.

Wouldn't need much more than that to learn about Dusty, too.

As long as I remained a fixture in the club's life, in my own family's, I'd be a distraction, a danger, a walking fucking target. If the mafia decided to hit them, or take someone like poor Lucy hostage…

No. I couldn't let that happen. I'd *die* before it did, and if I wanted to keep living some kind of life, then the time had come to disappear.

I cried for about a hundred miles, driving deep into the night, before I sent the last texts ever on my phone. I told the prospects to head down the highway, find the car, and clean up the mess inside, assuming the police hadn't gotten to it first.

The club had a knack for making things disappear. They'd do the same with the monster I'd dispatched inside the wreck. Maybe Dusty would find his father's knife somewhere inside, returned to its proper owner.

I didn't wait for a reply. My fingers tapped a message to Dusty next, the sweet, strong husband I didn't deserve, and whose life I wouldn't risk one day longer.

D, MY LOVE, DON'T WORRY ABOUT ME. DON'T COME AFTER ME. PATCH THINGS UP WITH HUCK AND LOOK AFTER HIS FAMILY. KILL ANYONE WHO GETS TOO CLOSE.

WE'LL MEET AGAIN SOMEDAY. THIS LIFE OR NEXT. LOVE ALWAYS.

Yeah, always. That word stung a hundred times worse than the whiplash in the wreck. It bored into my heart and wouldn't stop hurting while I sped up, rolled down my window, and threw my phone against the road as hard as I could.

Physical pain was something to hold onto, something tangible, but it always faded in the end. An hour later, crying myself to sleep in the beat up, cramped, no name motel room, all I could think about was how even the pain of tearing myself away from what little happiness I'd had would fade if I lasted long enough.

Nothing worse than the people I loved becoming a distant memory, and the man I adored fading day by day, until it became a struggle to remember his face.

I'd made a sick sort of peace with losing him. But losing his memory, his love, the way he held me and stroked me to sleep during those glorious months when we'd shared a single bed...

They had to go. They had to fade. They had to leave a

hole in my heart as big as a grave because if I didn't let go, if I didn't hold onto my own sanity, then nothing would keep the people I loved safe.

＊＊＊＊

Three Months Later

I hadn't cried so hard since my first night away from Dusty. Some days, it just hit me, like being cooped up in this lodge, watching the big, soft flakes rolling down from the mountains.

I'd missed Thanksgiving, Christmas, Valentine's Day, Dusty's birthday, and who the hell knew how many precious moments with Lucy. Being stuck in this room with a new laptop, a fake identity, and a lot of cheap freelance work humbled and hurt me like a dozen angry fists coming down.

I was somewhere in Montana, careful to avoid the little towns where the Grizzlies MC had a presence. Dust would've told his friends in their ally club to keep an eye out for me by now, and I wouldn't risk getting caught.

The morning sickness made it even harder. Fourteen weeks pregnant, give or take. Every day my body changed a little more like a grim reminder of everything I'd abandoned, everything I *had* to leave behind.

None was worse than his ring, though.

Once, I made it about forty-eight hours, burying it in my suitcase under my clothes, before the empty space on my finger became a steady, burning torture.

Couldn't sleep that night until it was back in its rightful place. Even then, the empty spot in the bed tormented me, as it did most nights.

I second guessed myself again, dozens of times. Had I really done the right thing?

Thinking about the brutal possibilities if I hadn't skipped town, everything that still *might* happen if I ever came back, told me *yes*.

The brain does strange things when it's under constant siege. I thought about the old Edgar Allan Poe Story, "The Pit and the Pendulum," where a man moved between different tortures until they drove him insane.

My heart knew his agony. My womb knew his pain. My soul ached and burned for my man, my family, my home, everything I've given up.

And now, I had one more innocent bystander to worry about, ever since I'd taken the test about a month ago, and seen the results staring me in the face.

This baby wasn't stopping for anything. The tiny life inside me didn't care about danger, guilt, or death. It only shared my heartbeat and will to survive. It deserved a better chance than the one I'd given myself, before everything fell apart.

I couldn't linger like this in limbo, indefinitely. There was one chance to save my child, even though it would rip my heart's remnants into even smaller pieces.

I'd already put distance between me and the old life, but I needed more. I had to keep going west, zigzagging along the route I planned, until I hit the coast. Just a few more months, and I'd have enough cash to leave. I didn't dare tap into my old credit cards or bank accounts since the first week I'd left Tennessee.

That was just asking for the club or, worse, the Sicilians, to find a loose end leading them straight to me.

I'd effectively surrendered everything I ever worked for. The bitter irony wasn't lost on me.

So, I'd cry a little harder, remembering the man whose ring still brought me bitter comfort, who'd given me a piece of him forever, no matter where I wound up on this ridiculous planet.

I'd start over. Raise our baby with a longing in my heart and tears in my eyes, but I'd never, ever look back.

I wasn't Hannah Grayson, or even Hannah Davis anymore. I was Kerry Simons – the name on my fake license and attached to my new accounts. Hardworking consultant, seemingly normal, soon-to-be single mother.

She'd live her life secretly protecting everyone I cared about. I'd go on hating the bitch for her lies, her mistakes, and her delusions.

XII: Halved (Dust)

Four Months Later

Losing a man's wife fucked him up. I drank when I wasn't on the hunt like the world's meanest hound, pouring over every damned clue I could, so fuckin' dogged and determined I gave Bingo a run for his money.

Booze didn't stop the dreams anymore. Neither did the optimistic words from my brothers, or Ma, who told me every day I'd be an idiot to give up.

Nothing shut up Early whenever I closed my eyes. I saw my destiny all over again, the night he'd decided to haunt my evil ass forever.

Why couldn't I see Hannah? Why the fuck not? If it could've been her ghost instead of his, I would've grabbed her, put my lips on hers, and told her what a fuck up I'd been not to follow her to the hospital that night. We could've stopped this shit from ever coming down.

Instead, I got my old man with his beard, his cold black eyes, his evil grin. Same dream, same memory, same reminder I'd wracked up a heavy fuckin' debt to pay. With

Hannah leaving, criss-crossing the country where nobody could find her, I knew the bitch called karma had come to collect.

Every time I closed my eyes, I remembered the precise moment everything was destined to go to shit.

* * * *

"Get the fuck down here, boy. You think hanging around the recruiter's office all day gives you an excuse to roll into this clubhouse an hour late?" Early puffed a thick cigar, shooting me a dirty look.

It was just him in the basement, and none of the other brothers, weird as hell. I wore my cut with the prospect patch over my new Navy shirt, something I decided I better settle into before I shipped off in a couple weeks to the Merchant Marine fleet.

"What's going on, Prez?" I asked slowly, taking the steps into the old storage cellar one at a time. *Prez* was the closet I'd get to calling this fucker dad. I hadn't used that word since I was twelve, almost half a lifetime ago.

"Your time to become a man, that's what." He grabbed my wrist as soon as we were down, stretched out my hand, and handed me a silver blade with the club's logo inscribed in the handle. "I ain't letting you ship out overseas 'til you remember what you're coming home to. And Danny, you *are* coming the fuck home. You'll be holding the gavel someday, making this club bigger and better than I ever did, assuming I can get your damned balls to drop."

I tasted sour, evil guilt on my tongue. Early didn't ask

me a second time, or give me anymore details, just pushed me toward the uneven opening under the clubhouse, a dark little hole I suspected he used to hide the junk he'd been selling outstate.

Tonight, the gap wasn't the pitch black, musty hellhole I'd been expecting. There was a flashlight glowing inside, and it lit the ugly, sweaty face of the man handcuffed inside.

"Ah, Jesus fuckin' Christ. You're really doin' this, Early? Sending a fuckin' kid to cut my throat?" The stranger bared his teeth when he looked up and saw me, revealing a few fresh, bloody gaps in his mouth.

"He'll do you clean, motherfucker," Early said behind me. "Show some damned gratitude. After what you did to Flap and Donny last week, I oughta feed your own balls down your throat, one tiny piece at a time."

That shut the man up. I took a long look at our prisoner, noticing the different patches on his cut. DEADHANDS MC, GEORGIA, they said, a rough crew we were running into more often than we liked.

"Go ahead, son. Show me you ain't a pussy. You know what this fucker did, yeah?"

"Yeah." I meant it, too. "I know."

The entire club was up in arms about it. Last week, Early sent Flap and old man Don down to Georgia to unload smack. Donny came back bloody and bruised, but he'd brought Flap home in a truck, both his hands missing, ending his Harley riding days forever.

"What're you waiting for?" Prez thundered behind me, annoyed with each second ticking by, while the fuck laid out in front me continued breathing.

"This ain't right. Him down here in the dark, cuffed like this, dying like a stuck pig. He's helpless." I watched Early's fist tighten out of the corner of my eye. He'd knocked me on my ass plenty of times, and clenched his rings into a fist a thousand more, before he laid into me or Ma over pure bullshit. "Prez, I know who he is, and what he is. I've got no sympathy. Still, I'm not into gutting this motherfucker like we found him caught in a bear trap."

"Fuck you, Danny. Should kick myself in the ass for thinking you'd know right from wrong." We locked eyes, as soon as I turned around.

On the ground, wedged in that little space, the Deads prisoner laughed. His jeering ratcheted up when Early took me by the throat, spun me around, and slammed my head against the wall.

"You know what, Mister Fancy Fuckin' Sailor? I think you need to learn why that point you're making is total horseshit. Tell you what, we're gonna do things your way tonight for once. Here, let me get this fuck outta his cuffs. We'll put him against the wall, give him a blindfold and a cigarette, and I'll hand you my gun to do the job."

What the fuck had I done? The bastard in the crawlspace twisted, craning his neck to look at me while my old man kneed him in the back, held him down, and jerked his hands up behind his back. I watched the little key slip into the lock, popping his cuffs open.

When I looked into his eyes, I'd expected anger, fear, or at least a mutual fuckin' understanding that I was offering him a chance to die like a man. Quick and easy.

Didn't see any of that shit. I saw nothing. No spark, no gratitude, no making peace with God.

I swallowed. "Dad, watch the fuck –"

Before I realized I'd let *dad* slip out, the motherfucker kicked my old man in the stomach, sending his head crashing against the edge of the low brick ceiling. Early went down with a grunt, and the freed asshole had his paws on my father's belt, going for his nine.

I fucked up royal. Before he could grab the gun and start shooting, I lunged into the crawlspace, kicking the prisoner in the knees. The fuck went down easy, probably too shaky and weak from being holed up in there for God only knew how long.

I landed on top of him, and we rolled, thrashing around in a space barely bigger than a grave, my knife searching for his face.

Shit, shit. Asshole nearly knocked the blade from my wrists, snarling the entire time.

"You stupid little cocksucker!" he roared, bouncing as hard as he could to hit me in the stomach. "Should've listened to your old man. Ain't no honor among enemies, asshole. You're mine. I'm gonna slit both your throats, kill every last fuckin' one of you, soon as I –"

I threw my whole weight into the next jab, and it found his mark. There was as sickening crunch, a splash of blood. We both went still. Early groaned behind me, halfway knocked outta the crawlspace by the scuffle.

Took forever to catch my breath. Crawling out, I threw

the bloody knife in front of me, standing on my knees while my old man leaned into the wall, nursing the world's biggest knot on his forehead.

"What the fuck is wrong with you?!" I screamed, starting to shake. "You knew he'd do that, and you freed him anyway, all just to make a fuckin' point?"

"Fuck you. Didn't have another way to make you understand. I'd do it all over again, too, if I still need to drill it into your head, Danny boy. You're about to set sail to help Uncle Sam with his law and order. Is it really so fuckin' hard for you to see I'm doing the same?"

I wanted to be sick. Law and order was about the last thing he'd done to this club, turning it into a violent, drug peddling slush fund for his retirement, which mostly consisted of special mods on his bikes, imported scotch, and gifts for the girls he fucked behind Ma's back.

"I've killed for this club. It's all I've known. I ain't going anywhere if that's what you're worried about." I stopped, looking my old man dead the face. "When I get back and sit at the table again with the brothers, let's get one thing straight. I will never, *ever* run this shit like you. Fuck your legacy."

"Calm down, boy. You're really running scared if you think I'm trying to remake you in my fuckin' image. Gave up on that a long time ago." He stood up straight, walked over, and put his dirty hands on my shoulders, squeezing so hard it hurt. "I'm trying to teach you some common fuckin' sense so you don't end up like the fucker bleeding out behind you."

As if on cue, I turned my head for a split second, noticing the dark red blood flowing against my boot. The life I'd ended wasn't just going to disappear without a few last ugly reminders.

"It doesn't have to be this way, Prez. You don't have to run shit this way. You could –"

"Danny, shut up. When you're wearing my patch, holding my goddamned gavel, you can turn this shit into a big biker beauty pageant for all I care. Trouble is, you still don't get it."

"What? What's so fuckin' important you dragged me down here for this?"

Sighing, he spun me around, forcing me to stare into the darkness at the man's corpse again. Early's face came close, his lips pressed against my ear, forcing me to feel his tangled grey beard against my neck.

"Ashes to ashes, and dust to dust, son. That's the only law worth a damn in this life. You kill the motherfuckers who deserve it as quick, as easy, and as painful as you can, or those motherfuckers kill you worse." Very slowly, he pulled away, making me shake from the sudden draft against my skin where his beard had been. "Congratulations, Dust. I'm gonna make sure that name gets stitched on your cut before you ship the fuck out. It'll help you remember everything that happened tonight."

Fuck remembering. Like I could even forget.

The last memory I had that night was standing down there alone, after he'd gone upstairs, yelling after me to clean up the fuckin' mess, and make sure nobody found the dead man's skin and bones.

I busted my ass scrubbing away his blood, bagging up his body for the truck, and hauling him deep into the Smokies alone. Feral tears scorched my face while I dug his grave.

My old man wasn't just a stone cold bastard. For once in his brutish life, the fuck was right.

If I hadn't jumped on the Deads thug when I did, we both would've been toast. I'd tried to show a little mercy, a smidge of honor, and I'd nearly gotten fucked over in the worst way possible.

Never again. Early taught me something that night, and I only resented my new road name because he'd thought of it before I did.

Dust. The final form of every living thing. Meant I'd kill anybody before they fucked with my club, or the ones I loved.

Ashes to ashes wouldn't just rain down to stop it, but they fuckin' *had* to. Losing brothers, lovers, or family was the only fear I had left, and I vowed that night I'd never let it conquer me.

* * * *

Except I hadn't conquered shit. I jerked awake in my bed, sprawled out, covering the empty spot where Hannah hadn't slept next to me for several evil months.

Like every morning since she'd left, I punched the emptiness, starting another fucked up day in a rage.

I rode to the clubhouse and sat down in my office, taking in the day's reports left on my desk by Joker. The

Veep fed me a lot of info. Held my breath flipping through those pages, wishing and hoping I'd find a lead to Hannah, the Sicilians, anything that would bring her home.

There were profit numbers from the latest gun runs we did for the Grizzlies and the Prairie Devils, going down to the coast. Another letter of condolences from some mafia fuck in Ireland, who'd assured us he had our backs when we finally tracked down Dom and his boys. The Sicilians wouldn't escalate their war with reinforcements, as long as they had to worry about reprisals in Europe.

Profit statements from the garages and the Ruby Heel. Our body work, dancers, and booze brought in more clean money than ever this quarter. Didn't do a damned thing to patch the black hole in my stomach.

When I got to the end of the reports, I sighed. There was nothing about Dominick Barone, and even less about Hannah.

I reached for the half full bottle of Jack in my bottom drawer. Nearly hit the ceiling when something long and wet slid across my hand.

"Fuck you, wolfie! You're gonna give a man a goddamned heart attack one of these days." Failing to see the huge wolfhound laying in the corner when I came in told me how fuckin' blitzed I'd really been.

Bingo pulled his head away and stretched, his mouth opening wide in a yawn, tail wagging because he didn't have a care in the world. I would've given anything for a taste of that attitude, right about now.

I pushed my chair over and stroked his head while I

poured myself a shot, listening to his heavy breathing. "You've only been with us for a little while, and you've already seen a heap of shit. Fuckin' shame, really."

The dog pressed his head into my hand, oblivious to the club's many struggles and fuck ups over the past year. Hadn't all been bad, of course. Half the boys were wed off or raising kids. Their stories had happy endings. I started to believe the same slice of heaven might be waiting around the corner for me.

Big mistake. Colossal.

My hand tightened on the little shot glass while I took a second hit from the bottle. This shit only did so much to numb the demon churning in my guts. It wouldn't be truly tamed 'til I brought her back.

I believed she was alive out there somewhere, ignoring the savage voice deep down that said I was wasting my time, and everybody else's, too.

The third shot was about to go down my throat when my door swung open. Bingo jerked up and walked across the room to make room for Firefly.

We'd shared an icy peace the last few months, ever since Hannah up and disappeared. Now, the giant stood over me, looking like a grenade about to go off, flatting his hands on my desk.

"You got something to say, or what?" I asked, looking back with daggers in my eyes.

"I believed you, Cap'n. Listened to every fucked up thing you said in church last week, when you swore up and down you were looking for her, giving it everything you had."

"Not sure what you're pissed about because I gave you the God's truth. What the fuck do you think I'm doing in here? Pulling my pud while I think about how much I miss her doing it for me?"

The whiskey had hit my system quicker than I believed. Words came out like bee stings on the tongue. Knew I sounded like an asshole, even if there was a bigger one standing in front of me.

Slowly, Firefly reached out, grasped the almost drained bottle, and gripped it in one hand. "I'm gonna give you one chance to tell me how throwing this shit down your gullet at ten o'clock in the morning helps bring my sis home. Half a minute. Go."

I stood up, tilting my face up, my eyes locked to his like knife on bone. Over in the corner, Bingo whined, sensing the storm about to break open in this little room.

"Whatever the fuck else you've got to say or do to me, just let the dog go. He don't need to be here for this."

Firefly grunted reluctant agreement as he walked over. He stroked the big grey dog's head 'til he stood up, and slowly ambled out the open door on four furry legs. I watched my big Enforcer cross the room after him, yank the door shut, slamming it so hard on its hinges the whole building shook.

"I gave you thirty seconds, Prez. You haven't said a fuckin' thing, which tells me you've got nothing."

"Fuck, we oughta add a detective patch to the club ranks for the fine work you just did," I said, stepping out from behind my desk, getting in his face. "We're missing the same woman for different reasons, so you deserve an answer that ain't just 'fuck off.' I come in here, morning after morning, looking for the day I see a scrap of paper that has a few answers on it. Every single evening, I go home, staying up 'til I pass out, combing over every file, hoping we missed something. Every fuckin' lead turns to ashes in front of my eyes, and then does it again when I'm stupid enough to double-check. That lead in Michigan last month that went fuckin' nowhere…the Grizzlies prospect who thought he saw her in Idaho…the drunken asshole at the Heel who told us she was right under our noses, two towns over, only to walk in where he said and find a bitch in a wig shooting up in front of her kid…"

My nostrils flared. That last incident a couple weeks ago really pissed me off.

The club called the good cops we knew as soon as we pushed the druggie bitch outta her house and got her kid to safety. Then I personally drove to the Heel, pulled the drunk who'd handed us the faulty tip out back, and put the fear of God into him for boozing so fuckin' much he thought a crank whore looked like my Hannah.

"So, you're giving up, Prez? That what you're saying?" Firefly snorted, shaking his head. "Fuck's sake. You know we're gonna get a hundred more false leads before we take a bite on one that's real. That's how this goes, and I'm doing my damnedest to keep my head straight, keep it clear, double-checking for anything – motherfucking *anything* – we might've missed."

"That's just it – we don't have goddamned time for a

hundred more fake leads. She's been missing for *seven* fuckin' months!" I pushed past him, hit the wall, and banged both my fists against it.

Seven. I counted them in my head every heartless night, right before I forced myself to blackout.

Some nights, Doctor Jack and Jim helped. Others, I got down on the floor, sweated like a hog, and did so many pushups I hit the floor with my arms half-broke, grinding my teeth angrily 'til I passed the fuck out.

Seven evil months without my Hannah. Seven months of darkness. Seven months shuffling through this life like a disembodied spirit.

"You're making excuses, Cap'n. I want her back just as much as you do," Firefly said, his grip on the bottle easing. His knuckles weren't pale white anymore. Maybe he'd gotten cold feet about bringing it down on my skull.

"Fuck wanting, Firefly. I'm bringing her back. Maybe you're right about the bottle taking too much away from me. It bleeds time, focus. Hours and days when I could've hit the shit in front of me a few more times, triple checked a few more leads. I hear you, brother, and I'm fuckin' sorry."

Apologies were supposed to help. This one tasted like ash in my mouth.

I kept my face to the wall, ashamed, wondering how I kept the boot off my own ass. Hated how it took this asshole behind me to admit I had a problem with the sauce cutting into these worthless leads.

"Don't apologize." Firefly laid a stern hand on my

shoulder. "Shape the fuck up, Prez. We just gotta be patient for a little while longer. Joker's touching base with the contacts we've got in Texas and Oklahoma, trying to sniff out anything new."

"Bullshit," I said, turning around to face him. Pulling out my pipe, I gave it a light, and motioned to the map behind my desk. The one with all the little rainbow tacks stuck in it, one for every place we thought we heard a rumor that wasn't total bullshit. "That's the trouble with all this, ain't it? Her route doesn't make sense. If anything we heard about her being in the Pacific Northwest was true, why the fuck would she give that up to go down to Texas? With her Sterner Corp ties, she'd be heading for Seattle, trying to get to Alaska, or fuck knows where from there."

"My sis ain't stupid, Prez. Last thing she'd do is walk right into a fuckin' trap." Firefly stared me down.

I never broke my gaze, but something inside me reached up, giving my heart a bitter twist. My Enforcer's words stung because she'd taken the bait. Dom and his bastards wanted her out there alone, by herself, where the club couldn't protect her.

And I hadn't stopped her. If only I'd gone to the damned hospital that night, walked her back to her car, throttled the motherfucker who ambushed her and tried to take her hostage before she crashed his shit on the mountain…

"Prez? What the hell's the matter?"

I closed my eyes, shoving my regretful demons back in their boxes. I said a quick, silent prayer in my head.

Lord, just a little while longer. Banish this darkness, send me a light, anything to bring my woman home.

I wasn't a religious man. Hard to be anything resembling that when you'd dispatched as many sick fucks as I did over the years. Still, I prayed, sent up my desperate hopes to a God who didn't owe me a damned thing.

"You've been pissed at me for months. I don't blame you," I said, stepping up to my Enforcer, putting my hand around his wrist. "If it wasn't for this shit between us, Firefly, she might be standing here today, safe and sound. She went to the hospital without me the night your kid was born because you couldn't stand having me around."

Firefly bared his teeth. Angry muscle bulged underneath my fingertips. "Now's not the time to dwell on the past. I always said we'd sort out our shit as soon as we brought her home. That's all that matters."

"We're sortin' it out now," I said. "Because as long as there's this quiet, toxic resentment between you and me, brother, we ain't finding her. Go ahead. Get it outta your fuckin' system. Maybe the blow to my skull will do me some good, knock some sense into places that need it."

My fingers dug into his skin. He tried to move back, but I wouldn't let him, holding on in a death grip 'til he moved that bottle high.

"What the fuck's gotten into you?" he said, his blue eyes going wide. "You're acting like a nut right now, Prez, and I –"

"You're pissed. You hate me for shoving my ring on her finger, and then letting her get away. And I hate you for hating it, wanting to spit in my face over the best fuckin' thing that ever happened to me. You thought I was too goddamned bad to put my lips on your little sis, have her in my bed, bury my dick in her, and promise her she'd be carrying my kid within the year."

I'd seen my boy's eyes glowing like hell itself a few dozen times in battle. They'd never been this bright, this hot, this pissed off.

"You know what you're asking for, Prez?" he snorted, clenching his teeth. "I'll fuck you up. Bad."

"Exactly. I *want* you to get this fuckin' poison out of your system so we can put it aside and find my wife. Don't give two shits if you refuse to believe me about going after her. I love her. I need her. I ain't giving up on her for anything, and I'll crawl through hell itself with a broken face if it'll stop the distractions, and put the energy you spend busting my balls into bringing her back."

The bottle in his hand twitched. I closed my eyes, bracing for a special kind of pain that'd probably knock me out cold, if it didn't do brain damage.

Instead of hearing the whiskey bottle colliding with bone, we both heard a dog in the newly opened doorway. Bingo yipped once. We both turned to see him standing in the hall, Joker holding him by the leash, squinting at the showdown in my office.

"Looks like I picked a bad time to pass out good news."

"News? What news?" I pushed past Firefly, frantically approaching my Veep, studying the smile on his face. It still didn't look quite right when he smiled, even though it happened a lot lately. The muscles must've needed practice to work right after all the years he spent scowling, loathing, waiting to avenge his dead brother.

"We've got ourselves a hit in some dusty little town in West Texas, Prez. Came in this morning. Warpath Nomads, riding down from Oklahoma, heading for Mexico."

My heart stopped pumping for five brutal seconds. The Warpaths were solid, only other outlaw MC in Dixie we trusted. Firefly stood next to me, taking in the news, while Joker went on.

"They think they spotted her driving into town for groceries."

I grabbed him by his cut, digging my fingers in, stepping over his boots and the dog laying down on the floor. "Think, or *know?* There's a big fuckin' difference."

"Know, Prez. They sent me these about an hour ago." He reached into his pocket and held up his phone.

The first pic had a license plate number I'd burned into my memory. Second pic showed her getting outta her car, those sweet locks I'd smelled and fisted in my hands a hundred times catching the Texas light. Third pic stopped my fuckin' heart for a whole lot longer than five goddamned seconds.

It was Hannah, wiping down her windows while she fueled up, beautiful as the day she left me forever. No, more beautiful than I'd ever seen her before, because her body showed one big difference from how I remembered it.

That bump in her belly, sticking out, could only mean one thing.

Firefly made a sound like he stopped breathing when he saw it. Shook me straight to my fuckin' core, so rough and sudden it was like catching a bullet. I gripped Joker's leather in both hands tighter, pulling hard, only support I had to keep me on my feet.

"Fuck…" One word rendered me speechless.

Joker sensed the earthquake rolling through my body. Veep's hands were wrapped around mine a second later, helping keep me up, walking me over to the beat up coach in the corner, across from my desk.

Nobody said shit 'til I was sitting down, with Firefly next to me, pale as a ghost.

"Christ, Veep, get them on her," he said. "You gotta –"

"Tell them to turn their fuckin' bikes around and pin her down!" I snapped, cutting my Enforcer off. "Block off every exit in that damned town. Don't let her out of sight 'til they know we're on our way. Find her a room in town, keep her cozy, as long as they're under her watch, I don't fuckin' care!"

Joker's face softened. "Like I said, brothers, I only got this shit an hour ago. They caught up to her about a half hour before that. By the time I got it, saw it, and texted them back, they'd moved the fuck on. I told them the same thing you just said, believe me. Unfortunately for us, they've got business south of the border. Big Dog told me personally they can't be bothered holding up for our missing girl. They did us a favor just reporting it."

"You're shittin' me." I gave him a hard look, but his eyes were honest. That dagger lodged in my guts for the last seven months gave me the sharpest twist ever.

"No, Prez, I wish I was. Ain't like we've got any authority over their club. They're our friends, and they've just given us a gold mine here. Best we can do is take that shit into our own hands, get on our bikes, and find her."

Joker laid down so much truth it turned my fuckin' stomach. I had to keep it together. "Get the boys together. Whatever the fuck it takes to bring them all here in the next hour, ready to go. Everybody except Tin and Lion, who'll hold down home with the prospects."

"On it." My Veep nodded. He stood, stroked his dog's head, and led the animal out. He never wasted time, a virtue that stuck, despite all the happy changes upending his life.

Me, I had one shot at tracking down my woman, and having something resembling the happiness I'd lost. Firefly looked at me, and I wondered if he'd want to pick up on where we'd left off after this punch to the guts.

"You've still got that thing in your hand," I said, looking at the bottle. "If you're gonna do it, let's get it over with, fast. I need to be on my feet and ready to ride, hoping to Christ we're not too late by the time we get to Texas."

Firefly stared at me. His hand released, and the bottle hit the ground with a heavy *thud*. "Prez...you just heard the same thing I did. Whatever the fuck my beef is with you, I'm too big a man to whack the bastard who put a kid in my sister's belly. And what you said earlier...fuck me. I hate it that you care about her, hate it that you're speaking from the heart, killing every last instinct I've got to put your ass through the wall. Fuck you, Cap'n. You've made me a believer, made me think you might not be total trash for my little sis. Only thing that matters is bringing Hannah home."

"Damned straight." We both stood up.

Only lasted a second before the big man threw his arms around me, squeezing me like a boa constrictor. That big, brotherly hug hurt like it was meant to. We'd been at each other's throats since before she disappeared.

Now, we forced that venom out, shed it in a bear hug mean enough to splinter bones. When he pulled away, so did I.

"Get your shit together, brother. We've got a long run ahead, and you know we're not stopping for any sleep."

"No breaks except for gas and coffee." He headed for the door, stopping once before he ripped it open to look back at me, a fractured smile on his face. "And Prez, if I catch you sneaking anything that's straight from the bar, I will kick your ass from coast to coast."

"I'd expect nothing less." We shared another nod, and he was gone.

I shook off the remaining booze in my system, tuned up my bike, and set to work packing up the guns we'd need to blow through anyone who got in our way.

Nothing, nobody, and fuck all was stopping me from finding my wife.

* * * *

One Week Later

Lady Luck wasn't giving us a damned thing without working us like dogs. The first day we rolled into that dusty little town just south of Odessa and couldn't find her, I nearly hit the roof.

I rode fifty miles further with just Skin and Sixty at my side, stopping at every ranch along the way. Had to bite my tongue 'til it was almost chewed clean through every time the answer came back the same.

No, sir, haven't seen anybody like her.

Don't recognize the plates.

You sure she's been this way? Hardly anybody takes this route if they're cruising to the coast.

That last reply, and every bullshit word like it, caused me to see so much red my brothers had to help me back on my bike before I shot the messenger.

She couldn't slip away from us, for fuck's sake. Not when we were this close, and it wasn't just Hannah I needed in my arms again to make me whole.

She was about to bring my kid into the world. *My son, my daughter, my flesh and blood I hadn't known existed for over eight fuckin' months.*

Before, I respected boys like Joker or Firefly when they got crazy about their pregnant wives, or their secret babies. After seeing that pic on my Veep's phone, I respected it a thousand times more, felt the pick digging into my brain every merciless second my wife and kid weren't with me.

I sat on the cracked patio outside my motel room, puffing my pipe like a chimney, trying not to chew clean through the stem. I was gone, too deep in dark thoughts, too distracted watching my old man's ghost laughing at me to notice Firefly 'til he had his hand on my shoulder.

"News from the scouts," he said. Soon as I saw his serious expression, I hopped up, studying his eyes. "Her car's been spotted at a hospital about thirty miles away. I told the boys to cruise every exit. Don't let her leave for anything."

"Fuck, what are waiting for?" We both went for our bikes, threw on our helmets, and peeled out of the lot so fast my head whipped backwards.

It was all open roads out here. Normally, a comfort, a zen-like blur I'd lose myself in when times were fucked, letting the growling engine and spotty lines on cracked asphalt bring me into a zone where I didn't have to worry about any bullshit.

Wasn't working today. I sweated in the cool winter air the entire way, wondering what brought her to a goddamned hospital.

Sixty, Skin, Crawl, and Joker waited for us near the main entrance when we rode up and parked at the small medical center. I started heading for the door, but the Veep grabbed me by the shoulders, pushed me back, holding me scary tight.

"Joker? What the fuck?!"

"Hold up, Prez. We've got company."

It took everything I had to look over his shoulder instead of knocking him flat, and then rushing in to find my girl. Too bad he wasn't bullshitting.

Over on the other side of the parking lot, several squad cars were parked along the curb, quietly blinking their cherry-blue lights. Far more cops than there oughta be at an out of way hospital like this on a normal day.

"What happened here?" I growled, my hands tugging at my Veep's leather.

"Don't know yet," Skin cut in next to me. "None of us do. We figured we'd let you decide how to approach the questioning. If we all go in there at once, it might draw more attention than we want, depending on what's gone down here..."

"They've got patrols out front," Crawl said, pushing his shaggy black hair away from his eyes. "Whatever it was, they put the whole hospital on lockdown. Nobody armed is getting in, or out."

I glared, sighing when I saw Skinny boy's face filled with concern. "You're right. Firefly, you're with me. The rest of you boys, stay put, and watch the bikes. Any of those badges come over asking what we're doing here, you tell 'em we're checking one of our crew in for nasty stomach bug."

They nodded. I headed inside with my Enforcer, hoping like hell we'd both be able to keep a lid on our emotions if the answers we got about Hannah came back ugly.

A panicked looking woman sat at the front desk. Had to slam my hand down flat in front of her to finally get her attention.

"Can I help you?" She sat up taller when she saw us, like a woman who'd just spotted a couple wolves roaming close by.

"Sure hope so. We're looking for Hannah Grayson. Should've been a pregnant lady who checked in here sometime in the last couple days."

The woman's fingers clicked across her keyboard. She chewed her lip, telling me either the system was fucked, or nothing was coming up easy.

"Try Hannah Davis, too," Firefly said.

I turned my head, staring him down. Hannah wouldn't use her fuckin' maiden name…would she? If she wasn't under mine, I had to believe it was something different, some alias that wouldn't shove my heart into the chipper for another round of pure torture, knowing she'd given up my name, like we never happened.

"No patients named Hannah the last few days," she said, narrowing her eyes. "I'm sorry, gentlemen. We're having a bit of a situation at the moment. If you can't provide more personal details about the woman you're looking for, I'm going to have to ask you to –"

"Mind telling us what happened?" Firefly stepped up with a lot more tact than I would've mustered just then.

"Oh…Jesus. You haven't heard? Guess it hasn't hit the evening news yet, huh?" She sat back, rocking the little chair on its wheels. We both shook our heads. "A group of really creepy men went after this pregnant lady who checked in last night."

"Pregnant lady?!" I spat both words, choking on my heart leaping into my throat.

Firefly laid a hand on my shoulder and gave me a look. *Just let her talk, Prez. Don't fuck this up.*

"Yeah." She sighed. "Really, really sad. They took her away before she even had her kid. Killed a nurse and roughed up a few doctors. The cops are hunting them down right now, calling for backup across the county. It's a full on manhunt."

Shit.

"Did you see them? What did they look like?" I asked, leaning over the high top above her, trying to talk like a rational human being.

"No. I was on break at the time when the crazy went down, thank God. It could've been me at the end of their knife." She paused, looked at me, and wilted a little when she saw the intensity in my eyes. "Um...I think I've already said too much. We're supposed to keep this to ourselves, seeing how it hasn't made it to the news just yet. Who are you looking for again?"

"Shit, look at this, just got a text on my phone." Firefly stepped in front of me, holding out a message from Cora on his screen, asking if he'd made it to Texas okay.

I cocked my head. What the fuck was he up to?

"This ain't even the right hospital, brother!" he said, grinning like a fool, before he turned to the receptionist. "We're real sorry for the trouble. We got mixed up. My sister's about to have a baby, and we thought it was here. Just heard she's a little ways upstate – siblings and all." He shook his head convincingly.

Very slowly, I stared at the receptionist and nodded, playing along. Thank fuck somebody was still using their brain. We didn't need more problems right now.

We had to get out of here, had to hit the road, and stay ahead of the swarming law before they caught up to the Sicilians before we did. The law wasn't cut out for a rescue op like this. If they found the bastards first, I might never see my wife and kid again.

"Well, if there's anything else I can do for you boys, just say the word." She went back to her screen, oblivious while we walked out.

One quick conversation with the brothers outside later, and we were back on our bikes, heading into a wintery rain on the highway. Cold ass sleet swept down my back, rolled down my leather in rivulets, bounced in front of me like God's wrath before it melted on the interstate.

I could've cursed nature, fate, the universe, everything keeping us from tearing down this road to bring my girl home faster. Instead, an eerie calm filtered through my blood, pulling the hot red sheet of rage off my eyes.

If I couldn't control what the fuck happened next, then I'd at least own the present.

Swore we'd see each other again. I'd taste Hannah's lips, push my fingers through her hair, hold her tighter than my own soul, tell her how fuckin' much I loved her.

I'd say it again. I'd say it a thousand times, pour it on again and again and again, 'til she was sick of hearing it.

These obstacles aimed to make it even sweeter when I got her back.

It was so close now. One big, beautiful, happy family. All the things I never knew I wanted before her. Everything I swore I'd have, or else die trying to claim.

We rode on twelve more miles before seeing that shitty hotel with the suspicious vans out front. I smiled like a maniac into the rain and the wind, grinned 'til Early's ghost staring back at me looked spooked as fuck.

What're you laughing at, boy? I heard him say, a quiver in his throat I'd never heard before. *Don't you know it's about to go to shit? Reaper's gonna take her, right under your fuckin' nose.*

"Yeah, old man, it's gonna be fuckin' awful for them," I whispered. "Haven't been so ready for a kill in my life. Hope you've got room on the other side for these motherfuckers."

Motherfuckers? Is that what you're calling your wife, your kid, the brothers you're about to get blasted in a shoot out over jack shit? You've already lost, Danny. Let them go.

"They ain't going anywhere but home. You know damned well who I'm talking about. Save a seat for Dom next to Satan after I rip his fuckin' throat out."

I've got one for you, Danny boy.

You're a bad seed. Only ones who deserve to be reunited down here are you and me. Not that poor woman you've kicked halfway to hell, and another bastard kid who's gotta carry our tainted blood.

Rain dripped down my face. I'd lost my mind about an hour ago, but talking to this sick motherfucker gave me something to do, besides riffling through the hundred ways I'd personally murder Dominick Barone.

"I'll be there, telling you to shut the fuck up for the next trillion years if it gives my wife and kid a chance. Hell, we'll hang out all fuckin' day while the devil spit roasts us, and I'll remind you what a worthless, cheating, boozing piece of shit you were to Ma, and how you ran this club into a ground. We can both look up at everybody still breathin', wearing our patch proud, families growing like grapes on a vine with the richest soil anybody ever seen. You can watch me smiling while I'm tortured, old man, because I know I've done well. And I'm gonna bring her home before I die. Long before I ever listen to another word of your miserable, sadistic, cowardly fuckin' shit."

I expected more hell shattering my head. Something about Hannah being dead, a ghostly scream so vicious it'd cause me to wreck, or maybe just his evil laugh, drifting through the sleet.

But it was quiet, lonely, magnificently desolate in this freezing rain, going down the final stretch.

For the first time in my life, behind the icy patter and the steady roar of engines, I heard a silence, dense as the thick sheet of grey clouds hanging over us. It was up to me to fill that void, wash it clean with blood, before I took everything I ever wanted, and never let go.

XIII: Scattered (Hannah)

I woke up in a sweat and smelled…pomegranate.

Jerking up, my stomach heaved. Just when it didn't seem possible, my body learned to hate the scent of that sickening fucking fruit more than ever.

"Hold her the fuck down. She moves too much. Bound to do some real damage if we let her kick and scream." Dom smiled, sitting in a chair next to me, switchblade in his hand.

I watched him sink it into the open pomegranate, pulling a juicy red seed out on the tip. Several goons put their arms on me, pushing me back onto the bed. Pain ripped through my lower abdomen.

I looked down and saw blood. Emptiness. Something torn from me while I was knocked out.

Oh, God. Where's my baby?

I squirmed frantically. One of the men growled in my ear, pushed me down harder, clapped his dirty hand over my mouth, before I could scream.

"Easy, peach. You're not doing anybody a favor, flapping around like a fish out of water." Dom's dark eyes focused on me while he leisurely fed more blood red fruit into his mouth. "You're wondering where he is, yeah?"

He? My heart skipped in my chest, confused, unsure if I should be celebrating my son if they'd murdered him.

"Will, go grab the kid, and show her." The other goon who'd helped force me down walked into the bathroom.

A few seconds later, he strolled out with a baby carrier in his hand, the soft, sleepy little life I'd brought into the world tucked into a blanket. I let my eyes take him in, oblivious to the horror around us for a moment, marveling at the miracle I'd created with the man I missed more than anything.

"Take a good, long look, peach, because it's gonna be one of your last. Soon as you can walk, we're hitting the road. Whole fuckin' highway's crawling with cops. You brought them out of the woodwork, making us get so rough at the hospital."

I looked at my baby helplessly. Why didn't this seem completely real?

Adrenaline swirled in my system, kicked my nerves every time I moved. But the pain, the happiness at seeing my son, and the hideous gravity of this situation painted everything in a surreal gloss. I lifted a hand, touched my head, and realized I was burning up.

Fever. Weakness. No wonder it didn't take much for the goons to force me down, no matter how much I tried to kick and scream.

"Please. Not Seattle. It's so cold this time of year…"

I started at my baby, more worried about keeping him

safe than catching pneumonia in the cold, gloomy Pacific Northwest. My infant son snuggled into his blanket, trying to bore down in the covers, hiding from the chill in the room. The bastards surrounding us were all wearing thick leather jackets.

It was cool here, but Texas was hardly a death sentence. Further north, that might be a different story, trapped with these reckless animals pretending to look after us.

Dom smiled. So evil, so smug, so vicious I wished I could just reach up, and tear his lips clean off his face.

"What? Why're you looking at me like that? Just fucking tell me," I sputtered, noticing how weak my voice sounded. He had to lean just to hear me.

"You're getting real flustered over nothing, peach. Lucky you, we're not going to Seattle." He paused, letting the mystery torture me. "We're heading for Miami."

"Miami?" I shook my head. "What? There's nothing any of us want there."

"Correction," he said, holding up another pomegranate seed on his knife. "There's a big black market for kids."

I glared through my weakness, rage filling my veins instead of fear. "Fuck you, Dominick. You're not even funny."

"Peach, peach, we've worked together long enough to know I'm no comedian. You might laugh at the buyer I have in mind. Funny little man with an accent, he talks a lot about this island out in the Caribbean where a bunch of rich freaks pay good money to dance around naked and dress up in Druid robes. Some kind of cult for bored, high class assholes. I think it's just one big frat house for spoiled fucks into voodoo. Anyway, they pay good money for the fleshbags they sacrifice there on the big night, before they get too deep in the drugs and fucking their whores. They'll pay *double* for kids. Can't say I give a fuck if my man's making it up – and maybe he is – all I know is he's paid me top dollar before when I sold off a few girls. He's an A-plus buyer. We've got ourselves a rare opportunity to collect on your debt in one sweet deal, and we're gonna take it."

I screamed, my strength returning. It took three of his goons to hold me down while I kicked, banging my head against their shoulders. I bit into one asshole's hand and tasted iron. Snarling, he punched me in the jaw, forcing my teeth off his skin.

They overpowered me eventually, cuffing one hand to the bedpost, high over my head. It wouldn't take long for my arm to go numb, preventing any more accidents.

"Fuck's sake, peach, you're acting like a brat," Dom said calmly, chewing more blood fruit. "You fucked me over, you understand? Got two of my boys killed. I'm man enough to let you live…in a sense. You'll be sold off for my time and suffering, but that funny little man I mentioned isn't interested. Broads with too much kick aren't really his type. We'll find you a buyer, peach, and you'll get to live out your days sucking, fucking, and maybe using your skin as an ashtray for your new owner. Pretty damned easy, considering a little fuckin' coding was too much goddamned work!"

He roared the last part. When I opened my eyes again,

he stood over me, glaring like the maniac he was. He slapped me, and the room spun.

I thought I'd black out. Maybe it would've been sweet mercy.

But my baby's crying kept me awake. "No!"

I reached out for the child I hadn't even named, helplessly moving my hands, crying out for Dusty as much as I wanted a miracle.

"Get that goddamned kid out of here. Spike the fuckin' formula, whatever it takes to shut him up." Growling, Dom hurled his half-eaten pomegranate at the floor. Seeds scattered across cracked wood and hit the walls like tiny shrapnel.

"More trouble than you're worth, bitch," he said, leering in my face. "Story of this whole fucked up arrangement I was fool enough to trust."

I stopped moving just long enough to realize he'd put his blade against my neck. *Slow breaths. You can't pass out again, or it's all over,* I told myself, forcing my eyes to stay open, fixed on the monster leaning over me.

"Don't make me regret keeping your ungrateful ass alive, Hannah. I'm not an evil man. You think I like this? Think I enjoy carving bitches up, or figuring out what pimp to send them to next, while I hand off their kids to get burned like a bag of fuckin' leaves?" He snorted psychotic rage in my face. "You forced me into this. Pushed me too far. Don't keep pushing, peach. You'll find out I'm approaching my limit *real* fuckin' fast. Keep kicking me in the balls, and I might decide you're not worth the trouble.

I'll take the kid, cut my losses, finish what fever's started, and leave you to die on the side of the road."

His eyes beamed hate, sick and brutally honest. Unmistakable evil.

He'd fed on enough pain for now. When I wouldn't give him anymore, he pulled away, his heavy shoe crunching a few stray seeds on the floor as he dragged his chair across the room.

I would have given anything to see Dusty's beautiful grey eyes one more time. Dom would kill me sooner or later, whatever gross incentives he offered in this game.

Regret ballooned inside me.

I'd made my mistakes, panicking and running when I shouldn't have. Hiding from the only man who ever loved me with his whole heart while our baby grew inside my stressed out body.

My life was about to be a total loss, and it killed me. Especially losing our baby without as much as a name to his little face. Much less a chance to let his father hold him, know him, love him.

More than anything, while I lay there tangled in the sheets, one hand cuffed to the bed, surrounded by these killers, I had one selfish regret.

I missed my husband's face more than my own life. Dusty's cool grey eyes, his expert lips, the salt and pepper stubble that used to scratch my face when he explored every inch of me.

I did everything I could to bleach it from my brain these last few months, on the run, and I'd failed miserably.

He was gone, but not forgotten. Robbed away by my own stupid actions.

Focusing on the mistakes wouldn't bring him back. So, I lay there in hell, struggling to remember every last detail of the man I'd loved with as much crystal clarity as I could get through pure delirium.

The next time Dom swore, barking an order to his men, I had a strange, sad smile on my face.

Dusty made me happy to the bitter end, and I wouldn't let anyone take that away.

The end was coming. I knew it the next time my eyelids fluttered open, and I heard a heavy roar outside, several loud engines, snarling and impatient.

Dom and his bastards moved around the room in a flurry. They were getting ready to load us up, and take us to the next world, one wicked way or another.

If there was any justice in the universe, it would be kinder than this one to me and my child.

XIV: Showdown (Dust)

I brought two guns to settle score. My trusty nine, which saved my life ten times over, and still might tip the balance for my crew when harvest time came. The other pistol hadn't been fired for a hundred years and…well, fuck, Dom would find out why soon enough.

I turned off the road, roaring into that beat up parking lot, as soon as I saw the two vans. Crawl pulled ahead, doing a quick survey, and radioed his confirmation.

They were there.

Very few businesses had tinted windows on their shit, especially out here in the sticks, where nobody cared if tools weren't strapped down according to code.

The cold rain picked up when we surrounded the main entrance. My boys fanned out quick, covering the soon-to-be battlefield like we'd done a hundred times, getting in between the fuckers and their vehicles so they'd have to go through us to leave.

Joker stood at my side. I turned to him, one hand on the nine tucked in my belt, ready for hot death if any of those doors in front of us popped up. "You go talk to owner,

Veep. Find out what room they're in. Tell them to take cover, and that there's ten big in cash waiting if they listen."

He took off running. This place wasn't huge, and probably hadn't been remodeled since the seventies. Maybe a dozen units, more than half unoccupied. I walked up to the one on the corner, just a few paces from the slots where the vans were parked crooked, giving the assholes the fastest escape route 'til we'd arrived.

Where the fuck's Joker? Firefly and I shared a look across the lot when the Veep didn't show. We were about to go after him when a maintenance door popped open. He stepped out with a gun to his back, clenched in the hand of a nasty looking fucker in a rumpled button down shirt.

Shit! As if worrying about my woman and kid being hostages wasn't bad enough.

The whole crew pointed their guns at the asshole's head, too close for comfort to Joker's. "Let him fuckin' go," I growled.

"We're just here to talk!" Crawl yelled, pushing his thick black hair away from his eyes. "Just wanna give your boss a message."

"Fuck you, Pistol cocksuckers. Why don't you tell him yourselves?" He yelled it, and the door we'd been swarming around opened a second later. "Anybody fuckin' shoots, this asshole's getting one right through his head."

Dom and several more mean looking motherfuckers came out through the new door. I kept my eyes trained on the asshole shoving his gun into Joker's head. Veep looked at me, angry resignation all over his face, silently telling me not to take any shit.

Fuck him, too. He didn't get to be so reckless. The boy had a wife and kid to worry about, same as I did. Even if he was damned near ready to give up his life, I wasn't gonna let that happen.

"Gentleman, gentleman, why don't we all lower our weapons and talk this out like men?" Dominick Barone was shorter and slimier than I expected. The evil glint in his eye was familiar, though, something I'd snuffed out in evil bastards like him dozens of times.

Before the day ended, I'd be doing it one more.

He walked toward me, ignoring the gun I kept aimed at his heart. Stupid sonofabitch practically walked into it before I lowered it. He stood in front of me, too damned close for comfort, a sickly sweet fruit smell rolling out his mouth each time he exhaled.

"You know why I'm here, *capo*," I said, his mafia rank bleeding sarcasm on my tongue. "Give me back my Veep, bring me my wife and kid, and maybe we can walk away from this alive. Ain't asking you again, motherfucker."

"Funny," he said, a sly smiling curdling his lips. "I'm not hearing much room for negotiation, biker trash. And this *is* a negotiation instead of a straight up shootout, correct?"

No, fuck face. I imagined ramming my nine into his jaw, knocking him on the ground, and burying a bullet deep in his brain. Too bad the people I loved would die if I went loose cannon.

"Name your price, and show me you ain't killing my Veep before we talk about anything."

"Three million, and not a cent less," he said coldly,

before slowly turning to the man at his side, holding his gun to Joker's head. "Will, you know what to do."

His chokehold on Joker came off. For a second, I thought the fuck was showing good faith. Fatal mistake, considering I always should have remembered animals like him had no honor.

No sooner than Joker got several paces, moving next to Firefly, the asshole who'd been holding him hostage fired.

Fuck! I watched my boy drop, blood coming thick.

Veep went down, screaming, falling into my Enforcer's arms while his leg gushed from the wound.

Everybody's guns were back up, primed, and half a fuckin' second from going off.

Goddamn, it'd feel good to finally pull the trigger on this bastard's skull, even if it was the last thing I ever did.

"Careful," Dom said softly, not even flinching when I rammed my nine's barrel into his temple. "I'm taking insurance. Your man is merely wounded. We could've killed him if we'd wanted."

"Asshole!" Joker screamed behind me, spitting through his teeth, while Firefly ripped through his jeans and bundled the denim tight, forming a crude tourniquet.

"Let's not have any hard feelings over this, Dust. This isn't about ego, whatever you think's happening between you and me. I want to talk."

"So fuckin' do it," I snarled, trying to keep my finger off the trigger. "No more violence. If one more bullet flies when it ain't meant to, I swear to Christ, I will kill you where you stand. Consequences be fucked."

"You want your woman and your son, and I named my price. Bring everything here in the next forty-eight hours, or there's nothing left to discuss."

Son? Fuck, my grip on the trigger weakened, temporarily taking my mind away from this psycho staring me in the face.

I had a son.

Four simple words that shocked me to hell and back, amping my consciousness to new heights when I got my shit straight, because now I had to live to meet my boy.

"We don't have that much, and I think you know it, asshole," I said. My eyes shifted to Skin.

"He's telling you the truth. I'm the club's Treasurer." Skinny boy stepped up, backing me up, neither of us knowing if we were digging ourselves deeper. "We might be worth three and a half or four with all our assets, but only half of that's liquid. It's taken all year to get back on our feet after our coffers ran dry."

I nodded. "We'll give you a million cash, and make payments, you piece of shit. You can come to Tennessee yourself to collect if you think there'll be any hangups."

The last part was a lie. I had no intention of letting this vampire drain the club dry and coming anywhere near my family ever again.

I'd find a way to kill him. If it didn't happen today, then several months down the line, when the fuckheads came for their money. If we had to part with a cool million to get him off our backs today, to let us all walk away alive, we'd deal.

Dom smiled, too dark and knowingly for anything good to happen next. "Ah, so you can just murder us later, right? I know how biker trash works, Dust. Your friends out west in the Grizzlies and the Devils up north have set too many traps, and I know you're working with them."

"I ain't Blackjack," I growled, secretly wishing I had some of the old man's magic right about now. The Grizzlies Prez made a fortune and kept his crew alive against the odds. "I'm a man of my word. You help us find some way where everybody walks away from here without more death or hurt, then we can do business."

Hurt like hell to say those words because I meant it. Fuck, I'd let them live to fight another day, if I just got Hannah and my son back in one piece.

Joker groaned behind me. Crawl leaning down with them now, applying extra pressure to the Veep's messed up leg.

"You're braver than I expected, but you're just as stupid," Dom said, yawning as he finally pushed away from my gun. "We have the upper hand. See that room back there?"

He laid his disgusting hand on my shoulder, squeezed it, and pointed. "That's where you'll find your wife. She's very sick. We delivered the kiddo just fine, but we don't have the fancy antibiotics and hygiene like you'll find in a hospital. Her baby seems healthy, for now. Whatever happens to him after today isn't our responsibility if we can't make a deal. That's on you, Mister Prez."

"Let. Them. Go." The words barely sounded human

when they left my mouth.

This time, I grabbed the motherfucker, shoving my nine against his ribcage, straight at his heart. Every one of his crew trained their guns on me.

Seriously contemplated pulling the trigger. I could kill him here, and give my boys a good fuckin' chance while they cut his crew to pieces, too busy filling me full of lead to fight back.

"We have the upper hand, Dust. Already told you. Don't be a fool," he said, digging his gun into my chest, too. "We gave our demands. You meet them, or everybody dies, including Hannah and the brat. We set the conditions. We set the timetable. We say fucking jump, and you do it. That's law when one group has more guns than the other. Remember: we're a multimillion dollar, international syndicate. You're a shit stain, drug dealing biker gang stuck in the hills. No fuckin' contest here."

For a second, I let my eyes wander, looking over the whole ugly scene. Joker continued bleeding on the ground, several brothers protecting him, aiming their guns at the mafia cocksuckers who had their arms trained on me.

Dom sneered in my face. Probably thinking he'd kicked me square in the balls.

That shit-eating smile on his lips didn't last long once I started laughing. He shoved his gun harder into my chest, his hand shaking slightly.

"What?! What's so damned funny?"

"You mafia assholes are all the same. Goddamned know-it-alls who never figure out they're in over their heads 'til the very end." I grabbed his gun, and pushed it off me. "You wanna fact check and tell me the lay of the land? Let's do it. You've got two fatal flaws in what you think you know, Dom."

His eyes were wide and rolling now, angrier than ever. He backed up, pointing his gun in my face. "Don't do anything stupid, redneck asshole. Are you high from that shit you push on the streets? Your little family won't make it out of here alive if you –"

"I don't deal junk. That was my old man, and he ain't been in charge for awhile now. That's mistake number one, and it proves you're pretty fuckin' out of touch," I said, walking forward, keeping the asshole on the move. He took a couple steps backward before he planted his heels in the pavement again, regaining his poise. "You talk a big game about your friends on the coasts and over in Europe. It's like you're clueless we've been making lots of new buddies, too."

"What? More biker trash out west?" He snorted, shaking his head. "You're really comparing the Grizzlies and the Prairie Devils, more worthless MCs, to a *world class* organization that's been doing business for the better part of a century? Listen to what you're saying, Dust. It's like you don't realize that even if your men get away untouched – and they won't – that they won't be putting their own lives and their families under the gun as soon as news crosses the ocean. There'll be a price on your heads so fucking high every bounty hunter on two continents will want to collect."

"Nah," I said. He stopped, and I put my hand on his

gun again, holding mine near his guts. "I'm talking about our friends further abroad. Trust me, the Irish and the Russians are *real* fuckin' happy with the money we're bringing in from the new gun routes going to the coasts. So happy, in fact, that they're not letting our little dustup spread to their home turf. Your Sicilian brothers overseas are smart. They cut a deal last week, told my friends they wouldn't interfere, whatever happens here. You're on your own, asshole."

Dom's face twisted angrily. Finally, my turn came to wear the ugly smirk, and I did proudly.

"Don't be mad, asshole. You've still got plenty of leverage. Just a lot less than you thought, considering you've been cut off at the balls by your own family."

"Fuck!" One of his men lowered his gun, off to the side, pacing in a panicked circle. "He isn't giving us the truth, is he, boss? Tell me he's lying through his fucking teeth!"

"It's true," Firefly said, standing up and moving over to the man. "I was there myself on the call when we heard your brothers give you up. Sure evens the odds. Our Prez is a genius."

"Shit...shit!" I saw another one of Dom's men turning pale out the corner of my eye. It was Will, the nasty looking fucker with the dark hair who'd put a bullet in Joker's calf. "Didn't know we were dealing with the Irish, or the Russians! Christ, I didn't sign up for this. I –"

"Shut the fuck up!" Dom spun, turning his gun away from me, aiming it at his own man. "It's a trick, you stupid, spineless cocksuckers. He'll say anything right now to stop us from marching back in there and feeding that fuckin' bitch scraps of her own dead kid. Fuck the negotiating, it's –"

Over? Yeah, it fucking is, I thought, finishing it in my head for him.

My gun went *off* before the asshole could say the final word. Not the nine in my dominant hand, but the old antique pistol I'd grabbed from my hip, hurling a fat ball of civil war era lead into the demon's spine.

Dom went down instantly, howling in pain. Several more guns barked, and I hit the pavement. Everybody fired at the bastard who'd tried to back up his soon-to-be dead *capo* boss.

The others took off, running as quick as their polished little feet would carry 'em. "Don't shoot! Don't shoot!" they screamed back at us, dropping their guns along the way, all but surrendering.

Sixty, Crawl, and Skin were on their bikes in ten seconds flat, revving them up, ready to give chase down the highway.

"No!" I screamed, putting my foot on the asshole's shattered back, making Dom squirm harder as he bled. "There's too many cops tooling around. They'll be all over the fuckin' place if we don't get out of here. We'll take the vans, too, if we can find their keys."

My boys gave me a sharp look. "You really want to let those cowards go, Prez?" Skin raised an eyebrow.

"No, no, he's right," Joker said weakly, struggling to pull himself up with the trunk of somebody's car. "Tried to talk to that owner before the asshole ambushed me. He looked pretty spooked, like the type who'll call 9-11, if he hasn't already. That shithead from their crew ambushed me, hiding behind his desk, but there's nobody watching him down."

Fuck. We had something else to worry about, and we had to move fast.

"You heard the Veep! Let's find the damned keys, get them out of that room, and haul some ass."

Nobody second guessed me. We burst into the room a moment later, and the rest was a blur.

I ran to the bed as soon as I saw her passed out, severing her handcuffs with one blow, pulling her up into my arms. Firefly walked out holding a bawling infant, the most beautiful fuckin' sound I ever heard in my life.

One second. That's all I gave myself to savor the moment, holding Hannah tight in my arms, thinking about how I'd finish the fuckface out front if his blood didn't run out first for keeping her in this dirty gown.

The boys were running in and out, finding the keys, loading up everything they could. Vans and bikes started out front, their engines rumbling together in a steady growl.

"Dusty?" she said, her eyes barely open, as if it took all her strength just to do that.

"Sleep, darlin'. We're bringing you home, and our kid, too. It's over, babe. It's all –"

We heard the sirens blaring in the distance about a second before Sixty came racing up and kicked open the door. "We need to go *now,* Prez! Hurry!"

Never ran so fast in my life. My heartbeat roared in my

ears, harder than any bastard slamming my head into the floor.

We were too fuckin' close to give up now.

I pulled Hannah into the back of the waiting van and held her tight. Firefly sat across from me, the baby carrier next to him, his big hands keeping it from moving too much while the vehicle jerked forward. We got about half a mile down the road before it rolled to a stop.

Then I saw the cherry lights blinking through the tinted windows, and I knew we were fucked.

A minute later there were voices outside. Men talking, cops shouting, probably negotiating our goddamned surrender.

Hannah was burning up in my arms. Still slipped my hand into her fingers, let them clench, and dipped my face to hers.

It wasn't a perfect kiss by any stretch. Her with a fever. Me and my boys about to be arrested for trashing several savage killers the law should've put away long ago.

Firefly's tense, frightened eyes were on me when I finally broke the kiss. Nothing like seeing a big, strong man who'd already been through hell several times crack to make you come undone.

"Prez, I can't go to jail for this shit. Cora, Lucy..." He drew a deep breath, the words he wouldn't say choking him.

"Forget it, brother," I said, grabbing his hand. "I'm stepping outside as soon as they give the word. Won't put up a fight. When they take me into custody, and start asking questions, it's on me. Everything."

His eyes flew open. Wide with disbelief, he looked at me while I turned my attention to my son, the fragile little infant I'd never get a chance to raise proper. He shifted in his blankets, somewhere between sleep and consciousness.

"Take care of my boy, whatever the fuck happens."

"Prez, he's my nephew. I'll back him up with my life, just like my Lucy."

"Yeah, fuck yeah," I said, giving his hand one more squeeze while I stood. "I know you will."

Every second ticked by, more precious than the last, because they were my last as a free man with my family and my brothers.

I kept counting in my head, expecting those doors to swing open any time, clearance for a dozen cops to pull me out and throw me on the ground with my hands behind my back.

Got to a hundred and twenty before I looked at Firefly. He was just as confused as me, whispering in the darkness while he stroked Hannah's brow. "What the fuck?"

The cops never waited this long if they suspected something was up. And with our biker convey roaring out on the road, in a town that just had a murderous rampage at the hospital, they had to by now.

What. The. Fuck?

I repeated it as soon as the van started moving. We were on the road again, heading down the highway.

For once, the prayers I hadn't even said were answered.

* * * *

We drove on through the night, only stopping for gas a couple times before we hit the Arkansas border, still a long ways to Tennessee. Didn't bother asking why we'd gotten away 'til we were filling up, roughly halfway home.

Found ourselves a hospital out in the sticks, where nobody would ask too many questions. Carried my girl in, told them to get on her, and waited with half the brothers in the lobby, holding my son for the very first time. The other boys helped Joker in, making sure he got patched up good and proper, faking a story about a hunting accident.

"Anybody gonna tell me why we ain't sitting in a cell right now?" I asked, trying my hand at giving the little man some formula.

"Bribes go a big way in the boonies," Skin said. "So does smooth talking truth."

"Truth?" My eyes narrowed, and I pulled the bottle from my son's mouth. "What'd you tell 'em?"

"That the bastards they were looking for fled on foot, up the road. Had them do a quick check on the Sicilian brotherhood. They'd never heard of our MC before, but there was plenty online about the mafia for anybody to see. Every Sheriff and his boys in these small towns wants their chance to play hero. I told him he'd find one dead bastard back in the parking lot and some property damage we'd be happy to pay for. Said we were no angels, and asked him if it really mattered who the fuck we were, long as we kicked a global crime syndicate outta their town."

I frowned. What he'd just done...crazy didn't begin to describe it. He'd effectively given them a full confession, something that would bite us big if the cops took the initiative to get the Feds involved.

"Wait. You're telling me they took the bait and agreed to keep their mouths shut, Skinny boy? How fuckin' lucky can we get?"

How much can we trust them to follow through? I thought, keeping it to myself.

He shook his head. "They didn't promise anything, Prez. But the older one, he said he'd seen a lot of shit before – used to be on the force in Baltimore. He'd heard about the big wolves running on his turf, seen plenty of evidence, and never caught any 'til now. Only took a few minutes for his men to head up the road and get the assholes who'd fled in custody. As for us, he didn't seem too interested, especially when I dropped fifteen-K for them to share."

"Christ, Skin. Bribery. You got any clue how damned –"

"Risky? You bet it was. And it saved your ass, Prez. Saved all of us."

How could I argue? We'd rolled the dice for the tenth time since we went off on this mission, and our winning streak held one more time.

"You know I wouldn't have gone this crazy if I thought there was another out. Didn't see any, especially with Joker bleeding in the backseat, next to that sick fuck still waiting for us outside. I wish there'd been another way, Prez. Really."

"Quit wishing. Come here, brother." I shuffled the baby over to one arm while I threw the other one around Skinny boy, hugging him tight.

We'd saved each other's asses plenty of times. This was one more, and I'd lost track of the tab a long time ago.

Skin pulled away, smiling, rifling a hand across the top of my kid's head. "Looks like he's gonna be strong, Prez. He's got your eyes." He paused, leaning in closer, lowering his voice. "What the fuck are we gonna do with mafia man, anyway? Wait 'til we're home to figure it out?"

I looked down at my son, who'd had his fill for dinner, sucking on the bottle just a little while ago. Hugging him tighter, he squirmed a little in my arms, slowly easing into a heavy sleep.

I'd get him checked up as soon as this place had an opening. He seemed healthy enough, at least. Thankfully, the jackals we'd downed hadn't done any lasting damage. But fuck, the scare they'd given everyone, plus the scars they'd left on my girl…

"Let me make sure my boy's ready for bed. Then we'll go out to the van, drive up the road, and finish this shit once and for all."

* * * *

Less than five minutes later, I rode with Skin while he drove the other van we'd commandeered, sitting in the passenger seat. We found ourselves a farm field about twelve miles up the road – abandoned, judging by the overgrown road leading up to the broken buildings.

"Stay put. Watch my son," I said, handing the sleeping baby off to Skin. Firefly took my spot in the passenger seat a second later, ready to play big uncle, pulling double duty so my kid would never be leaving our sight again.

I motioned for them to drive down the road. Not too far, but enough so there was no chance of my son hearing any screams.

Not like there was a lot of risk out here. We had wide open spaces, plus the walls of these vans were pretty thick. It wasn't a battle anymore, with Dom chained up like a dog in the back, awaiting his fate. Sixty and Crawl stood next to the van, near the back. They swung the doors wide open as soon as I nodded.

"No more. Please." Asshole raised his hand, still conscious and strong enough to protect his eyes from the flashlight I shined in his face, stepping inside.

He looked white and clammy. He'd lost a lot of blood. His legs didn't seem to work quite right from the nerve damage my shot did.

"It's not too fucking late," he said, speaking with a jagged rasp. "Don't be an idiot, Dust. We can forget all about the debt, the blood that's been shed, the stupid goddamned girl. I'll give you anything you want. There's almost eleven million in the bank and plenty more offshore. Easy to grab out of my Virgin Islands accounts. It's all yours, if you'll just let me go. Your club, your family…you could all be rich. Very, very comfortable."

I looked at him for a long, hard second. Never seriously considered the offer before I stomped his hand, pressing down with my boot, splintering several fingers.

"How many times did Hannah beg?" I growled, increasing my weight while I crouched down on my knees, switchblade in hand. "You think money even fuckin' matters at this point?"

Behind me, the boys gently laid down the tools I needed to give this prick a one way ticket to the next world. Dom stared at me in the darkness, his eyes wide and watery.

No surprise. The biggest, most merciless bastards always became dickless cowards in the end.

"It's never too late to negotiate, Dust. Come on!" He blinked slowly, licking his cracked, dry lips. "We've both been in this world for a long time. I made you name your price when I had the edge. It's yours now. Please, just tell me, how much to make this right?"

I brought out my pipe, gave it a light, and pulled it to my lips. Pushed smoke into his evil face 'til he coughed, while I reached for the pliers tucked behind me.

"Let's get one thing straight, motherfucker," I snarled, moving my foot on his hand 'til he groaned. "Soon as my bullet hit your back, you were done asking questions, or making demands. That's my job. I'm only gonna ask you about my girl begging one more time before I rip out your tongue – *how many times?*"

I needed to know how much he'd made her suffer. Had a damned good idea the answer was too much. And I'd make him pay for all of it, one meticulous, cruel inch of flesh at a time.

"Dozens, okay! Maybe hundreds. Honest. Now, can we make a fucking deal?"

I smiled grimly in the dark. This was gonna be good because he still had hope.

Half the demons we'd killed before went out defiant. They knew they were done, and they died like men. Went down snarling, fighting, spitting in our faces to the very end.

The rest whined like bitches, having their sick egos smashed before their bodies were bent and dead.

I thought about my son sleeping with my brothers, about a mile down the road. My woman, too, back at the hospital, slowly working herself up from hell with all the medicine they'd pumped in her system. They'd noticed the kid, the bruises all over her, the obvious signs that she'd just popped out a baby. We'd be paying plenty to shut the doctors up once we were done.

Primal anticipation churned in my blood, but it felt different than it always did before.

Sure, I wanted to kill this fuck. Make him suffer for everything he'd done, but I also wanted to wrap it up because it'd become a damned chore.

The last thing keeping me from my love, my family, was the pathetic, whimpering mess at my feet.

Fuck, this asshole would be crying for his mama before the night was through if I left his tongue intact, guaranteed.

I tilted the heavy pliers in my hand with a heavy sigh, turning my head behind me. "Give me some privacy, brothers. Start the bonfire for this asshole's bones where nobody going down the road can see."

Smiling, Sixty and Crawl nodded, then slammed the door shut.

I held the freak down who'd nearly ripped it all away

from me, shoving the steel pliers past his filthy teeth, grabbing his tongue.

No sense in mentioning what came next. A southern man doesn't torture and tell, even when it involves the most deserving sonsofbitches in the entire universe.

Dom suffered mightily with just the pliers and my raw knuckles. By the time I brought out my switchblade, the battery with the wires, and the acid shit they poured down factory farm drains to dissolve animal fat, the asshole was crying, screaming, blubbering one thing he couldn't pronounce with his fucked up mouth.

Mama.

* * * *

Hours later, after we burned Dom's body and scattered the ashes to the Arkansas winds, we were back at the hospital. I'd cleaned up at a quick pit stop on the way, and now I sat next to my woman, holding her hand, our son cradled in my other arm.

Outside, the first rays of dawn blinked through the cold, grey horizon. I was nodding off in the dead silence, next to Firefly, when her fingers stirred on mine.

"Dusty?"

"I'm here, darlin'. So's the kid." I picked her hand up in mine, brought it to my lips, and savored her skin. She already felt cooler, healthier than she had a few hours ago.

"I'm sorry I took off. I never should've ran. I was scared, terrified of hurting anyone. You, Huck, the baby I found out was growing inside me. I –"

"Forget it, sis," Firefly said next to me. "You need rest right now. We've got nothing to discuss."

"He's right," I said, laying my lips on her fingers again. "Past is the past, babe. Dom and his boys are gone. Ain't never gonna bother you again, and neither will anything else. Your job's getting well for me so we can go home. You rest, and we'll talk about the things that matter when you're good and ready, like naming our boy."

She smiled. It was one of those slow burning lip curls that would've caused any man's heart to do a dive, seeing it on his woman's face. Especially when the waterworks came a second later.

I brushed away the hot tears rolling down her cheeks with my fingertips. She'd cried enough for ten lives, dammit.

"Hank," she said softly. "That's what I want to call him."

"Hank," I repeated, rolling it over in my mind. "Hank Daniel Grayson's got a nice ring to it."

No lie. It was a good name, a strong name, and it lined up with a couple of my favorite country singers, too.

"Shit, darlin', it's supposed to be tougher than this. Now, what're we gonna knock around when you're well enough to have lunch?"

She laughed softly. Must've taken all her strength because one quiet minute later, I felt her slipping away again, back into the peaceful, happy place she went to for healing.

When I turned around, Firefly had a smile on his face, staring off into the distance. "What's the word, brother?"

"Good old Uncle Hank kept everything afloat when Ma ran

outta money. Huge honor if you're giving your boy his name."

"Didn't know him," I said, laying a hand on his shoulder. "But if he had anything to do with you and Hannah growing into the people I love and trust, I'm sold. We're brothers by blood. Not just patch anymore."

"Prez, a week ago, I still wanted to punch your fuckin' eyes out for dragging my sis deeper into this life. Just want to say, I was a damned a fool. She belongs in this club. Same way she oughta be with you, Cap'n."

I gave his shoulder one more firm squeeze before I brought both my big arms back around the baby, snoozing softly on my lap. Little Hank was part of this family, too.

I had a chance to give him the good, without the bad.

I'd shelter this boy from the violence, the evil, all the dirty shit that stained a man's soul. I'd watch him grow up with Lucy, Bingo, and Joker's Alex. All the brothers, their kids, their friends, and all the new women and babies to come for the boys who hadn't settled down yet.

Yeah, this boy in my arms was one tiny, beautiful blank slate who'd walk away from this life with nothing but the very best written all over him. Right now, all he had scrawled on him was love.

* * * *

Two Months Later

Winter loosened her grip. Bones and bruises healed. Dom's ashes blew to the seven winds, meaning nobody ever had to think about his evil ass again.

We were a family. Finally.

Nothing made me happier than coming home to that woman and my son, helping her along as much as I could 'til she healed up all the way.

Always heard babies were a lot of work, and the people who told me weren't lying. Still didn't feel like much after what we'd gone through to get here, changing dirty diapers and rocking him to sleep, holding my boy on the sofa with my woman curled up next to me.

Heaven? Fuck yeah, I'd arrived.

Only thing missing was a proper entrance. I set everything up in secret, rounding up Ma, the boys, and their old ladies.

It was just a couple weeks after we'd finished cleaning Hannah's massive house, and passed it over to the new buyers at closing. She'd let the mansion go to liquidate her debts and restart her career. She'd made off with plenty, and we'd be comfortable as hell once we found something nicer, without the stress.

For now, she didn't mind my place. It was familiar, easy to manage, somewhere she could focus on what really mattered, and who the hell was I to argue?

When I came in that day, winding down the icy streets through town, straight from finishing business at the clubhouse, she wasn't expecting a thing.

"Oh, great timing. I was just about to leave to get Hank from your Ma." She gave me that sass, perfectly timed to showing off the curve of her ass that made me want to forget everything, push her against the counter, and take her then and there.

"Forget it, darlin'. He's spending all night with grandma." I stared at her, propping myself up with one arm, leaning on the wall.

She froze. Turned her little eyes my way, the laughter all gone, studying my pose. Couldn't figure out why I sounded so damned serious, when I looked so casual.

"What's going on? We're not on lockdown, are we?"

I shook my head, hiding the smile trying to infiltrate my lips. "Go upstairs and change into your best that'll still let you on my bike. Meet me outside."

Didn't say another word. I left her standing there while I went outside and had a quick puff off my pipe.

This is it, boy. Biggest fuckin' day of your life, if tying the knot the first time and seeing your kid wasn't enough. You ready?

Hadn't heard that voice in my head for months. Early's ghost deserted me ever since I used the last few months' blood and tears to smooth things over.

I saw him coldly in the corner of my eye, looking as somber as the day he died in that wreck, propped up in his coffin, the hard demon edges he'd lived by subdued for once in his life. My old man looked on sadly, like he couldn't believe I'd done what he couldn't, and now I stood to reap the rewards forever.

"Ready? I've been waiting my whole life. Went through hell to have it, and I'll work like hell to keep it." I stubbed my pipe out and tucked it into my pocket, half a second before I heard the garage door opening behind me.

"Who were you talking to?" She stood at the edge of the

driveway, several feet from my bike, looking good enough to devour with her high brown boots, short black skirt, and purple top clinging to every raw inch I wanted to claim again. Preferably over and over.

"Nobody who matters, darlin'. You ready?" I reached for the spare helmet on my bike and pushed it toward her.

"I guess. Still can't say I'm a fan of the mystery going on here," she said, eyes narrowed playfully. She took the helmet from my hands, strapping it onto her head.

"It'll be worth it, babe. Trust me. There's a lot of shit I didn't do right when I should have. Today, I'm fixing it."

"Dusty…" She laid a hand on my back when we were both seated, my key in the ignition. "You don't need to impress me anymore. It's not like I'll ever forget you saved my life several times over."

She leaned in, pressing her lips to my neck. I didn't say anything, just revved my engine and slowly took us down the driveway.

Pretty fuckin' cute, really. She thought I was about to make her heart throb for the millionth time because I had some crazy obligation.

Bullshit. Love ain't work, and it ain't never a chore.

When we got to the clubhouse, she'd see how wrong she was. She'd see the only thing I ever wanted was to light up her face like the moon 'til she begged me to stop.

Sure, I'd saved her life, and put my own ass on the line to do it. Wouldn't stop 'til I went into my grave either, if any wolves were ever dumb enough to come sniffing around her ever again.

Salvation went both ways.

I saved her from psychos with knives and bullets. She saved me from myself. Put my life on the straight and narrow I'd sought for forty years without realizing it 'til I woke up to a woman I wanted in my bed, and a son carrying our blood.

Loving Hannah wasn't a chore, dammit. And if she thought it might be, I'd send those nasty thoughts spinning from her head so fast they went all the way to Jupiter.

Took every muscle I had not to start grinning like a fool when we were halfway to the clubhouse.

My poor, precious, clueless wife didn't have a hint what was about to hit her. If there was one thing I appreciated after surviving several ambushes, it was surprises that put a smile on people's faces.

* * * *

I parked the bike and put my hand on her back, guiding her round the side of the clubhouse, toward the back patio. Used my own money the last few weeks to have it fixed up, real nice and special for this occasion.

"Why's it so quiet here?" she whispered, flashing a cautious look over her shoulder.

"Darlin', you keep on walking. No questions."

"No? Not even if I'm going to guess I'm walking into some kind of surprise party? I know you do these kinda hijinks in the spring. Huck told me."

"Keep. Walking," I growled, shaking my head, prodding her forward a little more firmly with my hand.

She had the *party* right, at least.

"Give it a push," I said, putting my hand over hers when we got to the latch over the new gate. It towered over us, giving the club the privacy we'd always wanted, thick reinforced wooden doors attached to a ring of brick that'd stop anyone from coming in who wasn't supposed to.

Music started blasting the second the gate creaked open. My boys were all standing, and they came to attention the second we walked in, standing by the makeshift altar.

A neat row of fold out chairs formed an aisle. Cora, Meg, Summer, and Ma all smiled in unison, holding a whole new generation of kids born under our patch in their arms.

"Jesus." Hannah's knees locked up as soon as we stepped through, taking in the scene.

Bingo sat up next to us, and brushed her legs, happily wagging his tail. I reached down and stroked the big wolfhound's head, sharing a look even a dog could understand.

"What'd I tell you, darlin'?" I whispered in her ear. "Just keep walking. We ain't home yet."

Only had about fifteen steps to go to get to the altar. By then, she was turning red, hot tears raining down her cheeks when she realized the meanest version of *Here Comes the Bride* anybody ever heard was tearing out those speakers.

"But…we're already married!" she sputtered. Standing across from her, I grabbed both her hands in mine. She looked at the ring on her finger in confusion.

"It's called renewing vows, darlin'. Also gives me a chance to do things right, the way they should've gone down the first time, and have ourselves the reception we missed."

I let her cry it out, squeezing her sweet fingers in mine, while the music faded behind us. Preacher man stepped up to the podium, looking a lot neater than he had that first night I brought her in to make it all official.

Little Hank cried out in the chairs. His grandma hugged him tight, happier than I ever saw her.

We weren't the only ones up here with plenty reason to smile. Lord willing, I'd give my Ma a few more grins before the evening was through.

"Let's go," I told preacher man. "I've got my part ready."

"Friends, family, and brothers of the Deadly Pistols MC. Today we stand here to honor a husband and wife who hold the meaning of sacrifice heavy on their hearts..."

His spiel went on for a couple minutes. I let his flowery speech wash over me, too busy staring my woman in the face to care about poetry.

Hannah cried softly the whole way through. I held her hand, watching each tear roll down her cheeks, sweeping up my free hand each time to catch them, kiss them away.

Today, I did tender. Tonight, I'd do rough.

I did anything and everything that'd set her heart on fire, and I let the whole damned world know who did the kindling.

"...and if I may, I'd like to invite each person to say a few words. Dust, you have something you'd like to read?" Preacher man looked at me, genuine respect glowing in his eyes.

"It's all up here," I said, tapping my temple with two fingers. "Been memorizing this all week, so here goes…"

Hannah's fingers tightened on mine. Thought she'd rip my hand off before I finished, so overwhelmed with emotion. Off to the sides, all my brothers were smiling, elbowing each other like they couldn't believe I was pulling out my heart, showing it to everyone.

Wasn't doing this for them, much as I respected their shit-eating grins.

The only one who counted was looking back at me, waiting, and I wasn't holding her up any longer.

"Darlin', you're standing there, beautiful as the day we met, wearing my ring and my ink. Helluva lot happened these past few months. I gave you a second chance at life. You gave me a son. Love that boy with all my heart." I paused, watching Ma tear up out the corner of my eye, hugging Hank closer to her chest. "It's hard to offer much after we've given each other the moon, so I'm gonna make a pledge. Hannah, I'm not done yet. I'm gonna keep it coming. Gonna keep that smile on your face 'til we're both so old we barely remember what smiling's all about. Gonna keep you in my bed, on my bike, and in my heart. Gonna pull you close, hold you every night, just like I'm about to do now, and wash every tear off your cheek 'til there's nothing but room for that beautiful fuckin' smile."

I stepped up, bringing her into my arms, tugging her hand close to my heart while I put my lips against her cheeks, and then on her mouth. Pure, hot emotion flooded my tongue. Awesome and irresistible.

When I broke the kiss, had to hold on tighter because her knees were shaking. Behind us, a couple of the old ladies sniffled, either remembering their own weddings, or wondering when their boys would do something similar for them.

"I ain't much for speeches," I said, staring deep into her ocean blue eyes. "So I'm gonna keep it brief, with just one more thing everybody standing here with us oughta hear. I love you, darlin'. Simple as that sounds, it ain't even close. It's the biggest, most bewildering, goddamned beautiful statement I've ever made. And I'll keep making it 'til the end of my days. Love you, baby girl, and you'll remember how much every time I move mountains to taste your lips. I've done it before, and I'll do it again. Every day I need to just so you remember – you're *mine*."

I wasn't looking for a standing ovation. Got one anyway, a chorus of thundering claps and wild whoops ringing out around us while we locked lips.

Fuck, she tasted sweeter than before. Sweeter than ever.

I'd told preacher man several days ago not to put her on the spot. She wouldn't be saying much after the L-bomb I dropped on her heart, and I didn't want her to be embarrassed.

Still, the formal bastard prodded her. He laid his hands gently on our shoulders, easing our mouths away from each other, gently whispering in her ear.

"Hannah, if there's anything you'd like to say…"

XV: Live Free (Hannah)

No words.

I'd always been good with them, but now I was at a total loss. What can a woman possibly say to a man who'd delivered the heavens, the moon, and the stars in a neat little box?

My knees still hurt a little after the pregnancy and the rough treatment by Dom. I secretly hoped he was watching from hell. Looked up, saw us, and *raged* because we were alive, in love, and happy.

"Darlin'." Dusty clenched my hand, stroking my fingers with his thick fingertips. "If it's too much, you don't have to say —"

"I've got it," I said, standing up straighter in his arms, turning my head. I looked out over all our friends and family, men and women who'd made this crazy thing possible. "This is a huge surprise to me, and I'd like to take a second to thank everybody for coming."

Near the wall, Bingo let out a single yip, and everybody laughed. Smiling, I was thankful for the interruption, because it gave me just enough time to know exactly what to say. I had the man holding me to thank for it, and also the evil asshole he'd snuffed out forever.

"A minute ago, Dusty stood here talking a lot about love. I want to talk about another word that's close, and just as important." Everybody leaned in, listening intently in the fat pause while I sucked in a breath, precious air I needed to keep it together without breaking down again. "*Live.* That's what I willed myself to do when things were at their darkest, when I never thought I'd stand here with you, in my husband's arms, knowing I have a second chance to do better by myself, by him, and by our family. Live free – that's what I'm going to do, and I'll never take it for granted again."

I reached up, laying my palm flat against his rough cheek. His forehead touched mine when he leaned in, inhaling me while I breathed him. Divine, dangerous, and masculine as a pagan god.

"Dusty...you're the reason I get to go on living. If I couldn't live, then I couldn't love. I do, with every single shred of my heart. There's no way to say thanks in just a few words. No way to repay you except with all the kisses, laughs, and smiles I know are going to coming, year after year. Once, I thought I had it all, chasing money and running from my past. You showed me there was more, baby...so much more. If I ever waver, if I forget and make new mistakes, they'll be brief. I know it, because you taught me what it means to live and love. I've never been prouder to be your wife – the best thing I'll ever be as long as I'm alive. I love you, Daniel."

His name was barely off my lips before he pulled me in, smiling and eager, smothering me in another kiss. Naturally, it caused my entire body to smolder.

Applause exploded around us. Everybody cheered, if they weren't too busy wiping their tears, and preacher man said a few more words to finish the ceremony.

Neither of us heard them, though, because we were completely lost in our love.

* * * *

I remembered how fast Huck and Cora's wedding reception blurred by, the first night Dust gave me his kiss, and turned me into a total addict.

Now, I wondered where the time went by with my own. We sat at the biggest picnic table I'd ever seen, huge enough to seat everybody with plenty of room to spare, feasting on pulled pork with spicy barbecue, beer, fried okra, mashed potatoes thick as sin, and a dozen other rich sides I barely had room to sample.

Everyone came by to wish us well throughout the evening.

Skin and Meg. Firefly and Cora. Joker and Summer.

Lion, Tinman, Crawl, Sixty. Prospects whose names I'd only started learning. Dancers from the Ruby Heel, several looking like they couldn't wait to give the single guys some late night entertainment, after the families left the party to its dying embers.

Laynie came last, bobbing a very sleepy little boy in her arms. "I should really head out when you guys do. He's had his fill of excitement for one night."

"If he's tuckered out, he won't fuss later," Dusty said, laying his hand on my thigh, underneath the table. "You've got the easy job, Ma."

"And the best! Because now I get to be a grandma with a family who's finally had a proper wedding." She grinned, her old cheeks wrinkling when she looked down at us, real deep pride lighting up her grey eyes. "Oh, except for the dress. Next time you renew those vows, you let her wear it, boy."

"Well, if I'd had a little notice…" I elbowed Dusty gently, breaking into a smile. "Next time, I'll be honored, Laynie. I promise."

"She's got the ring, and it's staying right where it belongs," Dust said, his fingers digging into my skin deliciously, under the table. "Save the dress, Ma. Sooner or later, you're gonna have a granddaughter joining Hank. She'll need it someday for walking down the aisle."

Laynie laughed, and then narrowed her eyes, looking right at me. "Watch out for him, honey. He's on fire today."

"Lucky man. That's just the way I love it." I looked at my husband, feeding the lust boiling in his eyes with a quick, subtle flick of my tongue across my bottom lip.

His hand moved higher up my thigh, under my skirt, closer to the sopping wet mess in the middle. "Get the kid home and rest up, Ma. We're out soon. I think we've had our fill, as nice as this has all been."

She didn't need another nudge. Smiling, she stepped away, heading toward the front of the clubhouse. We lasted about another minute, sharing several quick bites off a decadent chocolate cake Cora made, and then we stood. Everybody waved as they saw us off.

It was still too crisp for a long ride into the mountains on his Harley, so we took the truck, strategically parked by a prospect, waiting for us.

"How long does it take to get down there?" I asked, knowing full well he had a little spot in mind, deep in the Smokies, a comfortable distance from the tourist thrills in Gatlinburg for the honeymoon we were due.

"'Bout an hour, maybe a little more going down these curvy mountain roads in the dark." Dusty's cool grey eyes were fixed on me, sending lightning up my legs. He leaned in, pushing hot breath in my ear. "Let's see if we can make it before I have to pull over, throw the seat down, and fuck you on the side of the road."

* * * *

We got about halfway to the cabin before his hand before his hand wouldn't be kept off my panties, and I lost my will to fight it.

Thankfully, this section of the mountains had all sorts of little paths leading into the forests. We took the first gravel road we found in his headlights, rumbling into the dense, dark growth about a quarter of a mile before he parked, and killed the engine. Huge piles of leaves swirled around us, the trees above just beginning to bud as winter relented.

Dusty looked at me while I folded my arms, searching for warmth.

"Forget the heat, darlin'. We'll make our own," he promised, shoving my panties aside with a single flick.

He kissed me while his stiff fingers pushed into me. I moaned against his tongue, giving him mine, opening my lips for the conquest I'd always welcome, my legs instinctively parting for his hand.

Fuck, he felt *good*.

He brushed my clit with his thumb, taking me to that *please, for the love of God, fuck me now* stage before drawing his fingers back. They grabbed my panties in the middle, jerked them down, and rolled them off my legs while I shuffled out of my boots.

Dusty reached underneath his seat with his free hand. His seat collapsed, making space for me to climb over him, and find my way onto his lap.

"Get on this dick, darlin'. *Now*." Thunder filled his throat, running into my skin when he pulled me onto his lap, pressing his stubble into my neck. "I've been waiting all evening, and I ain't wasting another second."

"Oh? Is that an order?" I asked, running my hands along his leather clad shoulders, grinding into the bulge in his jeans. I loved the smooth, rough contrast his clothes made with his stubble on my bare skin.

"Like you gotta ask. Fuck, darlin', I haven't had enough of you since I brought you back. Waiting for you to heal up wasn't easy." He lifted my skirt, holding it up, allowing him to see the PROPERTY OF DUST ink I had tattooed high on my lower belly a couple weeks ago. "Goddamn, I love seeing my name on you, babe. Never gonna get tired of it.

Never gonna stop missing it when you ain't naked in my bed, about to ride this dick for all we're worth. *Never,* Hannah, you understand me?"

Tell me about it. No sex for several weeks was the worst part about having a baby, and being tortured by those assholes.

Dusty pushed his fingers into my hair, forming a fist, moving my face until it was just where he wanted. Our eyes locked, frantic as jagged breath filled our lungs, the violent want beating in our veins.

"I missed you, too," I whispered, muscles turning taut when he pulled my nipple. "Jesus, I missed you so bad."

His free hand went down between us. I heard his belt buckle coming apart, and soon his cock was out, its angry tip rolling against my wet pussy.

"Nothin' like our honeymoon, making up for lost time. No more games, darlin'. I need to be in you, and if you think I'm gonna wait for sweet talk…" Laying his hand on my ass, he pushed me down, engulfing his length in one sweet, raging movement. "Think again."

"Dusty…"

I murmured his name while we started to fuck, the only thing I could on our second wedding night. Alive, in love, and lucky to enjoy it.

He filled me. So deep, so hot, so fucking good.

Outside, the early springtime mist coalesced around our truck. The Smokies offered us their majesty while we gave into our primal urges, nothing but our hearts and breath beating in our ears. The air was plenty cool, but we started to sweat within a minute, moving against each other faster, harder, needier.

"So fuckin' tight," he rumbled, quickening his thrusts. "Even after Hank. This pussy's getting another kid sooner than you think, darlin'. Count on it."

Holy shit. If there was any set of words priming me to come on command, he'd found them.

The craziest things sounded sane, sounded *hot,* whenever they left his lips. Our bodies thrashed and mingled at a base chemical level, and I'd come for this beautiful bastard whenever he asked.

Harder, he thrust into me, another sharp groan catching in his throat. Hearing his pleasure pushed me over. I clenched my teeth, riding him like mad, letting raw passion carry me up and down his magnificent cock.

A harsh moan slipped out my lips, telling us both what was imminent. His hand jerked my hair tighter, bringing my face to his. Dusty's mouth buried me in another kiss, his tongue probing deep, like he wanted to own the pleasure ripping through my body.

"Come already, Hannah. Come like every sweet inch of you is begging to." He growled the words into my ear, then sank his teeth into my neck, doubling his speed, pistoning into me.

No contest. No delay.

I came.

Boring down on his cock, clenching him tight, I held on and screamed. My pleasure cry pierced the dense, dark Tennessee night while climax owned me. His relentless cock fucked me straight through it.

I had about thirty seconds to catch my breath before he grabbed me with both hands, shifted my body under him, and kicked down his pants. He drove into me, pushing my legs apart with his hips, grinding his pubic bone hard against my clit. That little patch of hair above his cock burned like sweet sandpaper, forcing another moan from my lips.

"Please, Dusty," I whimpered. "Please come. Fill me. I need to feel you –"

Growling, he pushed a calloused hand across my mouth, a new arrogant quirk in his lips. "You know who gives the orders, darlin'. That game we started months ago at Firefly's wedding, trying to see who had better control?"

He thrust into me harder, making me squirm, my legs twitching against his with wild, wanton need.

"Never ended," he said, a wicked smile spreading his lips. "You're a wild one, Hannah. I'm one lucky sonofabitch. Get to spend the rest of my life taming every inch of you, making you come every which way I want, never giving you that seed you crave 'til you fuck it outta me."

Evil, beautiful bastard. I loved the challenge.

Secretly, we both did.

I pushed my face into his palm, probing his skin. My teeth dug into his hand. A love bite, perfectly timed to my hips rising to meet his. Faster, harder, ready to blow through another mind bending orgasm if it caused him to let go.

This wasn't human fucking anymore, not lovers on a misty, still southern night.

We were *animals*. We mated like possessed fiends, frolicking a little closer to delicious exhaustion every second.

His hand went up my shirt, shoved aside my loosened bra, and pinched my nipple. His fingers rolled it hard – just as hard as his next few thrusts, which shook the entire truck.

I thought he'd fuck me until the wheels came off when I couldn't hold back. My head tipped back into the leather seat, and I started screaming again, loving the rough tug of my hair his fist delivered.

This time, I wasn't alone. "You're a damned wildcat tonight. All right, beautiful. Here it fuckin' comes!"

My pussy seized, clenched, and sent its convulsions into every other muscle all over again when his cock swelled deep inside me.

Growling, bucking, sweating, cursing, we came together. His seed pumped hot, echoing the storm in our blood, our breath, our very souls. Dusty filled me with the same rough vigor as he'd injected his essence into my life.

Live.

Love.

Conquer.

Those stark words echoed in my head again and again, never fading until the bliss wracking my whole body began to wane. Dusty's fist in my hair became tender fingers again, stroking it, showering me in slower, sensual kisses as we came back to earth.

"Love you, darlin'. Love you so damned much," he spoke slowly, saying the words in between catching his breath.

"I love you, Dusty. Love you like nothing else. You and our kids are my everything."

"Kids?" He pushed his forehead to mine, quirking an eyebrow. "So, you're on board with six now like we talked about, right?"

He knew I'd only agreed to three, maybe four babies, tops. Laughing, I punched his arm, settling into his huge embrace.

He hadn't even pulled out of me yet. If anything, it felt like he was getting hard again. He'd probably demand a second round before we hit the road.

It might be early morning by the time we got into cabin, but so what?

This was our night. Our marriage. Our love, bigger and bolder than the infinite soft darkness all around us, and thicker than the mountain forest.

As long as I had eyes to see, lips to kiss, and ears to hear his wicked words, I'd never stop loving this man. Never stop loving it when he whispered in my ear, and said the word *mine*.

And maybe this week, just this once, I'd admit he had a little more control over this sexy business than me. A woman had to fluff her husband's ego sometimes, after all.

After everything he'd done for me, and everything still ahead, my outlaw man deserved it.

Thanks!

Want more Nicole Snow? Sign up for my newsletter to hear about new releases, subscriber only goodies, and other fun stuff!

JOIN THE NICOLE SNOW NEWSLETTER! - http://eepurl.com/HwFW1

Thank you so much for buying this book. I hope my romances will brighten your mornings and darken your evenings with total pleasure. Sensuality makes everything more vivid, doesn't it?

If you liked this book, please consider leaving a review and checking out my other erotic romance tales.

Got a comment on my work? Email me at nicolesnowerotica@gmail.com. I love hearing from my fans!

Kisses,
Nicole Snow

More Intense Romance by Nicole Snow

FIGHT FOR HER HEART

BIG BAD DARE: TATTOOS AND SUBMISSION

MERCILESS LOVE: A DARK ROMANCE

LOVE SCARS: BAD BOY'S BRIDE

RECKLESSLY HIS: A BAD BOY MAFIA ROMANCE

STEPBROTHER CHARMING: A BILLIONAIRE BAD BOY ROMANCE

STEPBROTHER UNSEALED: A BAD BOY MILITARY ROMANCE

Outlaw Love/Prairie Devils MC Books

OUTLAW KIND OF LOVE

NOMAD KIND OF LOVE

SAVAGE KIND OF LOVE

WICKED KIND OF LOVE

BITTER KIND OF LOVE

Grizzlies MC Books

OUTLAW'S KISS

OUTLAW'S OBSESSION

OUTLAW'S BRIDE

OUTLAW'S VOW

Deadly Pistols MC Books

NEVER LOVE AN OUTLAW

NEVER KISS AN OUTLAW

NEVER HAVE AN OUTLAW'S BABY

NEVER WED AN OUTLAW

SEXY SAMPLES:
OUTLAW'S KISS

I: Cursed Bones (Missy)

"It won't be long now," the nurse said, checking dad's IV bag. "Breathing getting shallower…pulse is slowing…don't worry, girls. He won't feel a thing. That's what the morphine's for."

I had to squeeze his hand to make sure he wasn't dead yet. Jesus, he was so cold. I swore there was a ten degree difference between dad's fingers in one hand, and my little sister's in the other. I blinked back tears, trying to be brave for Jackie, who watched helplessly, trembling and shaking at my side.

We'd already said our goodbyes. We'd been doing that for the last hour, right before he slipped into unconsciousness for what I guessed was the last time.

I turned to my sister. "It'll be okay. He's going to a better place. No more suffering. The cancer, all the pain…it dies with him. Dad's finally getting better."

"Missy…" Jackie squeaked, ripping her hand away from me and covering her face.

The nurse gave me a sympathetic look. It took so much effort to push down the lump in my throat without cracking up. I choked on my grief, holding it in, cold and sharp as death looming large.

I threw an arm around my sister, pulling her close. Lying like this was a bitch.

I wasn't really sure what I believed anymore, but I had to say something. Jackie was the one who needed all my support now. Dad's long, painful dying days were about to be over.

Not that it made anything easy. But I was grown up, and I could handle it. Losing him at twenty-one was hard, but if I was fourteen, like the small trembling girl next to me?

"Melissa." Thin, weak fingers tightened on my wrist with surprising strength.

I jumped, drawing my arm off Jackie, looking at the sick man in the bed. His eyes were wide open and his lips were moving. The sickly sheen on his forehead glowed, one last light before it burned out forever.

"Daddy? What is it?" I leaned in close, wondering if I'd imagined him saying my name.

"Forgive me," he hissed. "I…I fucked up bad. But I did it for a good reason. I just wish I could've done it different, baby…"

His eyelids fluttered. I squeezed his fingers as tight as I could, moving closer to his gray lips. What the hell was he saying? Was this about Mom again?

She'd been gone for ten years in a car accident, waiting for him on the other side. "Daddy? Hey!"

I grabbed his bony shoulder and gently shook him. He was still there, fighting the black wave pulling him lower, insistent and overpowering.

"It's the only way…I couldn't do it with hard work.

Honest work. That never paid shit." He blinked, running his tongue over his lips. "Just look in the basement, baby. There's a palate…roofing tiles. Everything I ever wanted to leave my girls is there. It was worth it…I promised her I'd do anything for you and Jackie…and I did. I did it, Carol. Our girls are set. I'm ready to burn if I need to…"

Hearing him say mom's name, and then talk about burning? I blinked back tears and shook my head.

What the hell was this? Some kinda death fever making him talk nonsense?

Dad started to slump into the mattress, a harsh rattle in his throat, the tiny splash of color left in his face becoming pale ash. I backed away as the machines howled. The nurse looked at me and nodded. She rushed to his free side, intently watching his heartbeat jerk on the monitor.

The machine released an earsplitting wail as the line went flat.

Jackie completely lost it. I grabbed her tight, holding onto her, turning away until the mechanical screaming stopped. I wanted to cover my ears, but I wanted hers closed more.

I held my little sister and rocked her to my chest. We didn't move until the nurse finally touched my shoulder, nudging us into the waiting room outside.

We sat and waited for all the official business of death to finish up. My brain couldn't stop going back to his last words, the best distraction I had to keep my sanity.

What was he talking about? His last words sounded so strange, so sure. So repentant, and that truly frightened me.

I didn't dare get my hopes up, as much as I wanted to believe we wouldn't lose everything and end up living in the car next week. The medical bills snatched up the last few pennies left over from his pension and disability – the same fate waiting for our house as soon as his funeral was done.

Delirious, I thought. *His dying wish was for us, hoping and praying we'd be okay. He went out selflessly, just like a good father should.*

That was it. Had to be.

He was dying, after all...pumped full of drugs, driven crazy in his last moments. But I couldn't let go of what he said about the basement.

We'd have to scour the house anyway before the state kicked us out. If there was anything more to his words besides crazy talk, we'd find out soon enough, right?

I looked at Jackie, biting my lip. I tried not to hope off a dead man's words. But damn it, I did.

If he'd tucked away some spare cash or some silver to pawn, I wouldn't turn it down. Anything would help us live another day without facing the gaping void left by his brutal end.

My sister was tipped back in her chair, one tissue pressed tight to her eyes. I reached for her hand and squeezed, careful not to set her off all over again.

"We're going to figure this out," I promised. "Don't worry about anything except mourning him, Jackie. You're not going anywhere. I'm going to do my damnedest to find us a place and pay the bills while you stay in school."

She straightened up, clearing her throat, shooting me a

nasty look. "Stop talking to me like I'm a stupid kid!"

I blinked. Jackie leaned in, showing me her bloodshot eyes. "I'm not as old as you, sis, but I'm not retarded. We're out of money. I get that. I know you won't find a job in this shitty town with half a degree and no experience…we'll end up homeless, and then the state'll get involved. They'll take me away from you, stick me with some freaky foster parents. But I won't forget you, Missy. I'll be okay. I'll survive."

Rage shot through me. Rage against the world, myself, maybe even dad's ghost for putting us in this fucked up position.

I clenched my jaw. "That's *not* going to happen, Jackie. Don't even go there. I won't let –"

"Whatever. It's not like it matters. I just hope there's a way for us to keep in touch when the hammer falls." She was quiet for a couple minutes before she finally looked up, her eyes redder than before. "I heard what he said while I was crying. Daddy didn't have crap after he got sick and left the force – nothing but those measly checks. He didn't earn a dime while he was sick. He died the same way he lived, Missy – sorry, and completely full of shit."

Anger howled through me. I wanted to grab her, shake her, tell her to get a fucking grip and stop obsessing on disaster. But I knew she didn't mean it.

Lashing out wouldn't do any good. Rage was all part of grief, wasn't it? I kept waiting for mine to bubble to the surface, toxic as the crap they'd pumped into our father to prolong his life by a few weeks towards the end.

I settled back in my chair and closed my eyes. I'd find

some way to keep my promise to Jackie, whether there was a lucky break waiting for us in the basement or just more junk, more wreckage from our lives.

Daddy wasn't ready to be a single father when Mom got killed, but he'd managed. He did the best he could before he had to deal with the shit hand dealt to him by this merciless life. I closed my eyes, vowing I'd do the same.

No demons waiting for us on the road ahead would stop me. Making sure neither of us died with dad was my new religion, and I swore I'd never, ever lose my faith.

* * * *

A week passed. A lonely, bitter week in late winter with a meager funeral. Daddy's estranged brother sent us some money to have him cremated and buried with a bare bones headstone.

I wouldn't ask Uncle Ken for a nickel more, even if he'd been man enough to show his face at the funeral. Thankfully, it wasn't something to worry about. He kept his distance several states away, the same 'ostrich asshole' daddy always said he was since they'd fallen out over my grandparent's miniscule inheritance.

All it did was confirm the whole family was fucked. I had no one now except Jackie, and it was her and I against the world, the last of the Thomas girls against the curse turning our lives to pure hell over the last decade.

A short trip to the attorney's office told me what I already knew about dad's assets. What little he had was going into state hands. Medicare was determined to claw back a tiny fraction of what they'd spent on his care. And because I was now Jackie's legal guardian, his pension and disability was as good as buried with him.

The older lawyer asked me if I'd made arrangements with extended family, almost as an afterthought. Of course I had, I lied. I made sure to straighten up and smile real big when I said it.

I was a responsible adult. I could make money sprout from weeds. What did the truth matter in a world that wasn't wired to give us an ounce of help?

Whatever shit was waiting for us up ahead needed to be fed, nourished with lies if I wanted to keep it from burying us. I was ready for that, ready to throw on as many fake smiles and twisted truths as I needed to keep Jackie safe and happy.

Whatever wiggle room we'd had for innocent mistakes slammed shut the instant daddy's heart stopped in the sharp white room.

I was so busy dealing with sadness and red tape that I'd nearly forgotten about his last words. Finishing up his affairs and making sure Jackie still got some sleep and decent food in her belly took all week, stealing away the meager energy I had left.

It was late one night after she'd gone to bed when I finally remembered. It hit me while I was watching a bad spy movie on late night TV, halfway paying attention to the story as my stomach twisted in knots, steeling itself for the frantic job hunt I had to start tomorrow.

I got up from my chair and padded over to the basement door. Dust teased my nose, dead little flecks suspended in the dim light. The basement stank like mildew, tinged with rubbing alcohol and all the spare medicine we'd stored down here while dad suffered at home.

I held my breath descending the stairs, knowing it would only get worse when I finally had to inhale. Our small basement was dark and creepy as any. I looked around, trying not to fixate on his old work bench. Seeing the old husks of half-finished RC planes he used to build in better times would definitely bring tears.

Roofing tiles, he'd said. Okay, but where?

It took more than a minute just scanning back and forth before I noticed the big blue tarp. It was wedged in the narrow slit between the furnace and the hot water tank.

My heart ticked faster. So, he wasn't totally delusional on his death bed. There really were roofing tiles there – and what else?

It was even stranger because the thing hadn't been here when I was down in the basement last week – and daddy had been in hospice for three weeks. He couldn't have crawled back and hidden the unknown package here. Jackie definitely couldn't have done it and kept her mouth shut.

That left one disturbing possibility – someone had broken into our house and left it here.

Ice ran through my veins. I shook off wild thoughts about intruders, kneeling down next to the blue plastic and running my hands over it.

Yup, it felt like a roofing palate. Not that I'd handled many to know, but whatever was beneath it was jagged, sandy, and square.

Screw it. Let's see what's really in here, I thought.

Clenching my teeth, I dragged the stack out. It was lighter than I expected, and it didn't take long to find the ropey ties holding it together. One pull and it came off easy. A thick slab of shingles slid out and thudded on the beaten concrete, kicking up more dust lodged in the utilities.

I covered my mouth and coughed. Disappointment settled in my stomach, heavy as the construction crap in front of me. I prepared myself for a big fat nothing hidden in the cracks.

"Damn it," I whispered, shaking my head. My hands dove for the shingles and started to tug, desperate to get this shit over with and say goodbye to the last hope humming in my stomach.

The shingles didn't come up easy. Planting my feet on both sides and tugging didn't pull the stack apart like I expected. Grunting, I pulled harder, taking my rage and frustration out on this joke at my feet.

There was a ripping sound much different than I expected. I tumbled backward and hit the dryer, looking at the square block in my hands. When I turned it over, I saw the back was a mess of glue and cardboard.

Hope beat in my chest again, however faint. This was no ordinary stack of shingles. My arms were shaking as I dropped the flap and walked back to the pile, looking down at the torn cardboard center hidden by the layer I'd peeled off. Someone went through some serious trouble camouflaging the box underneath.

I walked to dad's old bench for a box cutter, too stunned

with the weird discovery to dwell on his mementos. The blade went in and tore through in a neat slice. I quickly carved out an opening, totally unprepared for the thick leafy pile that came falling out.

My jaw dropped along with the box cutter. I hit the ground, resting my knees on the piles of cash, and tore into the rest of the box.

Hundreds – no, thousands – came out in huge piles. I tore through the package and turned it upside down, showering myself in more cash than I'd seen in my life, hundreds bound together in crisp rolls with red rubber bands.

Had to cover my mouth to stifle the insane laughter tearing at my lungs. I couldn't let Jackie hear me and come running downstairs. If I was all alone, I would've laughed like a psycho, mad with the unexpected light streaking to life in our darkness.

Jesus, I barely knew how to handle the mystery fortune myself, let alone involve my little sis. I collapsed on the floor, feeling hot tears running down my cheeks. The stupid grin pulling at my face lingered.

Somehow, someway, he'd done it. Daddy had really done it.

He'd left us everything we'd need to survive. Hell, all we'd need to *thrive*. Feeling the cool million crunching underneath my jeans like leaves proved it.

"Shit!" I swore, realizing I was rolling around in the money like a demented celebrity.

Panicking, I kicked my legs, careful to check every nook

around me for anything I'd kicked away in shock. When I saw it was all there, I grabbed an old laundry basket and started piling the stacks in it. I pulled one out and took off the rubber band. Rifling my fingers through several fistfuls of cash told me everything was separated in neat bundles of twenty-five hundred dollars.

I piled them in, feverishly counting. I had to stop around the half million mark. There was at least double that on the floor. Eventually, I'd settle down and inventory it to the dime, but for now I was looking at somewhere between one to two million, easy.

It was magnitudes greater than anything this family had seen in its best years, before everything went to shit. I smoothed my fingers over my face, loving the unmistakable money scent clinging to my hands.

No shock – sweet freedom smelled exactly like cold hard cash.

An hour later, I'd stuffed it into an old black suitcase, something discreet I could keep with me. My stomach gurgled. One burden lifted, and another one landed on my shoulders.

I wasn't stupid. I'd heard plenty about what daddy did for the Redding PD's investigations to know spending too much mystery money at once brought serious consequences. Wherever this money came from, it sure as hell wasn't clean.

I'd have to keep one eye glued to the cash for…months? Years?

Shit. Grim responsibility burned in my brain, and it

made my bones hurt like they were locked in quicksand. Dirty money wasn't easy to spend.

I'd have to risk a few bigger chunks up front on groceries, a tune-up for our ancient Ford LTD, and then a down payment on a new place for Jackie and I.

It wouldn't buy us a luxury condo – not if we wanted to save ourselves a Federal investigation. But this cash was plenty to make a greedy landlord's eyes light up and take a few months' worth of rent without any uncomfortable questions. It was more than enough to give us food plus a roof over our heads while I figured out the rest.

Survival was still the name of the game, even if it had gotten unexpectedly easier.

Once our needs were secure, then I could figure out the rest. Maybe I'd find a way to finagle my way back into school so I could finish the accounting program I'd been forced to drop when dad's cancer went terminal.

It felt like hours passed while I finished filling up the suitcase and triple checked the basement for runaway money. When I was finally satisfied I'd secured everything, I grabbed the suitcases and marched upstairs, turning out the light behind me. I switched off the TV and headed straight for bed.

I sighed, knowing I was in for a long, restless night, even with the miracle cash safe beneath my bed. Or maybe because of it.

I couldn't tell if my heart or my head was more drained. They'd both been absolutely ripped out and shot to the moon these past two weeks.

I closed my eyes and tried to sleep. Tomorrow, I'd be hunting for a brand new place instead of a job while Jackie caught up on schoolwork. That happy fact alone should've made it easier to sleep.

But nothing about this was simple or joyful. It wasn't a lottery win.

Dwelling on the gaping canyon left in our lives by both our dead parents was a constant brutal temptation, especially when it was dark, cold, and quiet. So was avoiding the question that kept boiling in my head – how had he gotten it?

What the *fuck* had daddy done to make this much money from nothing? Life insurance payouts and stock dividends didn't get dropped off in mysterious packages downstairs.

He'd asked for forgiveness before his body gave out. My lips trembled and I pinched my eyes shut, praying he hadn't done something terrible – not directly, anyway. He was too sick for too long to kill anyone. He'd been off the force for a few years too.

I lost minutes – maybe hours – thinking about how he'd earned the dirty little secret underneath my bed. Whatever he'd done, it was bad. But at the end of the day, how much did I care?

And no matter how much blood the cash was soaked in, we needed it. I wasn't about to latch onto fantasy ethics and flush his dying legacy down the toilet. Blood money or not, we *needed* it. No fucking way was I going to burn the one thing that would keep us fed, clothed, sheltered, and sane.

Jackie never had to know where our miracle came from. Neither did I. Maybe years from now I'd have time for soul searching, time to worry about what kind of sick sins I'd branded onto my conscience by profiting off this freak inheritance.

Fretting about murder and corruption right now wouldn't keep the state from taking Jackie away when we were homeless. I had to keep my mouth shut and my mind more closed than ever. I had to treat it like a lottery win I could never tell anyone about.

Besides, it was all just temporary. I'd use the fortune to pay the rent and put food in our fridge until I finished school and got myself a job. Then I'd slowly feed the rest into something useful for Jackie's college – something that wouldn't get us busted.

It must've been after three o'clock when I finally fell asleep. If only I had a crystal ball, or stayed awake just an hour or two longer.

I would've seen the hurricane coming, the pitch black storm that always comes in when a girl takes the hand the devil's offered.

* * * *

An earsplitting scream woke me first, but it was really the door slamming a second later that convinced me I wasn't dreaming.

Jackie!

I threw my blanket off and sat up, reaching for my phone on the nightstand. My hand slid across the smooth wood, and adrenaline dumped in my blood when I realized there was nothing there.

Too dark. I didn't realize the stranger was standing right over me until I tried to bolt up, slamming into his vice-like grip instead. Before I could even scream, his hand was over my mouth. Scratchy stubble prickled my cheek as his lips parted against my ear.

"Don't. You fucking scream, I'll have to put a bullet in your spine." Cold metal pushed up beneath my shirt, a gun barrel, proof he wasn't making an empty threat.

Not that I'd have doubted it. His tight, sinister embrace stayed locked around my waist as he turned me around and nudged his legs against mine, forcing me to move toward the hall.

"Just go where I tell you, and this'll all be over nice and quick. Nobody has to get hurt."

I listened. When we got to the basement door, he flung it open and lightened his grip, knowing it was a one way trip downstairs with no hope for escape.

Jackie was already down there against the wall, and so were four more large, brutal men like the one who'd held me. I blinked when I got to the foot of the stairs and took in the bizarre scene. They all wore matching leather vests with GRIZZLIES MC, CALIFORNIA emblazoned up their sides and on their backs.

I'd seen bikers traveling the roads for years, but never anything like these guys. Their jackets looked a lot like the ones veterans wore when they went out riding, but the symbols were all different. Bloody, strange, and very dangerous looking.

The men themselves matched the snarling bears on their leather. Four of them were younger, tattooed, spanning the spectrum from lean and wiry to pure muscle. The guy who'd walked me down the stairs moved where I could see him. He might've been the youngest, but I wasn't really sure.

Scary didn't begin to describe him. He looked at me with his arms folded, piercing green eyes going right through my soul, set in a stern cold face. He exuded a strength and severity that only came naturally – a born badass. A predator completely fixed on me.

An older man with long gray hair seemed to be in charge. He looked at the man holding my sister, another hard faced man with barbed wire ropes tattooed across his face. Jackie's eyes were bulging, shimmering like wide, frantic pools, pulling me in.

I'm sorry, I hissed in my head, breaking eye contact. One more second and I might've lost it. The only thing worse than being down here at their mercy was showing them I was already weak, broken, helpless.

They had my little sister, my whole world, everything I'd sworn to protect. No, this wasn't the time to freak out and cry. I had to keep it together if we were going to get out of this alive.

"Well? Any sign of the haul upstairs, or do we need to make these bitches sing?" Gray hair reached into his pocket, retrieving a cigarette and a lighter, as casually as if he was at work on a smoke break.

Shit, for all I knew, he probably was.

"Nothing up there, Blackjack." The man who'd taken me downstairs stepped forward, leaving the basement echoing with his smoky voice, older and more commanding than I'd expected. It hadn't just been the rough whisper flowing into my ear.

"Fuck," the psycho holding Jackie growled. "I like it the fun way, but I'm not a fan when these bitches scream. Makes my ears ring for days. Can't we gag these cunts first?"

Nobody answered him. The older man narrowed his eyes, looking at his goon, taking a long pull on the cigarette. My head was spinning, making it feel like the ground had softened up, ready to suck me under and bury me alive.

Oh, God. I knew this had to be about the mystery money the moment those rough hands went around me, but I hadn't really thought we were about to die until he said that.

Gray hair turned to face me, scowling. "You heard the man, love. We can do this the easy way or the hard way. I, for one, don't like spilling blood when there's no good reason, but some of the brothers feel differently. Now, we know your loot's not where it was supposed to be – found this shit all torn up myself."

Blowing his smoke, he pointed at the mess on the ground. I could've choked myself for being too stupid to clean up the mess earlier.

"You've got it somewhere. It couldn't have gotten far," he said, striding forward. "Look we both know me and my boys are gonna find it. Only question left is – are you gonna make this scavenger hunt easy-peasy-punkin-squeezy? Or are you gonna make all our fucking ears ring while we choke it out of you?"

I didn't answer. My eyes floated above his shoulder, fixing on the man across from me, stoic green eyes.

"Well?" The older asshole was getting impatient.

Strange. If Green Eyes wasn't so busy hanging out with these creeps and taking hostages, he would've been handsome. No, downright sexy was a better word.

My weeping, broken brain was still fixed on the stupid idea when Gray Hair grunted, pulled the light out of his mouth, and reached for my throat...

Look for *Outlaw's Kiss* at your favorite retailer!

Printed in Great Britain
by Amazon